William Haywood Henderson

NATIVE

A DUTTON BOOK

ACKNOWLEDGMENTS

I would like to express my gratitude for their friendship and support to the following people: Greg Miller, Jan Zimpel, Fred Leebron, Mikhail Iossel, Gilbert Sorrentino, Edmund White, George Stambolian, and my agent, Malaga Baldi.

DUTTON

Published by the Penguin Group
Penguin Books USA Inc., 375 Hudson Street, New York, New York 10014, U.S.A.
Penguin Books Ltd, 27 Wrights Lane, London W8 5TZ, England
Penguin Books Australia Ltd, Ringwood, Victoria, Australia
Penguin Books Canada Ltd, 10 Alcorn Avenue, Toronto, Ontario, Canada M4V 3B2
Penguin Books (N.Z.) Ltd, 182-190 Wairau Road, Auckland 10, New Zealand

Penguin Books Ltd, Registered Offices:
Harmondsworth, Middlesex, England

First published by Dutton, an imprint of New American Library, a division of Penguin Books USA Inc. Distributed in Canada by McClelland & Stewart Inc.

First Printing, March, 1993
1   3   5   7   9   10   8   6   4   2

Copyright © William Haywood Henderson, 1993
All rights reserved

Portions of this novel have appeared previously in other publications: The Faber Book of Gay Short Fiction, *edited by Edmund White (Faber and Faber Ltd., 1991); "What You Hear,"* QW, *40 (August 8, 1992);* Men on Men 3, *edited by George Stambolian, (Plume, 1990).*

REGISTERED TRADEMARK—MARCA REGISTRADA

LIBRARY OF CONGRESS CATALOGING-IN-PUBLICATION DATA:
Henderson, William Haywood.
Native / by William Haywood Henderson.
p.   cm.
ISBN 0-525-93574-6
I. Title
PS3558.E4944N38   1993
813'.54—dc20   92-23037
                                                          CIP

Printed in the United States of America
Set in Garamond No. 3 and Gill Sans

Designed by Steven N. Stathakis

To Kenneth Banks
and the memory of
A. J. Schott, Jr.

The wind, ripe with sage, rolled particles of mountain down each spine of the badlands, through gullies of flat washed rock, along trails scratched into the crust. From the highest parapet of badland, an antelope watched the moon fall from zenith. Below him, the earth plunged. Behind him, the bench rose across dark jumbles of sage, across open fields pocked with clumps of stiff grass and tundra slick at the edge of snowfields, and reached for pinnacles feeding on stars. The antelope lowered his head and rubbed his foreleg with his pronged horns. Then he raised his head, and his ears drew in sounds of wind, nothing else.

But there was something below the wind, something keeping him from turning away from the edge and joining his mates in the risings toward the peaks. He knew the trails laid out below him—the escapes down over the edge, the straight lines along wire to gaps, the passages through abandoned creek bed, along flowing water, across an open hillock where soil is white, licked for salt. He always skirted the wide trail dug hugely up the valley floor, a strip of ruined grass at its center, the trail that ate a steady swath of sage, that led in only one direction, regardless of the delicacies or wanderings to each side, the trail that troubled him, though he wasn't always sure of the reason.

Now, as the sound below the wind came clear, he felt the reason *quiver down his limbs. A truck, with stars at the front and fire behind, followed the wide trail. The truck wasn't fast—he could easily outrun it. It wasn't smart—it rarely left the trail, but usually lumbered up the valley on its black wheels in stupid pursuit of nothing, leaving the antelope to pause in his escape, safely up a ridge, and watch it disappear, seemingly unaware that its quarry had been left behind. He feared it because it moved unpredictably, sometimes unloading a man who'd shoot a rifle, bring strange luck—rocks would jump at the antelope's hooves.*

The antelope watched until the truck's fire had burned away around a curve of the valley, and then held his head high and cried—a sharp whistle that reclaimed the valley below and echoed as he sprang away to join his mates.

ONE

Severed heads—antelope, deer, moose—and the moving heads, I couldn't place them, not from outside with the red neon flashing, drawing lines through couples dancing. It surprised me, so many people. Clarence sat back there on the stage, one hand on his trumpet, the other on the piano—he'd accompanied the couples for years on Saturday nights. I pushed the door open and the sprung hinge creaked, a strained scraping sound, something I'd heard from the outside, passing on the sidewalk—it had been years since I'd heard it from within the doorway. But I stepped straight through as if I'd done it every Saturday night of my life, as if Mother's stories stepped with me.

Max pushed off from Sally and greeted me—"Hey, Blue." His scarred ear came around as he turned away, the ear scarred from that old, sad football team back then. Hardly worth a scar.

Albert took my hand, pulled me toward him, gave me a hard shake, and said, "How can you stay so invisible and still run that Fisher place?" He leaned closer to say, "I wish I could convince you to manage *my* ranch, young man."

"Thanks, but I'm pretty much set already." I returned a

good, solid shake, the proper gesture, pulled back out of his grip, and tried to find a way through the crowd.

The Talbots blocked me. Mrs. Talbot kicked her leg back on each spin, her skirt twisted and bunched and then flew out full again. They held their clasped hands straight out toward me in a large fist and smiled, broke their step, and as Mr. Talbot acknowledged me and headed for the bar, Mrs. Talbot approached, smoothing her skirt with her white hands. "Hi, dear," she said. Her fingertips landed on my hip. "Heard anything from that father of yours?"

"No, ma'am."

She rose up on her toes and pressed her lips to my ear in a soft kiss. "It's so good to see you out." Clarence, who had put his trumpet on top of the piano, set to playing more seriously, and his drummer took up his sticks and started to beat. "I love it, this song," Mrs. Talbot said, and as she wheeled around, looking for her husband, she reached back, touched me on the arm. "Call me sometime about dinner, Blue. We'll have you over. I've missed you. I've missed your dear mother, all these years." She wandered away into the crowd.

Everyone danced the same dance, the two-step—the women spun to the farthest reach of an outstretched arm and then snapped back close again. They all grinned, kept their backs straight.

I took a few more steps, paused, looked over the bobbing heads. Then I spotted Sam at the bar, standing with Derek—Derek of repaired rifles and swapped snowmobiles, planned wilderness trips, the memory of a single poached cougar still darkening what everyone thought of him. Sam was too close to him, should not have been talking to him, had maybe spent the day with him picking up who knows what kind of angry habits. But Sam seemed unchanged, calm, as if he'd forgotten what he'd said last night, that he might drop by to see me today, Saturday, first day of a free weekend. There'd been no sign of him. I'd spent the day up on the windmill, replacing the mechanism, watching each car pass on the road at the base of the red badlands across the valley. The grass waved in the fields, dark green and then suddenly a greenish silver. The cows lay in the sun like black rocks, and the calves ran in circles. No Sam.

Last night he'd told me about where he was heading, his voice strong, eager. He talked on and on about the places he'd worked, starting in the hot box of a factory making knives. He was glad to be in a mountain town, six months now and settling in, glad to be working on a ranch large enough that he could get far away, duck through a fence, walk to the shadow of trees, cool his feet in a creek, lie out in a patch of sun on a padding of pine needles, and feel the heat on his skin. He'd been heading higher, up off the plains, and he was getting closer. As soon as he had a chance, he'd be out on the trails he'd plotted on his maps, getting up to where he could see maybe all the way back home.

I'd thought, as I waited for him, that he might have already made up his mind to quit and move on. But I could give him something that would keep him around, an assignment I hadn't offered anyone yet. I'd phoned him—no answer. After dinner, I went out looking, wound up there in the bar. It was part of my job, to set things up. He could help me.

Now I came up beside them, said, "Derek," smiled down at Sam, thinking of the cow camp, twenty miles up at the first lush edges of altitude after all that dry road.

Sam grabbed my arm and shouted over the roar of voices, drums, piano, "Derek and me are buds." Sam, my recent hire with his mind on the wilds, just legal enough to drink. He waited for me, his round flat face without concern or humor, just open and pale, looked at me with dust in the creases around his patient gray eyes.

The cabin at the cow camp was unpowered, complete and rustic and far removed, isolated from unnatural sound. The barest thread of water flowed from the spring in the willows and carved a straight line behind the cabin, with a wooden box built over the water in which to cool cans of fruit, beer, a stick of butter in that iced water drawn straight from a wound at the base of the Ramshorn. The peak and spring snow hung like solid clouds over the cabin, the green roof. The view from the porch opened down to where the thread of water split and wove a marsh of tangled roots, where skunk cabbage leaves cupped white flowers beneath explosions of young willow branches.

Derek had hold of my other arm, and he shouted, "This here greenhorn shithead you hired is all right, Blue. He's keeping me company till Janeen gets here." They leaned toward each other and bumped foreheads.

The jolt of their butting bone went down through their arms and into their grip on my muscle, and I said, "Yes, he's fine."

"Bullshit—he's a bigger asshole than you, Blue," Derek said. "Where the hell you been? I ain't seen you out for years, you fucker. You looking for a babe?" He shook me.

Sam said, "Boss man," and he also shook me.

They laughed and swore at each other and butted foreheads again while I tried to back out of their grips, saying, "If you have a minute, Sam, I'd like to talk to you about something."

Derek mocked, "I'd like to talk to you."

Sam said, "Boss man wants to talk to me," staring up at me blank for a moment as if he were waiting for me to do something, to order him, but then he released me, both of them released me, and they bought me a beer as I waited.

Sam forced the bottle up against my chest, the glass cold through my shirt. I followed him away from the bar, through the dancing couples. Max and Sally whirled past. David danced with someone new, or maybe it was still Betty but with different hair, and he shouted, "Blue, I got the truck running. I'll move those bales tomorrow." His arm came up off his partner's waist, it *was* Betty, and he slapped me hard on the back as I passed. "Trust me, Blue." He hooked my arm and turned me back toward him.

"I trust you, David," I said. He laughed, eyes snapping back to Betty as she lowered her chin to his shoulder and got his free arm back on her. "You know I trust you."

We found the other wall and the booths, slid in, and Sam was straight across from me. I raised the bottle to my mouth, placed my lips over the open circle, and sucked liquid down into my throat, feeling the cold reach through me. I said, "Sam, I want you to man the cow camp up at the Ramshorn this summer."

Sam rocked his bottle back and forth, lifted it, tapped it on the tabletop. Then he glanced up at me, opened his mouth to speak, shut it. I took a long swallow of beer, thinking it might be best if I finished and got going—he could give me an answer later when his mind was clear. But he snapped his fingers at me, smiling broadly, pointed toward the far end of the room, got up, and walked away to piss, left me alone. I could wait.

There were many more people than I'd thought I'd see, and I ran through their names, watched their faces, wondered if they were surprised to see me. They all kept dancing.

Mrs. Hudson, the high school music teacher, slid in across from me. Her throat was flushed red, and her tortoise-shelled, magnified eyes ran over me and out into the crowd as she chuckled. "Leslie Eugene Parker, your eyes are blue as ever," she said. She reached across and patted the back of my hand, and her heavy fingers made my bones feel thin. "It's so good to see you out and around and getting so handsome. Smile for me, darling. I always liked your smile."

"I just dropped in to check on my new hand, Mrs. Hudson."

"You're working? Shame. Let's dance."

"Thanks, but I want to finish my drink." I held my beer out toward her and then took a swallow.

"Come on." Taking my hand, she pulled my arm out straight and lolled her head from side to side with the music. "I'll get Clarence to play something younger."

"I'm fine, really. Maybe later." I pulled my hand back and clamped it under my thigh on the bench.

"Okay, dear, but there's a lot of fun you're missing."

She started singing quietly with the music as she watched the couples churn past, their hips shifting with the beat. Mr. Kroeber held tightly to someone else's wife, and I knew the

9

words he whispered with cheek pressed to temple. Paulie, just out of high school, followed the lead of his taller sister, his arms held stiffly. Derek swung by with Janeen, her unusually blond hair shining down over her sweater, and he paused long enough to look back over his shoulder and say, "Get a load of the fucking squaw if ya got a chance." I roused myself and looked around to see what he meant, but then Sam slid in against me, and with the jolt of his body I pushed myself back into the corner, giving him room.

"Is this the business you can't set free for one Saturday night?" Mrs. Hudson said.

"Mrs. Hudson, this is Sam." They shook hands quickly across the table.

"Sam, sweetheart," she said, "you make sure Blue has some fun, okay? I leave him in your hands." She got up and left us, took a young man from the next booth, and danced out into the crowd.

"Nice old lady," Sam said, sitting beside me. He stretched across the table to get his beer, took a sip. "Tell me about this cow camp, Blue." He looked straight ahead, down the row of booths, as he spoke. "How far up is it?"

"Twenty miles off Horse Creek. Just below the Ramshorn."

His face came around toward me, and he said, "I'd like to do whatever you want me to do, Blue. What would I do up there?"

He sat close to me in the booth, his roughness softened by beer or something, his small sharp nose flushed pink. "We take the herd up there. For the summer. You'd stay in the cabin."

The night before, Sam had complained of his old factory job, saying, "All that dull shit just to make *these*," and then he unbuckled his belt. The tang chimed, the long end slapped leather down against his leg as he slid the sheath off and held it out toward me, wanting me to inspect a knife he had made in that factory. I took the sheath from him and turned it over, unsnapped it, pulled the blade from the leather, and the light of

10

flames from the fireplace licked the edge. It was sharp, I could tell, liable to cut by accident.

Sam leaned his shoulder into my upper arm, and his voice cracked and rose. "But what would I do?"

"You'd ride lines." I wanted to place him up there against the Ramshorn, place him in that green space above the marsh.

"Which horse would I have?" His weight rushed my pulse through my arm.

"Starwood. She's good on the rougher trails. You'd just keep an eye on things, watch out for strays and sickness."

He'd sit on the porch, hear the water running in the narrow channel behind the cabin, smell the tart funk of skunk cabbage, keep track of the herd in its high-country grazing, release a calf from barbed wire, lean back in a chair. The heat of late evening would evaporate in empty sky, walls of green discs would shiver above the ribbed white leggy aspens.

"Blue," Sam said, and he poked me with his elbow. "Blue, we have a guest."

A figure stood at the booth, fleshy, dressed in black jeans, turquoise buckle, baggy white shirt, obscuring the crowd. Squaw. This man stood there and looked down at us. His black hair was straight, long, and slick, and it played along his shoulders as he moved with the music, but it wasn't a movement I had seen, not like the couples two-stepping behind him.

His shoulders rose and fell, his hands came up. He descended into the rhythm, hips revolving. His head fell forward. He flipped his hair back over his shoulders and danced with eyes on us. He was a man without joints, loose and snaking. His smile pinched. He didn't know to turn his black eyes away, to act as if he weren't watching us.

He said, "Cozy," and we didn't move. I didn't look away from those black points. His eyes made the little shift back and forth between Sam and me. "Boys. Cozy." Then Sam seemed heavy against me, as if he'd been sleeping against me. "Someone needs to dust you two off and you'd be a fine pair." He laughed, a deep rumble, a laugh I didn't know, as if it were choked with honey. His face was brown and smooth as clean carved clay, his lips big, eyes Asian like the Indians get, and hair that moved down across his cheeks as if it were laughing with him. "It's the sugar in the alcohol that gets me every time. We don't break down sugar the way you white boys do." Then his laugh rose into a little chant, something I might have heard from the Indians in the ceremonies. His eyes closed for a moment. Arms over his head, he shook, spun, stopped dead where he'd started. He gave us a last look. "Fine pair."

He turned his back to us, stepped away, and people made room for his walk through their dance. Mrs. Hudson pulled her partner back with a hard maneuver of her elbow, the Talbots spun off in another direction. I watched the people watch him, saw their smiles flicker or go flat, and then I watched the man. He shadow-danced in imitation of each couple he passed, taking his time. He held his arms up in a feminine echo of each woman whose back came around to him. He might have been moving in those lines of Indian women, shuffling through those ceremonies down on the reservation. The old Indian women would come up maybe once a year to buy something at the mercantile, but they all had better places to go. It was rare to see a man, an Indian man, in this town. I couldn't remember an Indian ever talking as if he didn't know he could get hurt, as if he'd never heard the way a guy like Derek could say "Squaw."

And now Derek, it was his turn, Derek let go of Janeen and stood face to face with this man, mouthing something angry. The man should have known enough to turn away, should have known better than to sink into his loose dance, to let his chant slice through the music, should have known better than to reach out for Derek, take his wrists, and tug him around in a circle, a close circle, too quick for Derek to stop his steps. Then the man freed Derek's hands, held his own hands over his head, and closed his eyes, chanted again.

Derek clenched his hands across his chest, shouted something and whirled, stumbled against his girlfriend, pulled her arms around him. The Indian, whose chant had stopped with

Derek's shout, shook his hair back and continued toward the bar. The couples moved in behind him, and everyone whispered with lips close to ears before returning their full attention to the dance.

"Funny guy," Sam said as he held up his bottle, took a swallow. Bubbles rose through the liquid and burst. "Do you know him?"

"No, I don't."

"He can dance."

"He'd do himself a favor if he stood still."

"Beats me." Sam laughed. "I think he can dance."

"Not here."

But I could imagine the reservation, the cottonwoods big green clouds along the river, the earth dry. The stony men around the one big drum would pound, start the chanting, deep and wandering as if they were on their way somewhere. The women in white deerskin, fringe, beads, would begin to move out like a line of sadness, shuffling, hands clasped at bellies, heads down, shuffling and bobbing, as if something moved them all at once forward, then pushed them back a little, bobbing, playing with the beat, then forward again, in no hurry, never stepping off to the side, all moving directly into the steps of the one ahead. I could see the man moving with them, hear the chant, his hair down his back, hot black in the dry sun along the river, his feet in the footsteps of the women, his voice on the beat with theirs, his black eyes bold as a man's, his soft moves amplified and strange.

"So, what, I'll be riding lines?"

I leaned into the corner of the booth. The squaw was out of sight, over by the bar, or maybe he had come to his senses and left. Sam's fingers drummed, traveling across the tabletop, closer to me, away from me. "Yes. Riding lines."

"Any lakes up there?"

"Sure. Lots of water. Snowfields. Waterfalls. Anything you could want."

13

"But what else will I do? The day-to-day stuff?"

"Just watch the herd, like I said. I did it myself a few years ago."

"You'll teach me what I need to know?"

"Of course."

He nodded slowly and took another swallow of beer. "It's a deal, then," he said, and his lips tightened.

"Deal."

He reached below the tabletop, took my hand from my lap, pulled it up between us, and shook it. "Good." He smiled broadly and released me, leaned his shoulder into my arm, laughed. "You're a good guy, Blue. I mean it." His head came around and his nose brushed my sleeve.

"It's nothing."

He tipped his head away and looked up at me, his brown lips moved a little, a second of limp hesitation. But his shoulder bore harder against me when he said, "You're good. Setting me up in a place, way up high."

I could have left him there against me—he seemed drunk enough to be leaning like that—but Clarence stopped and people turned around, looking for seats. I sat up and Sam shifted away, went back to his beer. I sat there with my new ranchhand, and I drank from my own beer. "It's not easy work," I said. "It takes a strong guy."

"Don't worry." Smiling again, he leaned a little, and I pressed my shoulders square against the back wall. He finished his beer, started to peel the label, and recited some names he'd learned from his maps—"Battram Mountain, Pony Creek, the DuNoir."

We started in on new beers. A few people danced to the jukebox. After a while, Clarence started playing again, going from a long note on the trumpet to a fast riff on the piano, and the crowd filled the floor. I could have fallen asleep there, watching the people dance. Sam held himself upright on his elbows, drank from his beer in silence, nodded slightly with the music or smiled when he caught my eyes.

■ ■ ■

From down along the line of booths, the Indian approached. It's one thing to play a game once, but I couldn't figure why he would play it again when it could get him hurt. He had something to say to the people in each booth, and I watched his lips move, tried to catch his voice, tried to catch reactions, shouts, whatever, but the music drowned all but his movement. He laughed. He approached. Two more steps.

He danced at the end of our table, blocking things. Chanting at us, he tapped Sam on the shoulder. Sam sat up, looked at the man, turned his head slowly, loosely, toward me, and said, "Hey, who is this guy, anyway?"

"I don't know."

Sam turned back toward the man. "Hey, buddy, who *are* you?"

The Indian raised his arms, snapped his fingers out in front of his forehead, and spun himself around once with churning steps. "Gilbert." He slowed, leaned forward and supported himself at the end of the table on straight arms, his hips tilting and grinding, and his lips, tongue, worked around his words. "Gilbert fucking Richards. Some white guy's name. I'm changing it. Wagonburner, eh? Something with some guts. I'm gonna set something on fire, boys." Then he just stood there inspecting us for a moment as if he were waiting for a truck to run over his feet before he'd move. His face twitched with smiles, his eyes worked back and forth across us.

"Ha." Sam's head fell back, his face to the ceiling. "Isn't he funny," he said, and then he righted himself, watched Gilbert.

Gilbert started dancing again, kept his eyes on Sam. "You, boy," he said, his arms surging out toward Sam, pulling back. "Who are you, boy? Tell me."

"Sam."

"And him?"

"Blue."

"Sad? Baby. Sweet baby. Smile for mama."

15

"My *name* is Blue," I said.

I pushed Sam's beer into his hand and he took a few swallows, lowering the liquid, his shoulder drifting again toward me. I drank from my own bottle. This Gilbert character danced and watched us. He tossed his hair back. Sam watched him. Sam's head swayed with the same rhythm.

"Sam," I said, "are you all right?"

"Fine." He didn't look at me.

"Sam, maybe you should slow down." I grasped the neck of his bottle, but he held onto it, forced it to his mouth and took a swig.

"I'm fine, Blue. Trust me."

"Boys. Boys." Gilbert frowned and shook his head. "Tired? Cranky? Be good. Good boys. White boys. What's in store for you two?"

Sam laughed, and he waved Gilbert off. I watched the tendons shift as Sam's jaw worked. I watched the back of his neck, his hair cropped in short whorls. "Blue here is setting me up in a place. Real rustic. Way up high."

"Lovely." Gilbert reached out and took Sam's hand, pinched it between thumb and index, and pulled it up into his dance for a beat before letting it fall. "You've done well. Mama's proud." Then he looked at me, ran his hands up through his long, straight hair to clear it out of his face. I got it all, the black eyes, the thick lips pursing and working around his deep voice, the woman's skin on his sharp chin as if he'd never had to shave. "You, Blue. Lovely. What about you?"

Then Sam watched me too, he turned back to me, finally, for a static moment. His lips were wet with beer. I imagined him pulling his jeep off the highway, under the crossbar of the main gate, down the dirt road past the Fishers' stone house, a sharp turn with tight elbows and the jeep slides to a stop in the lot among the outbuildings, windmill, my cabin. Dust settles.

"I'm set fine," I said, and Sam nodded sharply and looked back to the Indian for his response, wouldn't stop looking.

"You are," Gilbert said. "Set fine. Yes. Envy's a foul thing.

I envy." He leaned far forward over our table, grasped my hand quickly, his skin rough, his grip strong, tugged at me for a beat, too strong for me to pull away without obvious force, without seeming that I had something against Indians, something against any normal Indian. He squeezed my hand—the unpleasant feeling of pressure on bones so close to the surface they're almost visible through skin. But he let go, leaned away unsteadily and grabbed the back of the booth behind Sam's head for support. His fingers twitched on the maroon vinyl, nearly brushed at the skin on the back of Sam's neck, the skin above Sam's collar burned lightly by days in the intense, high-altitude sun. Gilbert leaned down, and from what I could tell, his hair might have fallen across Sam's face. My hand rose, maybe to pull Sam back, maybe to push Gilbert's fingers off the vinyl. But Gilbert stood away, laughed, and looked at me hard. "Don't be frightened, white boy. You want to hide out? I got a room at the Pinewood Cabins. Number seven. I've got one night in you white boys' town, then it's fuck-you-all-to-hell and on to better parts. I've got high standards."

He made no sense. I'd never seen anyone go so soft, as if he had no bones to hold his shoulders square. He might have gone on forever it seemed, he might have babbled on until I could finally wrestle Sam to his feet and help him to his jeep, load him in the passenger seat, drive him back to his trailer.

But Derek came up to Gilbert and stood a foot away. Gilbert didn't retreat, didn't turn, just brought himself up and waited. Gilbert had an inch on Derek and more bulk. He seemed to be waiting for Derek to speak, as if he couldn't guess from the look on Derek's face what the message would be. But Derek didn't speak to Gilbert—he broke his stare away from the Indian and turned to us, to Sam and me, and his voice twisted out of his face as if it were hard for him to move. "What the hell are you assholes doing with yourselves? If you're not going to act right, why don't you go home?"

I would have gladly gone home, would have put an end to the game, would have given Derek a friendly fist in the gut if he'd pursued his anger any louder, but now three people were blocking my exit. I had to wait for an opening.

"Hey, bud. Hey, Derek," Sam said, motioning for Derek to slide into the seat across from us. "Have a beer. Sit. We're having a rip."

Derek didn't move. "Why don't you get out of here? Get some air? There's got to be something better for you fuckers to do with yourselves."

As Derek spoke, his voice harsh and tight, Gilbert watched him closely, watched his mouth move, darted his eyes to follow the descent of a dot of spittle forced out with the words. Then Gilbert's hand started to rise slowly, a finger extended, the nail flesh-pink at the tip. That pointed finger rose past Derek's shoulder, rose even with his jaw, and as Gilbert whispered, "There's nothing better for these boys," and as Derek snapped his head sideways to face Gilbert, he forced that finger straight at Derek, pressed against the lower lip, the nail sharp against the upper lip, pushed in. And Derek was gone, suddenly out into the crowd, walking with shoulders jerking up against his neck, with hands snapping out to the side as if he were trying to shake off water. He left Gilbert standing, unmoved, with white spit on the tip of his outstretched finger.

My own fingers are slender and long. Sam's are squat. Gilbert's are dark with blue veins obvious beneath the surface, and I couldn't be sure if the veins were from real muscle or if they were just tangled decorations, something fancy and untrue. Who could tell if he had any real strength, or if he was just art, a dark design on a clay pot. Designs are born out of something. I listened to him. Sam listened to him. Derek was invisible, silent, gone.

"I have things to give you, boys." He danced, soft and spinning, dead still, chanting, silent. "See me? You think I'm drunk? No. Magic." Sam tapped his fingers with Gilbert's beat. "Screw. Screw up your courage." Sam leaned back toward me, leaned away, his shoulders starting to tilt. "You can hear the music. Smell the sweat stirred up by firelight. Some young warriors.

Screw the berdache. Make the rain. Luck. Heal something. Berdache." He did a fancy turn, arms out, one hand up, one hand low. He chanted at us. He blocked everything behind. "Tell me I can't dance. Tell me I'm not something you could prize."

No one had to tell me that this man hadn't been in town before. What was to keep trouble away if he wouldn't get out quickly? What was to keep Sam out of trouble if all he could see was Gilbert, blocking everything behind? But I too watched Gilbert as if there weren't anything else to see, as if the faces I knew weren't there beyond him, as if his words had closed in over me.

"A real honor," Gilbert said. He danced, his moves fancy and loose. I wanted to figure him out, figure what would push him away. Sam leaned, the back of his head brushed me, and then he leaned toward the dance. Gilbert put out a finger and pushed Sam back toward me, frowned, said, "I want to dance. *Tell* me I can't dance."

His fingers snapped over his head. He lifted Sam's hand and tugged. Sam lurched, his head flopped, his eyes came around toward me sleepily, he gave a limp grin, said, "Blue. I've been drinking." Gilbert pulled harder on Sam's hand and got him to his feet and took him away.

I thought of Sam below the Ramshorn—black rosy finches passed through to the cliffs above timberline.

Lots of hands pressed on asses, the two-step, like before, and it didn't seem much different, except for an odd leaning, a swaying off the rhythm, as if they were all being pushed away from something dangerous, a wounded dog. Joanne Miller, her eyebrows skewed, lost a step as she snapped out from her partner. Jason Woodburn moved his wife away, keeping her back to it. The couples shifted, and I saw long black hair, straight, moving dead on the rhythm, snaking over shifting shoulders. Sam was supported and pulled through the steps by Gilbert's large hands. Sam's face drew up serious above his eyes, his forehead was wet, and he danced with Gilbert as if it were something to learn—a small rough hand, fingers spread, on the ass of a guy a foot taller with long hair and eyes half closed making a high chant like a woman in a ceremony we didn't know anything about.

I didn't get up to help Sam then. No one watched me. Sam would have done whatever I asked, whatever I ordered him to do. I could have taken him by the arm, said loudly that he'd had too much to drink, led him away, and then in a few days he'd have been at the cow camp, out of sight.

But then Derek was beside them. He reached out and took Sam by the belt loop and pulled him away from Gilbert, who reached to bring Derek into the dance too. Derek twisted his arm away and led Sam toward the door. Space opened through the moving people, and I thought I heard the scrape of the door over the noise of the piano, drums, voices.

Sam was outside now. Sam would be reaching into his pockets for his keys, in no shape to drive. But he was safely free from that dance. My way was clear to stand up, get out, help him home.

Gilbert stood alone, letting his movements slowly stop. I blinked hard to focus. The couples continued their dance, watching the floor, watching Gilbert, no one watching me yet. They were careful to leave a space for Gilbert, whatever direction he might turn, but while I watched for an opening toward the door, he walked toward me, toward the booth. People moved in behind where he walked, twisted their heels over where he stepped, John and Alex and Betty and Mrs. Hudson, all with a glance at me.

I didn't wait to see if their faces would calm, because I was on my feet and moving. I thought people might have been reaching for me as I pushed through, might have been trying to talk to me, but I was out the door and on the sidewalk. No one to touch me. The dead street, parked trucks, the bar noise muffled by the cool silence. I watched my feet through the red flashing on the sidewalk and stepped past the end of the bar building. The narrow empty lot opened out on my left and I heard voices. I looked over and saw two men circling, grappling, not a dance, a fight, every move falling into blurred shadow, a

20

hollow sound, dust, not clear, but understood, like a knife cutting—at first you see it cut, then you feel it, then you realize what it is you feel, and then you don't believe it, as if it's a mistake, and you run back through things, run to your truck, slam it into motion, drive away, off to somewhere high up.

After twenty miles of red dirt road, my headlights rocked sharply. The truck paused, lurched, and stopped as the engine continued roaring. Mud flew up on either side—I couldn't get the truck free. The engine rose into a last grind and died as I flicked off the lights and stepped out with the echo of the slamming door.

Standing beside my truck, I pushed at the door with a few fingers and waited for light to fall from the bright moon, the stars. I saw the pond, rimmed with grass, aspen, gray granite, with the spill-off running across the road, beneath my truck and its tires stuck deep in mud, and then down into the marsh. Something huge bounded through the pond water, hit harder ground, and departed, snorting and crashing with the scrabble of rock. Probably a moose. Then the noise snapped in, the bullfrogs crying from sponged moss and reed. Ahead, the square shadows of the cow camp rose from the clamorous night. I walked down the hill and stepped in through the door.

I struck a match and there was the hot rush of air before the small light made the cabin the place I knew and not just darkness. I found the lantern, touched flame to wick, and the kerosene drew into a thin line of smoke. I brushed away mouse shit from the table, opened the curtains, looked out toward the marsh, but with the light inside there was no light outside now. Lying down on the mattress, I felt the cold stained cotton hard against my back. The ceiling was low above me, lined with deep shadows, the beams holding up that handmade weather-tight sky. Forcing a button through its hole, I touched my chest. Warm in there, my heart beating. My eyes closed. White skin—clouds—moved away, wet and high, and the white flame ate ker-

21

osene, closing the cabin in around its bright consumption of fuel, dust, nothing outside.

The night before, with Sam in my cabin, I'd watched the blurred fire dance on his knife for a full minute before I forced it back into the sheath, ready to return it to him. But he couldn't take it, his hands were occupied. He had unbuttoned his pants and was tucking in his shirt. As I bent to place the knife on the hearth where he could pick it up himself I saw that flash of white, not cotton, flash of white skin, a black trail down the center, leading into shadow at the V of the jeans. I was over sitting down before he finished closing off that white skin, buckling it away. He sat across from me, looked at me in silence for a while, and left me to look at the fire or the sheathed knife in the firelight until he started speaking again. He asked what he'd have to do on the chores pending—the rounding up of a small herd above Wiggin's Fork, the repairs to the shed roof, stacking the irrigation pipes.

Wherever or whenever I had eventually caught up with him, that night or the next day, he would have agreed to man the cow camp, I was sure. Then, after a few days, he'd be up here, alone. He'd unbutton his shirt to the quiet breeze, his white muscles relaxed, rising, falling with his breathing, never startled, never seen by anything but the passing birds and the huge animals straying and grazing on the uplands through summer toward fall. For months, he'd be alone in the light of the kerosene lantern, the windows black around him. The light would be bright white, his skin just as white as he draped his shirt over the back of a chair, ran his hand up across his chest, gripped his shoulder, hung his arm there, the weight heavy across his flesh, pulled himself forward, drowsy. He would run his fingers along his belly above the line of his jeans, tuck a finger behind the leather through the buckle.

I must have slept. My jaw clenched and loosened, my eyes opened. In town, those voices and the music had been so loud I could barely hear my own voice. The cabin, silent except for my breathing, as silent as my own cabin on the ranch, shut me in, forced me to my feet, to the window, to look out. The couples had known me. I turned away from my reflection in the dark window and kept moving.

With a cupped hand I blew out the light, with a few steps I found the door and closed it behind me. Nothing would have kept Sam from taking this job, from stepping through this door, however I'd asked him. The porch creaked, and then the thick grass swallowed my footsteps. I buttoned my shirt, unsnapped my pants and let them fall around my boots. The cold air tightened me as I pissed, and I remained standing that way until the first shiver shook me. I pulled up my pants and felt each inch of cloth—the warmth of clothes—felt ready for the long walk ahead of me.

I guessed by the height of the moon that I had only an hour or two of brightness left, and dawn wouldn't be far behind the darkness. The road I'd taken up to the cow camp wound twenty miles back toward town before giving out to pavement. But the shortest route out of there was over the ridge and down through the DuNoir toward the mountain highway, where I might catch a ride. It couldn't be more than fifteen miles, ten of it on the dirt access road, and with luck I'd hit pavement after about five or six hours, sometime after sunrise.

At the edge of the woods, before following an animal trail up into darkness, I paused. White moonlight and shadows fell around the cabin, and across the hollow my truck rested, embedded in mud. The air throbbed, rippled by an assault of deep cries. I yelled, no words, just sound, and the frogs cut off. I turned toward the black of the woods, where I sensed my way toward the ridge.

Out in the moonlight again, the trail wasn't difficult. I stepped, stepped again, as if it were daylight. I wasn't in any danger of losing my way, not with the peaks like black arrowheads against the stars. The moon had fallen as I started down into the DuNoir, almost running in the darkness.

I couldn't think of anything that could cause me trouble. I could return to the cow camp tomorrow and rescue my truck from the mud with a good length of heavy rope. I could find my way out of anywhere in these mountains, in the dark. I could take Derek in an even fight, no problem. I had never gotten lost, had saved myself when I broke my ankle twenty-five miles in at Five Pockets. I had kept my mother company, listened to her stories, waited, had stayed on alone in this town after my father returned a final time to say he was off for Texas, New Mexico, Grand Junction, no reason now to come back to this town, a widower, an oil rig roughneck, a sometime truck driver. I had had enough smarts to take my job at the Fisher Ranch and turn it from ranchhand to foreman in just five years, had hired on the men I needed, had kept all that land and equipment and all those animals fit and functioning smoothly. And the latest, Sam—well-qualified, hardworking. But I kept walking, kept moving, unsure, as if I wouldn't be able to find the highway, catch a ride or follow the river back to town, back to the ranch, to my cabin, as I always had, wouldn't be able to sleep in my bed and hear the Wind River through the open window, the cold water rushing away.

The access road, broad and flat and wet, snaked among the low willows, and I walked at the edge where the ground was solid with short grass. I passed through a stand of trees for a while, with a corridor of sky running silver with stars over the road ahead. The Milky Way cut across—it stretched from horizon to horizon when I came out of the trees—the white streak wandered overhead as if it were leading somewhere through the black, but it fell in both directions, like water, always down. The edge of the world to the east turned the lightest white as if the Milky Way had broken and spilled. The night shifted west.

I'd never seen a man like Gilbert before, never seen someone who could touch a guy as if he didn't know he could get hurt, who could watch without acting as if he weren't watching. What would it be like to place your hand on what you wanted and take it with you, to stir up a crowd, to never return straight home?

The creek ran along the edge of the road, then off again into the marsh. I was sure that deer watched me, their color invisible off on the flats, waiting for me to pass, waiting for day-light to push them to higher altitude, out of reach. I thought that just a few steps through the water would take me across the creek, and a short run would get me up over the ridge. Or if I turned around I'd get going back toward the Ramshorn, and a day's hike would get me up on clean granite for sunset. From high up, sunset is drained of color at its conclusion, and a pure white line holds off the black.

There was no reason to run straight back to the ranch. My truck wasn't going anywhere, could be retrieved in a day or two. The hands all knew what to do, what was expected. When I neared home, I could cross the upper corner of the ranch, over the wooden bridge, up onto Whiskey Mountain. By now, the big-horns had left the broad slopes for their summer among the peaks, and I would be alone above the town, the grid of the streets laid out, the cars sliding in from down toward Crowheart Butte, driv-ing through toward Togwotee Pass. Whiskey Mountain, easy access—my mother and I had eaten lunch there occasionally, and she'd guessed at the driver of each glimmer on the streets below, told a story of the weight of a hand on her thigh, the voice against her ear, the offers to dance that led to the danger of something more, her retreat home, to me. She'd said, sometimes, that she wanted to get out there, to answer each offer, to become a couple, to let herself be pulled from hand to hand, spun, with my father on the road again, off on one of his jobs, but she couldn't. She laughed at the thought. Their breath is soaked with liquor, she said. Their wives must know their every line, every move. You think anyone could get away with anything in this town? Maybe Lander. Maybe I'll go to Lander for a night. She laughed.

Lights shone ahead, the Jankirks' A-frame at the edge of a stand of pines—Hanna and Gardelle up early. I pushed through the undergrowth and my breath made clouds on the window. Hanna held a kettle and looked at one of her paintings, three ducks in water, snow folded along the bank, bare orange lines of willows, all the colors just off the mark, as if she'd painted under artificial light. Gardelle sat in a high-backed rocker and ran a rag over a pistol, and then he held the gun metal up to the light as if trying to see his reflection in it. He held the barrel steadily in the air, advancing it until it touched the silver hair at his temple, and his eyes moved across and seemed to focus right on me as if he could see. He smiled, and the gun stayed there. Hanna stood at the stove. She closed her robe against her throat.

I ran along the road with daylight rising around me. Gardelle had told me of the days when he cooked for the tie-hacks, when they would gather, the Swedes all as tall and fair and strong as any men he'd seen, and they'd float in the thermal pools along the edge of the river, no lights from the camp off through the woods, no sounds but the murmur of voices and water, a simple picture, shivering and clean under heavy blankets, the lantern extinguished, the bunkhouse silent. And Sam at the cow camp, a simple picture. But Gilbert reached for what he wanted, wanted to take it away. I would be gone for a day, and if anyone looked for me, they'd find my cabin empty. If Sam knocked—but I was unsure now, for a moment, for a minute that spun me around, of what Sam looked like, of how he sounded.

Sam had left his home, plotted his travels west not by roads but by rivers—Missouri to Yellowstone to Big Horn to Wind River—and he might have found the branch to Horse Creek, to Pony Creek, to the spring at the cow camp, even before he met me. Water that flowed over his feet from these mountains now, that took the dirt from his soles, would take days, maybe weeks, passing through canyons, beneath stone bridges, shadows of cottonwoods and brambles, rapids, before feeding the fields that surrounded his daddy's place, before touching someone who recognized him, Sam, who knew his face so well that they could draw it in the dirt clear enough to make you know it too, real enough to touch.

Then I saw something coming from down toward the highway, a bobbing mass, low over the ground, moving as if it had no business being in the air at all, as if it should fall and crumble, but then it shattered, jagged, with a harsh cry like the death of something, and the black and white birds passed directly over me. I started counting—almost fifty magpies heaved themselves through the air, far from their roosts in the pines on Jakey's Fork, looking for insects, seeds, carrion, dragging their long tails behind like dull swords, patches of white flashing in their blackness. The air churned with their passing, like shadows broken out by a flash of red neon, flash of a raised fist, and the skin on black ground, and the noise of Sam falling.

I reached the end of the access road and faced the narrow highway. DuNoir Creek passed through a metal culvert, beneath the pavement, and rushed into the Wind River on the other side, shaded by tall spruces. With the sound of flowing water all around me, the sound kept close by the splintered wall of rock rising past the trees, I crossed the road. Light mist drifted over the river, cut among the boulders. Black and intent, a dipper disappeared into a surge of water, emerged miraculously a minute later a few yards upriver, climbed onto a log, and straightened his oiled feathers with his beak. The marshy scent lingered, had soaked into my clothing, but as long shafts of sunlight entered the canyon, the air seemed to clear slightly. With my back to the river, I sat on the low rock wall above the culvert, and the throbbing in my feet subsided.

Sam had dark hair, gray eyes, skin beginning to brown in the sun, short muscled legs. A week ago, he'd said it was his first time branding, but he could throw down a calf as if he'd been doing it all his life. He watched me do it just once, and then he was doing it himself. He hunkered down over the calf, nicked the ear, clipped the nubs of the horns, slit the skin and snipped off the little oysters. Not much blood. Hardly any. He'd hold it for the shots and the hot iron and then let it go, stand up, shake himself, just like the calf, only the calf would be bawling and limping and Sam would be shaking himself loose so he'd be ready to grab another and hold it.

The noise of mothering up—all those cows and calves

bawled as they tried to find each other when we put them together in the corral after branding. They always paired off, each
calf with its mother. All that noise and smell means something.

And then Sam was lying on the couch in my cabin, down-
ing a swallow of whiskey, talking on and on. He wouldn't stop
talking, wouldn't stop drinking, smiling, running his fingers up
into his tangles, wouldn't make a move to get up off the couch.
I had to tell him when it was time for him to leave or he would
have stayed until I couldn't keep awake any longer, and I
would've fallen asleep and dreamed as he kept drinking, kept
talking, maybe stole something or let the fire throw sparks on
the rug. I held the door open as he stepped out into the dark,
and I quickly turned off the lights, closed down the fire, stripped
off my clothes and lay in bed. I saw him grip a calf's foreleg.
Tendons shifted beneath the skin.

If I reconstructed the picture carefully, I could see Sam
move. He didn't seem to be at a disadvantage. He had real
muscle—I'd seen him work—he could lift his own weight. His
hand came up to deflect a blow. They both fell. Derek fell as
hard as Sam. Pressure forced both their voices out. I was sure I'd
seen Sam strike back.

Some vehicles passed on the other side of the road—a
motorhome, a station wagon, a motorcycle big as a sofa, all heading west from town toward Togwotee Pass, on toward the national parks and Jackson. I got to my feet and started walking.
The road emerged from a long curve and the valley opened out,
the irrigated fields thick with new grass. The pavement ran
ahead of me in an almost perfectly straight line for about three
miles, veering only when it encountered the pocket of badlands
at the far end. The river swung off to the right, and above it rose
the Wind River Range, first soft and pale green with sage and
grass, then dark with pine, spruce, finally gray and white with
the peaks, the Divide.

Nothing taller than a fencepost stood within a half mile of
me. Gilbert had gone into his dance, snaked.

Stopping for a moment, I looked back, scanned the north

side of the valley, over the winding edges of the intermittent badlands, over the benches tilted toward the rising sun, up to the peaks of the Absarokas, to the Ramshorn, the distant bulk of dark rock and snow in blue sky. I had come from the shoulder of that mountain, all the way through the maze of ridges, marshes, sheer drops, had come down to the road, to the fields and the widely scattered houses, a few miles from town. Soon I'd pass along the sidewalk fronting the long block of stores, glance in through the cafe window and recognize James and Mimi behind the counter. I saw the path through the thick grass, up into the mountains, but I headed on, downhill, approaching the passage through town.

Sam would probably spend the day running his fingers over his topographical maps, tracing the green up into white. He would need supplies. He'd need some teaching. I'd show him how to cut a calf from wire without causing extra harm, how to build a fire in the woodstove that would last through till morning.

Something blared at me. A green station wagon, heading out from town toward the pass, honked its horn, and I looked up too late to see the driver. The car had Wyoming plates and mud along its side as if it had been used for real driving. The brake lights flashed, and the car made a three-point turn, almost going over into the soft edge of the ditch, and came back at me. Then I saw who it was. You can't walk far enough. It was Gilbert, that Indian. He waved at me as he pulled to a stop, and his bumper almost touched my knees. Motioning me over to him, he rolled down his window, tooted the horn again.

There was nothing for me to do but to keep moving. I waved him back toward the pass and started to turn around. He lifted his sunglasses off his eyes, leaned out the window, and shouted, "Hey, don't be a fool."

The road was clear in both directions, nothing approaching. I could give him a minute of conversation, a final move. I walked to his window. He seemed rested, not surprised to see me, as if nothing had happened.

"Walking off a hangover?" he said, and he shook a finger at me as he laughed. His voice came out purely from between his calm, fluid lips, no music to confuse the depth. It seemed strange that a voice with such an even tone could have tightened into a piercing chant. His long black Indian hair caught lines of sunlight.

"I had a breakdown with my truck."

"I always said you can't trust anything mechanical." He revved the engine, and his eyebrows went up with the increased volume, came back down as the engine settled into its soft rumble. "So where'd you run off to last night?"

"I had to be somewhere."

"I missed you."

"I've got to get going." But I didn't move.

"Climb in. I'll give you a lift back to town. I'll buy you a cup of coffee."

He would park on the main street, and when he'd finished his cup of coffee, when a dozen patrons had passed through the cafe, he'd reach out to take my hand, to shake it, to say goodbye. His hand would hold onto me, his grip strong, and I'd have to use force to pull away, would have to seem as if I had something against a man like him, someone with such slick dark hair. "I'm not going to town."

"Where are you going?" He waited for me to answer.

If I said "home," he'd take me to the ranch, let me off, and David would watch him drive back out the long dirt road to the gate. He was offering to help me. He'd leave me if I refused him—he'd head on to some unknown destination. "I'm just walking. I don't need a ride. Where are *you* going?"

"I'm going to Jackson. Why don't you come along?"

His fingers went up into his hair and held it off his face. His eyes stayed on me, the dark points, as if I hadn't made any progress since I left him the night before. But he was different now, he was slow and steady.

I heard a car enter the straightaway from up toward the pass—the sound of the engine came clearly across the wide space.

Turning slowly to look down the road, I said, "I don't have to be anywhere." I shaded my eyes. As the car neared, I took a step toward the front of Gilbert's car and pressed my legs against the metal. Hardly swerving over the center line to give me room, the car roared past, and the wind buffeted me, filled my eyes with grit. Gilbert leaned out the window again—I saw him through my wet eyes as I rubbed them. He reached for me, almost caught my belt. Maybe he wanted me closer, wanted just to shake me, but his hand hung there without making contact, wavering, no further effort to grasp me, maybe no effort in the first place. He wasn't talking crazy. I turned and leaned my butt against the hood. He was talking calmly as if I'd stand there and listen to him, as if nothing had happened. "I can't go to Jackson. I have responsibilities. I have to get back to the ranch. I'm in charge."

"Everything will be fine for the day. You ever seen a cow who didn't know grass when he saw it?"

"A cow's a she," I said. He stared, without expression. He seemed to think that whatever he said was right, that whatever he wanted he could have. But you can't go on with things as if nothing had happened, as if you had no responsibilities. Thinking that he would finally shift his eyes off me, I said, "I have to check on Sam."

He grinned. "Check on Sam? Your little friend? He's fine. Fine boy. He got into a slap fit in the dirt. Nothing more than a bit roughed up—it looked good on him. Will you get in the car already?"

My legs ached. "Sam?"

"Trust me. I saw him. Nothing happened. Come on, Blue, let me give you a lift. To town?"

I felt heavy against his humming car. I felt thirsty, ready to sleep. No clouds had risen from the west, over the pass, and it was sure to be a hot day. He could let me off at the side of the road by the upper fields. I got myself upright and walked around the front of the car to the passenger side, waited for him to reach across and release the lock, and then opened the door and settled onto the slick green vinyl. A window crossed the roof just behind the front seat. I let my head fall back onto the headrest, and I looked up through that tinted window at the sky.

"Vista Cruiser," Gilbert said. "The perfect car if you've got claustrophobia. It was cheap, and cheap is good if it runs." Putting the car in gear, he let up on the brake, and we drifted out onto the pavement. In a minute or two, we'd reach town, in ten minutes we'd be running parallel to my fences. I slouched down to get comfortable, leaned my head against the door. Gilbert drove with one hand draped over the bottom of the steering wheel. He glanced at me, pursed his lips, and said, "Here we go."

He turned the car, and we stopped. I looked forward over the hood. We faced a barbed-wire fence, a "Posted" sign, a quarter horse standing dumbly fifty yards away, his tail limp, rump to the sun. Then we lurched backward, gained the pavement again, and Gilbert headed west, moving fast. I sat straight up, and as we passed the rock wall I'd rested on just after sunrise, I finally said, "Where are we going?" We covered new ground, left the section of spruce woods and rose over rounded hills dotted with sage.

"To Jackson. You want to? By the looks of you, you could use a vacation. A little pick-me-up to a place with more than one corner. I hate to go alone. After Jackson, I'm thinking of Craters of the Moon. I got a pamphlet on it. Here." He took it off the dash and slid it into my lap. "Blue pentstemons and purple lupines on the old hard lava flows—it sounds lovely. And these empty lava tubes run along beneath the surface—you can climb down ladders where the roofs have caved in and walk through the rock tunnels like you're headed for hell." He landed his hand on my knee and squeezed a few pulses. "You can hold the torch while I scratch on the wall."

"No, I don't think so." I leaned my knee away.

"But you *said* you didn't have to be anywhere today, didn't you?" He grasped my shoulder, shook me, and made me look at him. His eyes worked on me while they darted at the increasingly winding road. "Are you feeling all right? I thought this would be fun for you. Come on. Be a sport, boy. Be a good boy. No whining." Then his hand snapped to the wheel, and with the sound of flying gravel he swerved back fully onto the pavement.

"Okay, okay," I said, and I watched the road, watched his hands as they controlled the wheel. In Jackson, there would be plenty of opportunity to catch a ride home. As he put miles behind us, I gradually settled down into the seat again. "I guess I really wasn't going anywhere in particular."

"It didn't seem so."

"No one will be looking for me. They know what to do."

"I hear you, boy."

"Nothing can go wrong over just one single day. Nothing can go seriously wrong."

"Of course not."

"I mean, how many years have I kept an eye on things without taking a step away?" He glanced at me, smiled sympathetically, and waited. The noise of the engine came into the silence. "I just think," I said slowly, "that a ride to Jackson would be all right."

"Good. Good for you." He reached back over the seat, flashed his head around for a dangerous moment, and then pulled something from a paper bag and handed it to me. "Drink this."

I opened the ginger ale and took a swallow, drank it quickly. Gilbert reached back again and produced an apple. He rubbed it on his pant leg and handed it to me. "Eat," he said. "Good boy."

I took a bite, another. As we rose toward the high meadows, approaching the pass, Gilbert began to drive more smoothly, the car straining up the incline. The Wind River was an icy creek, a black line across the scrub.

"Isn't this nice," Gilbert said. "I tell you, boy. A clear day. A road. You get away much? Ever go to Jackson?"

"Not too often."

"Too bad. I think it does a man good to get away. Finally. Forever. You've never traveled?"

"I hike."

"With that friend of yours? Sam? He seems like the type who'd hang close to your hip and build a good fire."

"No. Alone. Sam's new."

"Fresh?"

"He's a new hand."

"Good for you. And me." He snapped his fingers in front of my face, and I looked at him. "I'm a new hand. Aren't I something you could prize?" He tapped the dash and let out with a clipped, high moment of his chant. Glancing from the road to me, he smiled broadly, shifted his shoulders in an awkward imitation of his dance of the night before, the bold dance. Watching him try to perform while strapped by the seat belt, I thought that now, sober and brightly lit, he might be amusing.

The trees were becoming shorter, stunted. Heavy patches of snow still clung to south-facing banks, but flowers were bright where the sun was full. The Pinnacles came up on the right, the massive rock cliffs split into towers at the top.

"I tell you," he laughed. "I got plans. Get away. Stir things." He slapped his thigh, whistled sharply when we reached the summit of the pass and started down. "Keep going till something stops you. Love. Luck. Change something. White boy."

He talked with a rhythm, softly and gradually without words. I must have fallen asleep sometime before the sharp young teeth of the Tetons came into view.

I awoke to an empty car, the engine vibrating silently. Sitting up, I tried to place myself. Shadow fell across the car from an overhang, and there was a wall of mirrored windows, credit card symbols—the Teton Crest Lodge, in Jackson, seventy miles from home.

It was nearing noon, and the day was still clear. A couple with daypacks wandered past on the sidewalk. I picked up the empty ginger ale bottle from the seat beside me and started to peel the label. The car was warm, the space close around me, the engine soothing. It would have been difficult to have suddenly thrown the door open, jumped to my feet, made a run for it, difficult for a man with little sleep. Easier to wait for Gilbert's return, and then I could say my good-bye and spend some time in town before looking for a ride home.

With the window rolled down, I inhaled, the air tinged with exhaust but still with the spark of spring warmth. I slumped back into the green vinyl. David would have loaded the bales by now, and he'd be in town looking for Betty. Maybe they'd pack a lunch and hike up to Louise Lake, across the logjam above the waterfall, squint across the lake toward the ice, cirques, cliffs above. And Sam would be resting, sitting at the edge of the creek behind his trailer, his eyes closed, thinking of granite forced to great elevation. His hand might land on his ribs and press, testing the location of a bruise, something he'd have to point to twice when he showed it to me, soon as I saw him, tomorrow. "Blue," he'd say, "where were you yesterday? I called. I wanted to come over, show you something I found on my maps. Here. Is this a lake? I'm not sure. Seems to me that the ink might've bled where the stream takes a sharp turn. Tell me."

Straight ahead, over rooftops, the ski slopes cut through the forest on the hills close to town, bright green grass in steep meadows. In all my life, I'd made it to Jackson just a few times a year, in no need of the skiing, the galleries, ice cream, traffic. Red lights make you stop, always the joke, and why stop? But sitting in that car, the engine idling, I felt warm, not ready to move yet.

I pictured the rancher or logger or tourist who would agree to drive me home, the darkness that would fall on the ride over the pass, the green glow of the illuminated dashboard, the radio pulling in faint rock and roll from Los Angeles, and, finally, the brief stretch of orange streetlights through town, then darkness again, the ranch. No telling who had missed me, whose knuckles had pounded on my door, what images had come to mind as they wondered where I'd gone.

Gilbert stepped from the motel office, smiling, his hand

35

flying high over his head. He held a room key out and shook it as he approached, enjoying himself, stopped beside the car and stretched, his head rolling back and around, his chest thrust forward. He put on a show for someone. No one passed on the sidewalk.

He pulled the door open, his turquoise belt buckle at eye level, and bent down. His hair fell straight away from his face. "Be a good boy," he said with his rich laugh. "Sleepyhead." His hand gripped my shoulder and shook me gently. "Poor thing. You look dead." My feet were tight in my boots, my thighs heavy. His eyes blinked slowly. "Park the car and bring in my bag, will ya, boy? Room 25." He said it straight, his voice slightly raised, like a mother with eyes on something else. Then he walked away, his shoulders shifting forward, back. An unusual softness about him, not purely soft.

I pulled the door closed and slid across the seat, put the car into gear, and parked it. It wouldn't be much just to carry his bag. A few more hours and I'd be home, nothing to keep me from sleeping right through the night.

When I stood at the open doorway with his bag, he was closed off behind the bathroom door. The two double beds with white covers sat side by side beneath huge blue glass light fixtures, with fuming Old Faithful framed above one bed and the solid square face of Mount Moran above the other. Dropping the bag, I pushed the door closed with my back. The room smelled of pine and cigarettes. Water ran in the bathroom, pulsing and gurgling down the drain. I pictured Gilbert scrubbing his face with a tiny bar of flowered soap, the bubbles sliding over his skin, clinging in airy clumps to the tips of his black hair.

At the desk, I watched myself in the mirror, my eyes wide and red, watched the reflection of the bathroom door. When the water cut off, I stepped to the front door, opened it, squinted into the bright sun, and then turned back around and leaned against the doorjamb, waiting to see him again, to say good-bye.

The bathroom door squealed on its hinges, and Gilbert faced me, hands on his hips. He shook back his hair and puck-

36

ered his lips. "I feel like a new man. Try it. Jump on in." Stepping forward, he paused at the mirror, looked at himself for a few long seconds, and glanced at me. "Please. Come in out of the sun. Wash your face. You *know* you want to. You *know* you feel dirty."

He was right. I felt dirty. Reasonable. True. Moving past him and into the bathroom, I hunched at the sink, washed my face with cold water, watched the dirt darken the porcelain, took a few deep, sucking swallows from the faucet, and dried myself on a stiff towel. With my skin chilled and tight, I felt better.

He lay on the Old Faithful bed and looked at the ceiling, his hands behind his head. Before I left, I wanted to say something, make him look at me. But I also wanted to take off my boots, roll down my socks, rub the soles of my feet. I tried to think of something to say, something he might say, something he might try to shock me with, tried to imagine the shape of his mouth around the words, but I struggled.

Gilbert raised his head, patted the mattress, and said, "Better? Lie down." He wriggled, and the bed quivered slightly, the only sound the flap on his open hand on the white bedspread.

As he lay there waiting, I lost whatever thought I'd had, whatever words I'd begun to form, and I took a step, said, "Good-bye, Gilbert."

"Oh, please." He rose to his feet and stood between me and the door.

"I have to find a lift home."

His hand landed on my shoulder, and I gauged the pressure—firm. His tongue tipped out and wet his lower lip. "Okay, boy. I'll walk you." He tugged at my elbow, a gentle guidance toward the door. Pulling back from his hold, I followed him outside, out where he moved, I moved behind, in bright sunlight. We walked the back streets, passed the motels, vacation houses, a brick apartment building, trimmed bushes. He had straightened himself into a regular man with long strides, and even though his hair blew down against his shoulders, I thought that he could probably cover a lot of ground on legs like that,

that he might not tire easily, had possibly hiked all the miles he could on the reservation and now wanted to find something different.

"You don't have to come," I said. "I'm just going to look around for a while, and then hang out at a gas station to find someone going east."

"Hang out at a gas station? Tacky. But resourceful. I approve." In step, he reached back, tapped my arm, nodded, continued. "I'll sightsee with you. Okay? I'm heading on tomorrow, myself, after I see what trouble I can get into. You could come along. You want to? You could run away with me. Ever thought of just running off without telling anyone?"

The highway curved west with the Snake River, into the brief jumble of Idaho Falls, and then flat out across the Snake River Basin, steep mountain ranges like green stone clouds passing to the north, and the sun falling off toward a cold ocean still a thousand miles ahead.

"I've never thought of running away," I said.

"Of course you haven't." Pausing, he looked at me without blinking, full on me. "But this is your opportunity. A good one."

"Things are fine. I'm fine."

"Good for you. Yes. I'm sorry. You do what you want."

He walked faster, and I hurried to keep up, to watch his steps, the swaying of his hands at his sides. We came to the Jackson town square, antlers piled in arches at each corner of the green, a bronze cowboy, a stagecoach offering rides, blinkered chestnut mare in harness. Gilbert crossed the street to the grass, and I followed. The air was warm and even, almost skin temperature. Traffic rumbled, circling the square, the lines of cars driving north to the Tetons and Yellowstone or west into Idaho. Beside a fat spruce, Gilbert sat himself on the grass and patted the ground. "I hate good-byes," he said. "Sit and tell me something. Tell me a story." His eyes were back on me, and then they closed.

A few yards away, a tourist in a red running suit stopped and focused his camera above us, taking in the cowboy statue and an antler arch and the storefronts—the poster gallery, lunch shop, clothing boutique. If he'd lowered the lens, he'd have seen me, no ten-gallon on my head, no chaps, just jeans worn shiny at the crotch from the saddle, mud in the crook of my boots, and eyes focused not on the great wide-open West, the mountains and the herd, but on this plumpish Indian sitting at my feet. In the slow warmth of the afternoon, with Gilbert waiting, I sat down, faced him, and felt the coolness of the grass press into my palms and through the seat of my pants.

"I don't have any story, Gilbert."

His eyes opened. "No story? Nothing? A man like you, out walking the highway first thing in the morning? There's a story there, I'm sure of it."

"I was just walking."

"Then you're a sorry case. All revved up with nowhere to go. Why don't you come with me?"

"I have to get back."

"Leave it."

"I have to get back tonight. At a certain point, people count on me."

"Everyone's their own man. Now, me, I'm going to Craters of the Moon. You should come along."

"I have a job."

"A job." He paused, leaned toward me, slid a foot into the shadow of my bent legs. "I'm going to Craters of the Moon to get out on the lava fields, and I'm going to find the circles of boulders, the windbreaks left by people like me, years ago. I want to sit in one of those circles and light a fire. Burn some candy wrappers and tissues. If I hear any spirits, I'll hang around and listen. The spirits would say, 'Rise up, child. Go out into the world and heal someone or make corn grow or be fruitful.' Something like that could make a guy think twice. Keep him from stepping in a hole."

Then he was silent for a minute, watching the cars pass, before he lay out fully on the grass, his eyes roving beneath closed lids. His lips shifted to the slight curve of a smile.

I had been places. I had been to Five Pockets, the valley with the gray cliffs and the five waterfalls like fingers rising from a green palm. After high school graduation, stripped of my clothes, lying in the summer grass and burning myself deeper and deeper brown, I had been up there for a week. At night, I sat beside a small flame and felt the warmth of my clothes as a luxury. I hadn't thought of descending to town. Not yet. My body didn't crave anything.

I heard my father before he arrived. He had tracked me up the valley. My horse, hobbled and deep in grass, raised his head high, froze, and then whinnied, a shrill, sharp echo that seemed close to cracking the sheer granite walls. Then an answering scream from down past the opening of the valley. Gradually the echo of hooves on the rocky trail moved me up onto my elbows, onto my side. I ran my fingers off through the damp grass and caught hold of my pants, pulled them on slowly, replacing the prickle of grass with the warm denim, closed myself off. Falling back, flat, I watched the broad orange heat of the sun through closed lids, listened, dozed.

My father arrived. I opened my eyes, sat up, and he dropped my shirt into my lap. "That's enough," he said. He laid out lunch—cold fruit, cuts of cheese and salami, bread ripped from a thin loaf—and we ate slowly, attracting a gray jay that caught bits of food in midair. "This is it," he said. "I got you a job at the Fisher Ranch. You start tomorrow. It'll be no problem for you. I'm packing up. I'll be gone in a week. It's up to you to keep our name in this town."

I watched Gilbert. He might have been asleep. Sam had watched him, Sam's shoulder against me, leaning into me, saying yes to the marshy meadow and the white stars of the skunk cabbage blossoms and the long steady bullfrog cry.

Five years of treks farther and farther out into the narrow granite valleys that held dark water and golden trout and lichen and me naked in the sun, the last five years alone. At night, I curled my sleeping bag into the lee of boulders and listened. Maybe I heard what Gilbert would hear. Maybe something I heard had caught up with me. Three years ago, when I'd broken my ankle, far back in at Five Pockets again, I'd waited out a night, in pain, sleepless, thinking I could leave town anytime, go anywhere, any state, any city, but where? I always ended up far from light, solitary, miles into mountains on familiar trails. Sam, too, wanted to be far back in the high country, far from light. Gilbert wanted to build a fire on a plain of black rock and listen for voices to tell him what to do. Lying awake, with my broken bone throbbing, I hadn't thought of anywhere to go but out where I'd be alone, up high, above it.

"Tell me where you're going," I said.

Gilbert sat up. "Going? Craters of the Moon. Are you coming along?"

"I mean, where are you going after that?"

"I don't know. Far. But maybe I'll crash my car tomorrow. Maybe I'll slit someone's throat. How do you think I'd look in prison gray?"

"I mean, what do you want?"

"I just want to get away." Lying back again, he shut his eyes tight, and his breathing slowed. I counted the breaths, watched his chest expand, fall.

His voice, silent now, edged me, continued in my ears like a river droning outside a window, but it wasn't like running water—water flows along the lay of the land, but Gilbert didn't follow a course. Now he was sleeping. I pictured him combing his hair. I thought of costumes that could wrap him, give him a place in a ceremony, a performance. Feathers to lift his weight, beads to distract from his dance and his song. His tongue clicked. He danced in a line of women. But he wasn't a woman. His clothes trailed behind his limbs as he proceeded, the cloth swayed and moved, delayed, making him hazy, indistinct. Then his hands flew up, clapped. The men beat on the large drum with long sticks, droned in their deep voices. Gilbert might have been chanting with their buried song, but then his voice sliced up through the ceremony, alone above it all. His fingers snapped. His blue veins laced his knuckles.

41

With the cars circling the square and Gilbert close to me on the grass, I lay back. It reminded me of something I must have always missed—the sound of someone breathing as I dozed, heavy and drained.

I thought of the first and only cougar, two years ago, a line of prints in the soft ground along twenty yards of the Glacier Trail. Chuck Smith had been up at the glacier for a few days, painting simple watercolors, the pale blue water of the glacial lakes diving to darkness beneath the ice. Leading his packhorse down along the trail, he paused to examine the tracks, laid his hand out fully on the imprint of the paw, held it there in the damp brown soil until a chill began to tighten his flesh. He told a few friends—me, Alison, Hanna and Gardelle, Christy, Doug. The cougar wandered the trails we had known throughout our lives, traced our steps for a few yards before turning off, catching a scent, following its own invisible, unimaginable instincts. It drank from water that would rise through our wells. It found shelter from rain that pelted our roofs. It stalked bighorns, deer, a young elk. Its jaws tightened, blood rose into its mouth, its throat.

Derek heard about the cougar—an accident—news travels. He came down out of the mountains with it draped over his packhorse, tied on among tent, grill, lantern. The taxidermist mounted the carcass. Derek had tracked the animal, centered it, shot.

When I awoke, with the sun low and Gilbert standing over me, after having slept in the open square for what must have been hours, my head cleared. Rising onto my elbows, I tried to focus on Gilbert. He shifted, the sun behind him, and darkened, turned faceless. I imagined him dancing, pulling Derek around, pressing his pointed finger past Derek's lips, sending Derek away. Gilbert had moved with ease, snaking, chanting on and on as if he'd memorized it all as part of a game. I wondered where his game came from, if I could pin down the moves, if the moves were anything I needed or could learn. I should have left then, should have pulled myself to my feet and gone home. Listening for his voice, I heard only the engines of the cars that circled us. If he spoke—perhaps he'd been speaking to me for hours as I slept—I knew his voice would seem familiar now. He'd say something about luck, about fire. Knowing I should move, not wanting to rouse myself, I watched his shadowed face carefully, wondering what steps I could take to send him away without caring.

"I want a meal," Gilbert said. "Can I buy you dinner? I want to treat you. Something special. Celebrate. I'm so far from home. You, too." With his hands on his hips, he leaned forward over me, nudged my leg with his foot. "Something sweet in your stomach. Something cold." He messed with my hair, pushed my head from side to side roughly. An odd figure, extra flourishes, he walked away, kept talking. "Here. Or here. We eat. Take care of that and move on to something else. Boy. Come on."

The salad arrived, and we started eating. I watched Gilbert's loose hold on his fork, watched a crouton fall to the tabletop and bounce out of sight, and Gilbert's lips closed quickly over the tines and glistened with a few spots of vinegar and oil. He'd been telling me about how he and his mother had moved off the reservation to the edge of Lander when he was young, how he'd visited his grandmother and uncle occasionally on the reservation over the years, how he'd moved to his grandmother's house after college to live with her and his uncle. "My Uncle Gordon was the gentlest man you'd ever want to know." His hands moved distantly in the air. First lifting the carafe and holding it against the light, tilting it from side to side, he poured himself another glass of wine, replaced the few sips I'd taken from my glass. "Drink up, boy."

It was getting late, and I knew that I should be moving soon. Gilbert was oddly subdued. I wondered how long dinner would take. I was hungry, but I wanted to get on the road. And then Gilbert reached across the table, laid his hand on mine, said, "Hear me, Blue?" He pulled his hand back, watched me steadily, in silence for a minute, his eyes held open. "My uncle always wanted me to live on the reservation with him," he said, careful, smooth, "but we'd soured our luck."

Gilbert's mouth, open, the wet red and darkness straight down into his throat. His teeth clamped across the black in a quick, white smile. His hand sliding toward mine, stopping, his attention locked on me, back on me.

"My uncle died a short while ago," he continued. "He was in the hospital for a few days before he went. I brought Gran to see him. She rubbed the backs of his hands as they talked, their own language, never harsh. When he died, Gran loosened her braid and her hair came out in a wavy mass on her shoulders. She kept patting his hands. She cried when I drove her and the body back to her house, the house by the gully in the outwash plain, below the mountains. She cut her hair and ripped a sleeve from her dress, then laid them both at the foot of Uncle Gordon's bed. We dressed him in his Sunday suit, a dark brown cotton with wooden buttons, put his whitest shirt on him, and his red tie with the American flag clip. Handsome, the same suit he wore at my college graduation—in the photo on his dresser, I cooled our eyes in the shade of my mortar board. After a day of waiting—my mother wouldn't come onto the reservation—Gran and I took the dead body up the hill to a hole I'd dug. When we got him down in there—Gran put her cut hair in his suit pockets before we closed him off—we piled on rocks and some thorny branches to keep the coyotes from digging. Then Gran and I walked along the foothills to the hot spring and took a swim, rubbed each other's backs and arms with black dirt from the bottom, rinsed off and then dried in the breeze.

"We sat at the grave each day and Gran cried. At night she burned some leaves in a clay pot. She made only a little food. No one came to visit. One morning, when she had finished crying, she brought me a bowl with thick red liquid in it and asked me to paint her. I spread the color on her face and hair. She sat out in the sun all day. Then she braided what was left of her hair."

His hand pulled back, eyes closed slowly and came open. I

could picture each step they had taken—I knew the country, knew the steepness of the hills, the moist ground that stayed cool in the depth of gullies, the rusted cup of rock that held a hot spring—but I was unsure of why Gilbert's eyes had toughened, set straight, when he'd spoken of lowering his uncle into the ground. My own mother, beneath short grass and rocky soil in the cemetery above town, was likely to make my eyes twitch, at least once, when the burial came to mind, was likely to soften me.

I drank from a glass of cold water and watched the waitress hurry among the tables, watched the families with infants in earrings, and waited for the wagon-wheel chandeliers to grow brighter as the daylight faded. Gilbert raised his wineglass to his lips and held it there, and his eyes darted across the other customers, then back to me briefly, before he took a swallow. "Sad story?" he said. He grasped the carafe and tried to give me more wine, succeeded only in spilling a few drops on the back of my hand as I blocked my glass. "You take hold of what you can reach," he said. His hand came toward me again, his tongue pressed against the back of his teeth.

The waitress brought the main course, and Gilbert pulled back. She put our plates on the table and stood waiting for us to speak. Looking from me to Gilbert and back, she smiled, and her head lolled to the side. She was probably a kid who'd come in to work for the tourist season. "You tell me if you want anything, gentlemen," she said, her voice drawn out with extra syllables, an edge of Southern. I thought she might talk long distance each night to a sweetheart, or might write a daily letter. She wouldn't leave us until I took up my fork, and still she looked back at us, at me for a longer second, at Gilbert for a last glance.

He pulled himself up, finished his wine and poured another glass, and started to investigate his food. "We're here to have some fun, now, aren't we, boy?" he said. "A good meal."

"Sure."

"And then we take the next step, whatever that is. Yes?"

"I'm going home."

"And I'm going somewhere—I don't know. I want to do something with my body. Listen to this—this is what I want—" He sliced across his steak, and his fork sank into an inch of fat and pushed it aside. In the air before him, his knife kept rhythm with his voice. "I want to sit in the back of a Greyhound bus at night and roll a rubber over my prick while everyone sleeps. Leave the used thing in the sink for some sleepy-eyed boy to stumble back and find. Let him push it aside and get some of me on him before he's even realized what it is or what he's done. He'd never know me. I'd know *him,* keep his fingers and arms and ears and chin in mind all the way to the end of America. That's not asking too much, is it? A simple ambition." His fork darted across the table and tapped the edge of my plate. "Come on, dig in."

Things happen too quickly. I would have taken some time to conjure his uncle, to decipher the funeral ceremony, but it was lost and I was faced with his increasing volume, new looseness, slipping back toward his game. I took a few bites, cutting my way into the center of the steak. A voice raised harmlessly outside becomes a shout inside. We all sat in our seats at the tables, eating and drinking, listening to the piped music made vague by the voices, the scrape of silver on plates, none of us going anywhere until our meals were consumed. "This is what I want," I said. "I want you to keep your voice down, please."

"Dear boy," he whispered loudly, shaking a finger. "Be good."

"Just try to keep quiet, please," I said. "That's all I want."

His face hardened, and I waited for him to break, to start in on another of his stories, but he said, "You're serious? I'm just *talking.*" His face turned slowly away, and his final word went out around the room.

A woman at the next table brought her bluish face toward us, then turned back to her table and rearranged her silverware. I focused on the center of Gilbert's chest and sat forward. "Please."

His utensils clinked out of his grasp. With his voice lowered, he said, "Be a good boy. I'm celebrating. Let a guy have some fun. We're on the verge of something." He held his glass up toward me and took a swallow. "Either you're coming with me, running away, or you're going back to your hermit den. I know you'll choose right."

I thought of my cabin standing in plain sight among the buildings on the ranch. I had my pine chest, the rows of true white socks, fireplace, window open to a hint of river chill, door unlocked if someone should stop by. "I'm not a hermit," I said, and I heard the short edge to my voice.

"Let me guess then. You're a murderer. You killed someone with a hot poker. With a branding iron. You beat someone with one of those things till he died. Look at me and tell me you didn't." He stared at me, hard and serious, and his knife stabbed toward me in the air.

"I didn't," I said, holding my hand up flat toward his knife.

"Then what the hell's your problem, boy?" He tapped my plate again with his fork. "You follow me around. You look like a spark would blow you away. You won't stay, you won't go. You've got something unpleasant going on in your head. Am I safe?"

"I'm fine. I've always been fine." I'd never been a danger to anyone, not one day of my life.

Gilbert's fingers drummed on the back of my hand, the nails pressing a dull red line onto my skin. "What is it, baby?" he said. "Tell me." His hair drooped forward from his face as he leaned to get his voice closer. "Tell." His eyes closed us away together.

Sam sat at the edge of the creek. His maps were cleanly folded. As the sun began to set and the air cooled beside the water, Sam rose, walked to his trailer, watched darkness fall, listened to cars on the road, music from the other trailers. Maybe he reached for the telephone, dialed, prepared to ask me a question about riding lines. "You said Sam wasn't hurt?"

Gilbert sat back heavily. "Don't worry about him. I told you. Everything's fine."

47

"But what happened?"

"Listen, dear, you're miles away. It's all over. You're safe and happy with me now. So take what you want. You want the rest of my potato? Something to drink?" There was a solid blackness in his steady eyes, locked hard across the space between us, set like quartz in the ridges of his face, above the fissure of lips.

"Please," I said. "Be quiet."

His face softened, went blank, and he relaxed. "Be a good boy and eat your vegetables."

I pulled my feet straight under my chair. Maybe I'd eaten enough, but as he worked at finishing his meal, I found myself eating more, everything. Keeping my eyes off him, I watched the headlights pass outside the window. A woman and two tall children, all in matching T-shirts, peered in at the window, read the menu, and headed on around the square. Who might be driving over the pass at this hour? A trucker, maybe a local, probably too late for tourists. A moose or deer would stand frozen in the beam of the headlights, then leap into brush, run a few yards, pause to look back and watch the passage.

The waitress left the check. "I've got to get going," I said as Gilbert dropped some money on the table. "Thanks for dinner."

"Don't go."

"It's getting late."

"Wait a minute," he said, waving me back down into my seat as he took the carafe, poured out the last half glass, and toasted me. "You're a sweet guy, Blue."

"Thank you."

"I mean it. You've kept me good company. Tell the truth, I'd like you to fuck-it-all and come with me. Partners. But I'm being silly, eh, white boy?" He swallowed the rest of the wine, put down the glass, and held out his hand to shake.

I took his hand, shook it. "You're being silly, Gilbert," I said, but as I smiled and tried to back out of the handshake, his hand suddenly opened, slid forward, and took my wrist. He held me.

48

With his free hand he pushed my plate, and the cold curved rim slid over the edge of the table and pressed into my chest. "You want to know what you want?" he said, and one eye closed halfway as he grinned slightly. "I'll tell you. You want to get that little Sam boy down and give him the once over. You want to screw him, probably by the edge of a rushing mountain stream. I know that's what you want. Anyway, I think you're missing a hell of an opportunity with me. I mean, I know what I'm doing. We could get some luck going. I know what I want." His grip tightened, and he pulled my fist toward him across the table.

I looked up at the chandeliers, and the lights were bright white. It seemed forever since I'd lain beneath stars—the scent of a pine, the lee of a boulder with the fire dying a few feet away. I pulled against his hold on me, and as I rose an inch, leaned toward him, I said, "That's the end, Gilbert. Good-bye."

"Okay. Sorry." He released me, smiled, rolled his eyes, waved me off. "Bye-bye."

I walked among the tables, toward the door, out onto the sidewalk. I had to think for a minute which direction would be best, where I could find what I wanted, a ride, but as I watched cars pass, bright lights and red tails, someone, Gilbert, linked his arm through mine, put his chin on my shoulder, and said, "Be a good boy—I don't want much." He took my hand, turned me to face him. "No hard feelings. Have a drink with me. One drink."

"No."

"Please. Boy. I'll be alone from now on. Help me postpone."

"No."

"Twenty minutes." He held his hands at his sides, palms flat and facing me, and took a step back. "I'll be good."

If I threatened him, would he fight? I was sure I could push him off with a single shot. He stood absolutely still, silent, waiting for me to act. Something he'd said returned, something I'd only half heard as he'd rambled about his youth, or it might have drifted out then, on the sidewalk, from his calmed, smooth face—"I remember walking down from the hot spring with my uncle. I placed my arm around his shoulder and brushed my lips against his ear. There were broken veins that formed a sort of web on his nose. Aluminum glinted along the creek." There were other details. I stood facing Gilbert, eye to eye, close in the darkness, with the sounds of traffic and the night air cooling. "He loved a boy who played on the green fields behind the school. He would follow the kid out along the dirt roads. He got courage and caught up with the kid one day and told him that he had money, that he had come up with a magical name for him, that he could cook and weave. The kid beat him. Maybe it was my fault. Gordon and me had no business being together, uncle and nephew. The kid couldn't have known that Gordon was a prize."

I could make little sense of what he said—yes, he spoke then, eyes moving over me. I imagined his words, leaned forward to keep his voice close, to cut him off. Sam, he'd say. You want something from Sam. But he said, "Won't you come with me?" He turned and walked away.

No magic. I could push him away. I followed. He turned off the square, a half block, and passed through a door beneath a bank of white lights. Inside, a dim room, music. I'd never seen such clean hats. Along the bar, posted on stools, men in crisp ten-gallons drank beer, and a few women sat in a booth. A man and woman danced with arms linked loosely around each other, leaning from side to side with the beat. Above it all, set among lines of green neon, black-and-white photographs hung, blown to huge proportion, unshaven faces in the shadow of sweaty rims, dull stars pinned to their clothing. Gilbert kept his momentum going right up to a barstool, landed himself, and patted the empty stool beside him without looking back at me. He waved to the bartender and shouted for two beers.

Standing at the end of the bar, I propped my foot on the bottom rung of the empty stool. "I'm not thirsty."

He twisted his head around and looked at the couple dancing at the back of the bar. "Move, girl. Give him what he paid for." His face came back around slowly, and his mouth prepared, his chin tightened. "Every man should get what he's paid for, don't you think?" He slid a beer toward me. "I've been nice. Haven't I been nice? Calm down. I'm not going to hurt you."

He pulled money from his pocket and dropped it on the bar, took his beer and downed half of it in a few swallows. He leaned far over toward me, pushed my beer into my hand, raised it to my lips, tipped it. More beer went down my chin than into my throat. Taking the beer from my hand, he sipped from it himself, then placed it next to his mug, rolled the mugs together, the handles clinking. He drank, pushed a mug into my hand again.

"I don't want any beer. I don't want anything."

"I'd like to think we're friends."

"There's nothing."

"Fuck it. Of course there's something. Now drink. I bought you a drink and you're going to drink it. You're not leaving until it's gone. Be good."

"You're drunk."

He looked away, looked back, drummed his fingers loudly on the bar. After a frozen second, his mouth forced open. "My people, I've seen them drinking hair spray for the alcohol. Think about that, boy. White boy. You spray that stuff on your beehive and it'll hold you pretty perfect in a tornado, but when you sit down and drink a can, maybe with crushed ice and a twist, you might feel a little better, but your beehive ain't gonna do you no good because you can't get up off the couch—it's like you've been sprayed onto the cushions. You can go where you want, boy, but don't call me drunk, even if I am. I drink. I shouldn't. I know. I've got places to go.

"There was a time when my people had a clear view of things. They'd set up the ceremony for me, for any boy like me, start a fire in the brush, I'd take the grinding stone, step away from the flames, leave the arrow behind. I'd sleep with you, bring you luck. I'm a prize. Supposed to be. Screw it. Of course you fall to drinking and tearing the boards off those houses the government slaps up—those houses all bowl-cleaner blue, salmonella pink, shades so strong they'd knock you blind."

He went silent, drank again, seemed angry, but he smiled. "You want some luck, some magic," he said.

"I don't want anything from you. I have everything I need."

"Sure you do. I envy you for what you think you have. None of us has what he wants. You have to know that by now, or you wouldn't be watching me. You must know the way things were, the way they ought to be, the way it was before you white guys twisted what was natural. If you don't understand me, then why do you listen to me?"

He ordered another beer, cupped the mug in his full hands when it arrived, drank deeply. "You see," he said, "to get right down to it, there was this thing called a berdache, not a thing, a person, a sort of male squaw, and they were nothing odd, they were even kind of sought out, and they'd dress like they weren't male and they weren't female, and a man would take this berdache as a wife as if it were something special, a real honor, a real thrill in the crotch."

He pushed my beer into my hand and curved my fingers around the glass. I managed to free myself and drink on my own. "Gilbert," I said, and my foot dropped off the rung of the stool. "I don't want to hear your story."

"But that's just it, boy. You don't want to hear it. You white guys ignored it, like it wasn't a story at all. Fuck it. These berdaches weren't just different. They were magic, the center of ceremonies, making rain, healing, spiritual power. You see, if you want a good crop or some rain showers, you take a berdache, at night preferably, knowing that darkness always adds to even the dullest events—but this isn't dull, it's great in the dark—and you light a fire and put this guy in the center of a circle and you bring out the warriors, start the drums, young warriors, and they start dancing around the berdache, and then they screw the berdache to make the magic." He shifted far over toward me, held a finger across his lips, removed it, sat up square again. "Not like I've ever made it rain or gotten banged by a war party or

brought anyone luck. It's not like that anymore, not since berdache became faggot." His voice trailed off, and he finished his
beer, reached for mine and downed the last inch in the bottom.

"I have to go," I said. "I want—"

"What do you want, boy?"

"I want to get home."

"No. I have what you want. You aren't gonna get what you
want from that Sam—he's nothing, he's a cute child. You aren't
gonna get what you want till someone like me makes something
of you. I'll give you luck. Don't you want to be what you want
to be?"

"I don't want to be anything like you."

"Then I was wrong. I've wasted my time."

His profile fell behind his hair as he leaned forward and
touched his tongue to the lip of his mug. Then he slid along the
bar to the next stool, brought his knees against a man's thighs.
What was to keep him from forcing his fingers behind the man's
buttons? What was to keep me from the clear path to the door?
I saw Gilbert and Sam dancing the night before, back in the bar
in the mountains, back home, their hands on each other, Sam
trying to keep up, off-balance. Gilbert moved in grand sweeps on
a beat I couldn't find, moving like he was somewhere else, somewhere outside his man's body. His hair couldn't have been more
liquid or more black.

Gilbert's hand moved in the air behind the man next to
him. His fingers played, stretched, then pressed firmly into the
flesh of the man's lower back. The man's shoulders tipped away.
The bartender stopped, his hand on the draft tap, and his eyes
rested on Gilbert, lips drew thin. Gilbert removed his hand,
raised it slowly, placed it on the man's shoulder, tipping him
level again. Jerking out from under the touch, the man grasped
for his hat as it fell from his head to the floor, and then his hand
shot to Gilbert's upper arm, gripped him, Gilbert's white shirt
puffing softly above and below the man's tight fingers. Gilbert
looked back over his shoulder, his eyes hard on me, reflections of
the overhead lights.

In the motel, Gilbert stepped from the bathroom, paused, and slowly turned around. He was almost completely without hair except for sparse black tangles at the crotch and hidden away beneath his arms, and the long slick black that fell in excess between his shoulder blades. Unmarked. Nothing to break the deep supple tan of his skin, as if nothing could touch him. His nipples, slack and large and slightly protruding, disappeared beneath the loose muscle of his biceps as he pulled his arms in tight and covered his crotch. With a flimsy smile, he said, "Don't look," and then his hands went back up and he spun. "They doused you," he said. "I bet we could wring a few good swallows out of those clothes. Come on. Strip down. Nothing worse than being all clammy with beer."

He reached for my buttons, but I stepped away a half turn, unfastened them myself, slipped my shirt off and let it fall. Gilbert came up behind me, and his hair brushed the small of my back as he dipped to grab my shirt. "Come here," he said as he walked into the bathroom and dropped the shirt into the sink. "We'll assess the damage." He ran the water and held the cloth beneath the stream, swished it and squeezed. "Now," he said as he wrung the shirt out and draped it over the towel rack, "now let's see about you, boy." His fingers grazed my ribs, and his touch stung where the skin had scraped away into patches of hardening blood.

In the bar, a balled fist had taken Gilbert on the shoulder, and he lay on the stained floorboards, his feet tangled in the rungs of the stool. As the sharp toe of a boot pressed into the flesh at his waist, his eyes sealed shut.

My hand took the man's arm below the elbow and clenched it tightly as I watched his hand spread wide and retract gradually into a fist again, a fist that thrust toward my gut as the man reeled to face me. I knew the feel of it, had faced guys one-on-one before, part of every boy's life in a town where you know each face, each name, and they all know you, where you all shift from friend to fight and back again in long cycles, no avoiding it. So it was a familiar rush of blood up the back of my neck that straightened me, a tightening of my gut to receive the blow, and then the rapid advance into the fight as our fists made quick work and pushed off. The man's sweat rose in a line of beads above his eyebrows and shook free. His eyes flashed, white, and we were finished. But before I could take Gilbert's hand and get him to his feet, some other guys advanced on me.

As Gilbert slept, his breath rumbling, unsteady, I dragged his suitcase into the bathroom and dug through stacks of pants in black and blue, shirts with red parrots and delicate turquoise stripes, boot socks, hand-painted T-shirts, black leather sneakers. No underwear. The shirt smelled of perfumed soap. His pants were too short by an inch, too broad by a few, as I cinched them with my own belt.

TWO

I caught a ride in a pickup headed east toward home, sat in the back among boxes and overstuffed chairs all the way over Togwotee Pass, slid through the silent town under the stark orange street-lights, rode on in the first hint of dawn, still far ahead across the plains beyond Crowheart Butte. When I tapped on the cab window, the driver stopped, and I stepped onto the gravel at the edge of the road in front of the main gate, Fisher Ranch.

I took a length of heavy rope from the workshop, pulled the dirt bike from the shed behind the granary, kicked the engine started, and headed back through town, up Horse Creek Road, and accelerated over the twin dirt ruts toward the cow camp. Over the narrow valley floor, the sage lay in a silver-green coat, and its rich leaves slashed at me, its heavy smell clung to my pants as I leaned the bike into the turns. The Anderson homestead, choked and crumbled among thorny branches, flashed past through the thickening pine forest. Then I rose over the final ridge, passed the row of white aspen pillars ring-ing the pond, and came into the hollow at the head of the val-ley. I jumped the edge of the road and let the engine die in the grass beside my truck.

In the silence of the windless dawn, the quick beats of my footsteps seemed close. I hurried to fix the rope to the winch on the truck's front bumper, scrabbled over rock to find a tree trunk or boulder where I could anchor the other end of the rope. The truck's engine roared, I flipped the switch, the winch started to grind, and I freed the truck from the mud I'd driven into in darkness.

Loading the bike into the back of the truck, I drove on down the last two hundred yards toward the cow camp, stopped beside the cabin long enough to jump out and scoop a handful of cold water from the channel that ran from the spring, long enough to swallow it and feel it tingle my empty stomach. I turned the truck around. As I headed up the hill and skirted the mud, I caught the cabin's green asphalt roof in the rearview mirror for a second before descending from the high country.

At the intersection of Horse Creek Road and the street through the center of town, I paused beside the taxidermist's blank side door and leaned forward over the steering wheel to glance left and right. A few trucks and cars lined the sidewalk in front of the mercantile and the cafe. They were mostly tourists, but I recognized two vehicles. That would be Alan Miller stopping for a bite before the long drive up to the fish hatchery, and Henry Rich pausing to chat or eat or buy new sunglasses before opening the gas station just a few harmless minutes late. I turned east and drove straight through town and down along the Wind River.

The worn ridges of the badlands along the river sat in deep relief against the early angle of the sun. I lowered the visor. John Zimpel's home-built A-frame stood peeling beside his mucky corral. The holes for the upper windows were still covered with plywood. John, raised here like me, had always been focused close—the walls of eroding badlands and the sharp peaks beyond were like air—nourishing, part of him. He didn't need to look at them.

Then the ranch's fields opened out, flashing behind the posts and poles of the tall fence. I passed beneath the crossbar of the main gate, my tires roaring on the steel pipes of the cattle guard, and drove straight toward the five spindly spruces and the river-stone mansion with its curtains all drawn. The Fishers were off to the Andes for a month to look for temples and gold. I wove among the outbuildings—the main barn with the twin doors cracked open, and David already at work, coming out with a bucket and shovel, giving a quick wave, and then the loading chute and the tangle of high fences, the bunkhouse, and the high square wooden base of the windmill, the blades stock-still against the sky. I pulled to a stop near the river's edge and crossed the short stretch of dusty grass to my cabin.

The light followed me in through the door, and I glanced back to where, far across the lower fields, Sam would soon pass through the gate, fresh from checking the pump and the water tank on the property seven miles east along the river. That had been my last instruction on Friday evening before he took off for his trailer in town, before I'd seen him in the bar. He'd speed his jeep around the edge of the fields on the gravel road, park in the shade beside the long low empty bunkhouse, glance at my door, and wonder if he should start something on his own. He'd wait long enough for me to catch sight of him from my window. I'd set him to making preparations for his summer at the cow camp—a list of provisions, the horse trailer, his saddle, the flatbed truck for transporting the cattle. He would want some books to read, batteries for the mouse-nibbled radio, bullets for the .22. I kicked the door shut.

In the mirror over my dresser, I stood in foreign clothes—Gilbert's black pants and blue shirt. With the shirt off over my head, my chest seemed young and stark white against the small brown bumps of my nipples. Turning sideways, I lowered the pants. My eyes had sunk out of recognition, deep in red. I smelled my shoulder, my arm, and there was my own strong and familiar sweat fouled slightly by nerves, and the flowered perfume from the discarded shirt. I scooped the clothes from the floor and tossed them on the bed, where they splayed out. The legs twisted, and the shirt folded over on itself, the sleeves opening empty holes toward me. I grabbed them and aimed for the trash basket in the shadow beneath the window, but I thought how they would fill the basket, poke up into sight, and continue to smell. I stuffed them into the duffel hanging on the nail beside the bathroom door.

In the shower, with the hard stream of hot water flowing over me and my eyes closed against the steam, I slowly leaned into the hardness of the tiles. I saw Gilbert in a different ceremony, not along the river or dancing with women, but up on Crowheart Butte. A bonfire of dry sage crackled, red in the wind, and Gilbert lay on the dirt. There might have been a drum beating, or it was footsteps on the flat ground as if it were hollow below, as if the fire might burn right through and open them all out to nothing. The young warriors moved out with heavy steps, knees raised high and brought down on the ground like a punishment, the men twisting, spinning in on their own progress, circling.

I turned the water cold for a few seconds to wake myself fully, get my blood moving, and then shut it off and stepped out. With the steam wiped from the glass, I faced myself in the mirror, stood up on the edge of the tub to get a full view. My hair was up like horns, cheeks dark with stubble. Dropping the towel, I approached myself, ran my hand up over my chest and tried to gauge the heft of my muscle. The scrapes on my ribs stung as I stretched the skin around them.

In fresh clothes drawn from the closet and dresser, I sat on the edge of my bed, pulled on long white socks, and reached for the warm, sweaty leather of my boots. My fingertips moved over the delicate swirls of the ornamental stitching.

In the motel room, I'd stood wrapped in a towel in the bathroom doorway, my clothes rinsed and wrung out and draped on the shower rod and the towel rack behind me. Gilbert circled around the room, poking through his suitcase, arranging the covers on his bed, leafing through the Bible and dropping it back into the drawer. He hadn't found anything to put on—no shirt or shorts or pajamas, not even a towel around his waist. Falling onto his bed, he lay flat, hands behind his head, and talked to the ceiling. "You'll catch your death out there," he said. "Death or a damn nasty cold. I say you don't tempt fate. You've tested your luck enough for one night. It banged you up. You rest now, boy. You get into your bed and rest. Tomorrow is plenty close."

I climbed beneath the covers and pulled them to my throat. Gilbert rolled onto his side to face me, reached his hand into the gap between the beds and let it hang there, limp and swaying. I didn't move. I looked at his hand, at his feet, at the far wall. I tried to breathe steadily until he rolled onto his back again with a long sigh.

He told me of a man who had not eaten for many days, seeking visions. The sun warmed him, but at night he shivered as he curled naked on the short grass, on the wide plain. He slept with eyes open. Women moved out in a line beneath full moonlight, turned in a circle, their legs long and stepping high, their bellies soft, their hair black as the man's dreams. The women lolled their pink tongues toward the grass as they leaned forward, and their eyes rolled up into an edge of white. They had no mind for anything but the thunder of their circle and the luxurious dust they stirred. The man learned the Buffalo Dance.

Gilbert was up again, standing at the window, parting the curtains to peek at the parked cars and the rooftops and the face of the mountain hazy with the town's glow. He switched off the bathroom light, moved in darkness. His bed shifted and settled, shifted again, and I felt my blanket slide an inch off my shoulder. "Don't, Gilbert," I said, and I heard nothing, felt nothing, until his voice returned, he was moving around the room, had switched on the bathroom light again and sent his shadow here and there. Stories.

He brought something from his suitcase and held it close to my eyes. "A medicine bag," he said. His fingers ran over the beadwork design. "This stripe down the center is the buffalo path. The green part of the stripe is the buffalo. The crosspiece at the top is the bow. The black V's are arrowheads. These are the barbs in the flesh. This is a tall blue sky."

Darkness again, and the drone of his voice. He wouldn't touch me now—he'd pulled down his covers and climbed in, secured himself beneath the blankets. "Listen to this," he said. "Listen to me—" And I did listen, thinking that I could slip away as soon as he passed into dreams. Nothing he could teach me could get me what I wanted. Stories from another world, somewhere far away, something that could only get me hurt.

So in my cabin, home, watching myself in the mirror, I pulled my boots on, stood to settle my weight down into them. My hair, with its slick comb marks, shone like fresh black creosote. Except for my eyes, I might just have woken up and gotten dressed for the day, Monday, with Sam due to arrive and things to be done.

I pushed my keys down into my pocket and took the few long strides through the living room and out the door. My eyes tightened against the glare. David stood away from the barn across the yard, where he'd leaned in the shade, and approached. "Here you are, Blue," he said. "I was thinking maybe you had some trouble now so I started early." His careful whisper. His face came clear against the light, and I saw the long kinky red hairs lining his jaw and the flat broad bump of his nose. His lips were gray with pressure.

"Trouble?"

"Derek's back," he said. "Sheriff let him go last night. Where you been? You been off checking on Sam? Lord knows I like the boy. We was just getting him broke in."

Sam's mouth gaped, his tongue wandered with his raspy breathing. The skin of his face was unbroken, but purple and blue shadows lay clearly beneath the surface like something newly killed beneath a thin layer of snow. The whiteness of the room, the crisp sheets, the limp hanging cloth walls, sharpened his uneven sucking at the air.

I couldn't watch him as I waited for his eyes to open. So I stood at the window and looked across the rooftops of Lander to the mountains, tracing the line of the peaks northwest across the reservation toward the Wind River, the ranch, my cabin, ninety miles of flat-out road away. In the parking lot directly below the window, my truck sat among the other trucks and jeeps and station wagons, the dirt bike still lying on its side in the bed.

A nurse entered the room. I watched her hazy reflection in the window, watched her brush Sam's hair back from his face and hold her palm on his forehead while her other hand moved quickly to adjust the needle in his arm, straighten the sheet, and smooth his green gown around his neck.

The sun slowly fell to meet a line of deep blue thunderclouds. It rained. Huge drops bounced off the roofs and the cars like hail. Sam's head rolled to the side, and a few minutes later it rolled to the other side. His mouth closed and opened in silence. When the storm had passed, I inched the window open to inhale the air. Sam spoke.

"Boss man. Blue."

I turned. Tendons stretched tight in his neck as he held his head up off the pillows. I took a few slow steps to the chair beside his bed. "Don't strain."

"When they unwrap me," he said, "I'll show you my stitches." His pale gray eyes flickered for a moment and then closed. His hand rose, crossed his body, and lay on the needle in his forearm. "I swear this thing's been poked in me forever. Right from the start, on that bumpy fucking ride down here, I've been wanting to rip it out." He opened his eyes and looked at me. "What if I yank it?"

"I don't think you should."

"You think I'd die?"

"They must've put it there for some reason."

He left the needle alone and tried to sit up, working his shoulders and legs side to side. Glancing at me, he kept working, and then paused. "Gimme a hand, huh? It's not like I'm full of zip."

His narrow shoulders felt cold beneath the thin green cloth. I tried to pull him upright as he wiggled, his eyes closed, face

65

taut, but we made only an inch or two of progress. Releasing him, I said, "Sorry," and sat down.

His breathing slowed and his eyes opened again. He rolled his head to the side and smiled, one eye squinted. "Try harder next time," he said. "Where you been, anyway?"

Coming around the curve into the center of town, I scanned the vehicles along the curb. Even on Mondays, there were always a few clustered in front of the bar. The grayed top of Sam's jeep poked out from behind the cab of a pickup. I parked a few empty spaces from the first truck and stepped out. I'd snatched Sam's keys from his bedside table after he fell back asleep, and with them jammed in my fist I walked along the sidewalk toward his jeep, my boots catching red neon reflection. Stepping down off the curb, I yanked the canvas-and-plastic door open, pulled my feet in after me as I settled in the seat, and worked the key into the ignition. The engine started after a few tries, and I pulled the headlight knob and watched the speedometer needle vibrate. As I moved my boot to press the clutch and get in gear, the flimsy door fell away from my elbow and a body stood there, backlit by the neon.

"Blue, good to see you're taking care of this, moving his vehicle. How is the boy?" It was Max—his high, tight voice and the gouged shadow of his ear.

"He's not good at all."

"Oh, I know," he said, and then I heard the same story David had told me that morning.

After I'd left the bar, Saturday night, some guys went out and pulled Derek off Sam. He was at Sam like it was in his blood to draw blood from that boy. No one knew what Derek was doing, no one *ever* knew what Derek was doing. Sam didn't move for a while, and someone said he thought maybe he was dead. Derek started puking in the dirt against the building, which made it hard for the guys trying to hold onto him. If the town hadn't gotten a medical clinic the year before, there wouldn't have been anyone to keep Sam going until they got him to the hospital in Lander.

"Ruptured spleen, huh?" Max said. "I guess he's gonna make it fine. We like that Sam all right. But we've always had trouble with Derek, eh? With all the beer we'd been drinking, we were fed up with him, and some of us thought maybe we should lynch him—or something like that—but no one had any rope and he was smelling so bad with his own puke that no one really wanted to handle him, so we just kept him cornered with some long sticks till the sheriff came and took him off our hands. Shit. We don't need that kind of stuff around here—a fight's fine, but you don't go nearly killing someone. They charged him with battery and let him go this morning. Fuckin' stupid to let him go. Someone saw him walking through town with a pistol on his hip like he was some fucking John Wayne maniac. It gets to the point where a guy should be locked up away from people, or dead. He ain't doing himself or anyone any good. He's looking to do more damage, I'm sure."

Sally Jeffries came up behind him, and as she circled his waist, her red fingernails clicked on his belt buckle. "Blue," she said. "Blue, dear. Tell me how you're handling things. I mean, a man short. You think I could help you out?"

"Thanks, Sally. Things are running fine."

Max twisted to press himself flush against her hip. "Any of us could help out. With the lumber mill closed temporary, we're all a little slow."

"Things are fine. David will take the cow camp. Jake's driving him up tomorrow. Jake and I will be fine down here."

"I don't know," Sally said, and she reached out and drummed her fingers on my shoulder. "You're in a bad situation."

"Nothing will go wrong."

"Well, no," Max said. "But you know any of us will give you a hand. You watch yourself, Blue." He reached forward and pinched my arm.

I pulled out into the road, stopped past the bar, zipped open the window enough to look out, and faced the empty lot where the fight had taken place. Gilbert had said nothing much happened, as if he'd seen it all.

I rolled to a stop in the gravel lot beside the creek, where Sam's half-size silver trailer and two others clustered beneath thick cottonwoods. Purple TV lights shifted against the closed drapes in the pink trailer—Melvin and Tracey and their round slow daughter would be lounging, dozing to a sports program pulled in through their satellite dish. And in the wood-sided trailer, Ricky and Noel would be pacing the room, trying not to block their reception of the single Casper channel from the translation station on Whiskey Mountain. Across a few open backyards, one of their parents or grandparents could look out into the darkness and spy these trailers and their lit windows.

Sam's key slid into the lock, and the metal door swung open. In the dim light from the other trailers, I felt for a switch on a lamp. One long room. I checked the stove to see that the propane was off, wiped a damp sponge across spots of tomato sauce on the knobs. Then I went ahead and stacked the dishes that were piled in the sink, filled the sink with hot, soapy water, and washed them.

Books and magazines lay open on the tables and on top of the refrigerator—*High Country, Teton Outfitter's Catalogue, Birds of the Rockies.* He had circled a dome tent. The green, white, and delicate brown topo maps of the Wind River Range and the Absarokas were all mixed in, spread out together, folded to special lakes, and marked with pencil x's. I ran the orange nub of an eraser up valleys I'd hiked for almost twenty years, circled the lakes stocked with golden trout, and rose to the head waters of the highest streams. On a scrap of paper, he'd written, "Horse Creek to Pony Creek. Timberline?"

The bed was made, but a jumbled layer of dirty clothes circled it on the floor. I picked them all up and piled them on the bed. Some of the shirts had been rolled into twisted lumps, and the pants retained Sam's shape at the knee. It didn't seem worth the effort to fold them all, dirty as they were, so I rolled them into a mound at the foot of the bed and drew down the covers. The sheets looked fairly fresh, but when I held a pillow to my face, I caught the scent of dusty hair.

A car passed on the road, and the curtains brightened. Dropping the pillow, I followed it down onto the bed, curled onto my side with my head padded. My ribs throbbed, a dull ache, and I rolled out flat on my back, closed my eyes to the harsh circle of light on the ceiling. Gilbert had told me a story, talking in darkness as I held off sleep, waiting.

There was a woman whose eyes wandered to the men's deerskin breeches and the tunics of porcupine quills. She dreamt of hides against her loins. She dreamt of running with the young men.

A war party was started against the Pawnee. The woman circled at the edge of the firelight as the young warriors prepared. They placed dangerous designs on their skin. They danced in tight spirals. Letting her robe slip from her body, she crept in among the men, applied paint, dressed herself for war, and found the rhythm of their chanting flowing from her lips.

Men's voices rose through the blood and dust of battle. She held her horse in the grip of her thighs. Death flew from the mouth of her gun.

Victory was made. She had killed many Pawnee—their bodies lay like fallen cairns along the path of battle. When they rode back into the village, a dance of celebration was performed. As the woman exulted with the other warriors, her father recognized his daughter. The dance stopped. Her clothes were taken from her, and she faced the tribe undisguised.

"I have caused shame to my father and my mother," she said. "Although the Pawnee cannot harm me in battle, any one of you could easily kill me. I invite any man to kill me."

The tribe chose a man to execute her. Her father brought from his tent his finest clothing for his daughter. He attended her as she dressed as he had always dressed. She smelled his body

69

on her, and it seemed to be her own body. Her fingers ran along the seams of the cloth and hides, and they found nothing strange.

She stood in front of her father's tent and calmly looked out over the faces of the tribe. The executioner raised his rifle to his shoulder, centered her, and shot.

Her father knelt beside her body. He thought that she was a beautiful child, a delicate woman. But her legs emerged from his breeches like the legs of a runner, hardened and sleek. He thought that she was a courageous warrior.

I shook Sam's pillows from their cases and pulled the sheets off the mattress, then stuffed the sheets and Sam's dirty clothes into the cases. Slinging the laundry over my shoulder, I flicked off the light and locked the door behind me.

From anywhere on the sparse grid of streets, it was only a few blocks back to the bar, and I could either walk straight or cut over a street and pass Derek's cabin. I took the turn. His lights were on, the porch lit yellow and the windows bright white, and his truck was there, alone—Janeen and her white Camaro were probably out at her duplex along the canyon road. I stopped behind a young bushy pine, lowered the stuffed pillowcases to the ground, and watched for a few minutes. Derek crossed in front of the window, paused, stood squarely behind the glass. He turned his head left and right, stretched, his arms tight in his T-shirt.

Those arms, I'd watched them at the Pack Race, watched him heft the loose dead weight of a duffel with one hand and sling it onto a mule. He pulled a rope tighter and the canvas puckered beneath the strain.

And when Walter had sat in a booth at the bar a few years back and asked Janeen to lend him a hundred dollars, and when Derek had seen the exchange from the shadow of the doorway, I'd heard that the impact of Derek's steel-toed boot in Walter's gut sounded like wet mash plopped onto the ground from a height.

Derek drew the curtains.

I had the strength to keep someone off. In the bar in Jackson, it had taken only three good punches to put that first guy out. Then as I stood over Gilbert, he looked up at me as if I should help him, take his hand and pull, as if it was expected and my effort meant nothing. Maybe it did. Mean nothing.

A door opened, and Derek stood with a hand shading his eyes. He stepped forward, crossed his arms, pinned his fists tight against his sides. Reaching for the pillowcases of laundry, I turned to continue along the street.

"Blue," Derek said. "Stop, you asshole."

I stopped. "What is it, Derek?"

"You know what I'm up against, buddy?"

"No, I don't."

"I could get jail. Locked up with a bunch of ding-dongs and retards. You heard?"

"I hadn't heard."

"You want to help me out, bud?"

"What?"

"Come to the hearing and tell 'em I was provoked."

"I don't think so."

"Don't go weird on me, Blue. You saw what happened. You was in the middle of it. I could get my lawyer to make you tell what happened."

"I'm not going to help you, Derek."

"I'm asking you. All you do is tell 'em about the squaw and that squirrel of a ranchhand of yours and how they wouldn't leave me alone to the point that I had to do something. I need you on my side, buddy. Don't be an asshole about it. Don't go weird on me." His clenched hands came out of hiding and lowered to his hips.

"That's not what happened, Derek."

I turned, but paused long enough for him to say, "I guess

what I been hearing about you is true, huh? Help me out, buddy, or it's true."

I didn't turn back, but I said, "What?"

"Nothing, Blue. Not a fucking thing. Help me, Blue."

I started walking.

"Blue, you keep away from that Sam. Hear me? I see him again, I'll have to hurt him harder, you know that. You do anything for him and you know I'll have to hurt you too. You know that, buddy. You must know that."

The sidewalk in front of the bar again, the red light on my palms as I held them up, and in through the broad pane a single man crossing the dance floor toward the door. I wanted to get home, to lie out flat on my bed and feel my weight settle through the springs, the gentle creak of the frame, but I waited as the door opened and a man, it was Max again, stepped up to me. "Blue," he said, his face close, looking up at me and then glancing to the street, to the window. His fingers tapped on the glass. "You got Sam's jeep back to his trailer?"

"I did."

"That's good." He turned and leaned barely back against the window, crossed his arms, tapped the heel of one boot against the toe of the other. "Come in, Blue," he said, and he touched his chin to his shoulder, toward me, looked somewhere around my gut. "People been wanting to know the story about what's doing with that boy of yours, that Sam, now. Will you have a drink? I'll buy." His eyes came up to look at me squarely for a second before he cracked a smile, turned away, said, "Get your butt in here."

The jukebox played a grumbling country song that backfired every few measures with a sharp slam of drums. I could feel it through my soles. We walked across the vacant room, stopped behind the five people sitting on the row of stools. Sally, Dolores, Tim, George, and Bruce all leaned forward with their elbows on the bar. I dropped the sacks of Sam's laundry at my feet. The bartender, Susan, pink with a new sunburn, was saying, "So this guy from Wells gripped my ass and wouldn't let go. Threw me into the ice chest. Shit. I won't go into no dark places. I want me a man with blond hair, blue eyes, big, tan, with intense thighs, and he's got to be easy. Shit. You find me a guy like that, I'll stop drinking. Even stop swearing."

"Sue," Dolores said, "you might as well shoot yourself right now."

"No. I been having too much fun with the rejects."

They all laughed as she ran her hands up her sides and hung her head forward. Then, as her head slowly came back up, as her hands found her hips and pushed out of sight into the taut pockets, she scanned her friends—ranchhands, loggers, beautician—before settling her flush gaze on me and keeping it there, her eyes widening and contracting in a calm rhythm. "Blue," she said, and she turned away, her back full at me, her upper arms squeezed by the elastic of her short sleeves.

Susan—she'd sat behind me in high school and read her poems to me over my shoulder. Her stringy brown hair was now almost a pure yellow and full of cylinders of stiff curl. She shifted bottles behind the bar and dropped ice into a tall glass. She'd always had a hard joke aimed at me whenever we'd met over the last few years, always something about the time she'd wasted writing poems for me or the fun she was having that I would never taste. I could laugh at her, passing in the drugstore, in the mercantile, but when she slid a drink toward me across the bar and said, "Have a Dirty Mother, you little skunk, or was it an Orgasm you wanted me to fix," I watched the other faces come around, and I couldn't bring up a smile.

Dolores handed me the drink, and I held the wet glass, looked down at the dirty milky liquid opened out by the squares of ice. "Tell us, Blue," Dolores said, "tell us what the deal is with Sam."

"Yeah," Susan said, slapping the bar, and they all turned to look at her. "You mean to tell us he'll be back soon enough to keep you from hiring on some help temporary?"

"I need the work," Max said.

"I got time on my hands," Sally said.

Bruce punched me in the arm and said, "Down on Albert's place, if I lost a guy, I'd be hard put not to get some help."

"Shit, I seen the boy," Tim said. "I seen him after the fight when they got him in the ambulance. Derek did some mean work on him."

Dolores shook her head slowly. "I thought for sure he was gone."

"It ain't right," Sally said. "You'll need some help, Blue."

"How the kid got himself in that mess, I'll never know," Susan said. She motioned for me to drink up, but I didn't raise the glass. "Shit, Blue, what happened? You must know. You was in the center of it."

My bedroom window was pushed wide open, the curtains flapped and settled, the river water and the wind rushed among roots and branches, down through the valley, pulled out to the plains. I lay with the covers rolled to the foot of the bed, lay naked on the sheet, head sunk in the pillow, black ceiling overhead, no constellations or guidance of any kind. A chill gripped my chest, my arms twitched against my sides, but I didn't take cover.

When I was a boy, I'd gone with Gardelle up through the canyons, early January, to walk among the patches of snow, move in silence, count birds for the Audubon Bird Count. Up Jakey's Fork. His eyes were fading, even then, lost in the shadow of his bushy gray eyebrows. I'd spot some movement off through the trees, tell him the color, the pattern of flight, the song. He'd pin it down and write it on our list. Dipper. Magpie. Gray jay. "Good job," he'd say. "You've got sharp eyes. You'll get somewhere, with eyes like that, when you're a man."

Up out of the snow, we lounged on a south-facing boulder and rested. The silver thread of the Wind River, far below, wove with the gray road. A car sparkled. Gardelle slept, his breathing grainy and slow. Something large swooped overhead. I shaded my eyes, listened to the sharp cry, and made an entry in the log. Bald eagle.

When Gardelle awoke, I showed him the entry. He smiled, rubbed my back with his open palm, and said, "That's right, Blue. That's the way it should be." His hand stayed on me as he talked, slowly at first.

When he came west, he said, the road was nothing—it picked its way around the ravines. It was more than a day's drive up from the next town of any size, Lander, east. He stopped in the shade of some cottonwoods, where there was a well for a cup of cold water and a homestead with sod on its roof. A woman— she couldn't stop talking at the sight of a human face—fixed him a lunch of biscuits and gravy. He ate, headed on, and when he glanced back she was still watching. But she was the last woman for a while.

He drove past the red cliffs, past the badlands, up along the river. Men stood on huge jams of squared logs out in the water, pulling and poking with barbed poles, resting in the meadows, trying to hurry the logs away on the spring runoff. All those men. Tie-hacks.

Swedish tie-hacks, way up here in nothing but all these mountains, working to cut ties for trains that never rolled anywhere close to this high country. They showed him the flume down from Union Pass. You can still see what's left of it, the poles and boards leaning here and there across those deep meadows, along the cliffs of the canyon, down to the river. It cradled the ties smooth as a greased bullet all the way down. They gave him an ax, figured out he had limits, and set him to cooking instead, cleaning up after them. No one from home found him. A thousand miles? Two? He didn't write. Never thought of it. Scrubbed those huge iron kettles.

He didn't always know what they said, couldn't get their English, gave in to the murmur of their talking as they ate in the light of a few lanterns, their hard work smell, spooning onto their plates the food they'd showed him how to make. They sang sometimes, out where the pines opened over the creek and the stars were bright, they sang songs he didn't know, songs they taught him. They drew their shirts off their arms, left their trousers in a heap, stepped into the thermal pools where the water swirled away from the fast current. Their hair was silver like stars at high altitude. They laughed at him and called him to join them.

Their skin like gray shadows bobbing sometimes into sight at the surface of the water, they floated in the dark. No light from the camp off through the woods, no animals rummaging—just the sound of air and water flowing, breeze in the pines, warm water, the breathing of the men, sometimes faint, sometimes closer.

There were eagles then like something magic. He sat with a friend when the camp had closed and the men had mostly all moved on, sat and watched through field glasses a bald eagle perch on a fallen log across a meadow. The eagle watched them watch him, watched them judge him, guess his height and his span. He finally rose, lifted in spirals until he seemed to hang still against the belly of a thunderhead, a speck against that mass of danger. They heard his cry—it made them shudder—strange that such a sad cry should be so loud and sharp. He fell. He came down at them like a bolt. They pushed against each other and waited. His wings finally opened, snapped out flat and huge, and he swept above their heads, his strong body calm and dark, his whiteness so pure it seemed harsh, almost hard to watch. He was over tree tops and out of sight too fast, and they were alone again, trying to remember, trying to judge him. They talked about it often over the months before they finally parted.

"*You* know Sam," someone in the bar had said. "You must have some idea of what got into his mind when he danced with that Indian."

If I had been Gilbert against that line of faces, each face and each life would have been unfamiliar. I'd know nothing of Susan and the deep lines around her eyes, the flaked red of her nails. Never know that George had lost his first child to a kicking horse, that he still loaded that horse each year during hunting season, cinched it tight with the weight of tent, stove, tarp, ammunition. No idea that Dolores had married a man who didn't love her, wouldn't touch her, wouldn't divorce her. That Sally had had her first child at sixteen, gave it up for adoption, had another a year later, kept it, loved to square dance, wanted a degree in physical rehabilitation, once thought she'd move to Denver. And that Bruce, manager down at Albert's place, had come in from Casper after a time on a spread in Montana, got his limp from a motorcycle crack-up, was once in a cigarette ad, his thick brown mustache and long nose in profile beneath his gray hat, the snowy hills above East Fork in the background against the darkening sky.

"Was that Indian someone you knew?"

All I'd said was, "I didn't know him. No one did." And they all nodded and looked at each other and waited for me to say something else.

But Gilbert would've reached out, tapped their shoulders, tried to tip them all together in a tight cluster, and said, "Now, what do you want to know? You wonder what kept Sam and Blue listening to me? Shit—with all you dead-asses around here, who *wouldn't* listen to me? I've got something going. And, I tell you, those two boys—" He jumped back a step, and they all flinched. He crouched, held his clawed hands forward, made his face fierce. "Those boys can't defend themselves." He rose to his full height, smiled, shook the danger off his limbs, and stepped up to them again. "They don't have a clue." If he'd laughed then, his eyes closing, a flash of his teeth, they all might have thought of returning his smile, watching as his body went soft.

Sam lay on his back, eyes closed to the red neon, red light across the line of his brow, light at his neck, red on his hands. Now he lay in white, with someone, some mothering young woman, to enter the room, fluff his blankets, keep him warm, window closed to the wind off the mountains, off the mountains above the reservation, someone to brush his hair up off his forehead and leave her hand there to test his temperature.

On that same hall in the hospital, in a room facing the same view of brown mountains over rooftops, I'd stood, years before, at the window with my back to the light, my shadow out flat across the bed, Mother's legs barely causing a wrinkle beneath the pale green blanket. The drip of painkiller into her arm seemed almost audible. Straight across from me, at the door, my father appeared, stopped, forced his hands into his pockets, and brought his shoulders up tight against his neck. "Honey," he said, "I got here. Twelve hours on the road straight here." His hand twisted in his pocket and he hunched forward to look at his watch. "Twelve straight hours." Twelve hours, after I'd stood there, or dozed some, through thirty-six straight, watching her sleep or wake up, watching the nurses and doctors pause on their rounds to attend, prescribe, wash, listening to Mother say to me, "You'll be fine, Blue. You don't need to worry about a thing. You go on out, walk around. I'm taken care of."

When the time gets near, each year, I take the first-calf mothers down to the property at Red Willow. Safe from winter, they all stand in the barn, eat from a long wooden trough of grain, alfalfa, hay cured in the dry summer sun. Myself, I medicate them, administer the vitamins and vaccine through the thick, translucent syringes. No pain, no stress. Watching them, I lean against a wall in the dim high-ceilinged barn that shifts in the wind, or the night man watches them—we switch off. The time comes, and if she has trouble, if an hour goes by as she struggles, I take her into the warm room, the room with white-washed walls and heat up to a hundred degrees, and I ease her through it, do the pulling for her. She can't get too weak, her calf can't get too weak. In the warm room both are fine as I watch for the small eyes to focus, as I inhale the scent of bloody straw. The mother will breed back fine next year, now that she's been cradled, coddled. She has given me a heifer with dark eyes and dark udder. She will be a good mother through eight more calves, now that I've helped her with the first.

I talked with Gardelle—winter, months ago—a man I needed to see. Stepping from my truck, I passed between his two vehicles, shocked the snow from my boots as I knocked on his door. Hanna answered. Dressed in a heavy coat with fur-lined hood, bulky mittens, she was on her way to town on errands, and she greeted me briefly as she shuffled past and allowed me into the warmth.

"Hey, Gardelle," I said.

He sat in his usual rocker, head back, black eyes toward the open rafters. Propped on easels, hanging from wires midair, Hanna's paintings surrounded him. A doe's hindquarters were tilted under strangely. A raven's lush black held false reflections. "Blue," he said, bringing his eyes down in approximation. "Blue. I'm glad. Sit." His hands waved me closer. "Tell me things," he said as I sat in a chair beside him. "Tell me how that job of yours is working out. That whole Fisher place *yours*. That's big shit. Big time."

"I'm handling everything."

"No question about it. How many head you running?"

"Seven hundred."

"Hands?"

"Three. Losing one soon. Janice Seever is taking off for a spread in Colorado."

"No loss. I know the gal—hard worker but a real tight-ass. Argues with every right-headed idea."

"I inherited her."

"You're a free man. Shake here." He extended his hand, and I reached and took it, squeezed it hard. "Congratulations. Glad you stopped by. You got a real life going for yourself." He released me, sat back, and his head drifted to the side, a remote smile.

"I'll tell you something," he said after ten minutes of flat silence. His head rested limply against the back of his rocker, and his fingers wove together and fluttered. "You find yourself a hand you can trust, someone you think you know. I used to know some men who would do a real job for you. Some guys who would stick with you and think your thoughts. After the tie-hacks moved on, I had every bit of these mountains to find,

79

to keep me busy, every mile of trail, man-dug or animal trail, over the last sixty-odd years. Me and Benny Chubb, we was a pair. It was different."

He told me of acquiring golden trout fingerlings from California, packing them in to high lakes in tin drums, releasing them into strange water. "They swam away quick, like little sparklers in the sunlight near the surface. They stayed in groups for as long as we could see them, then they was in pairs, or alone. Then nothing. A year later you might see one rise—not see it, really, but see the circles of ripples opening out from where it had been a second before."

He leaned forward in his chair, listened, continued with his voice hushed and rapid. "We had years up there. Pack in for a week, sleep in a tent if rain came, or in the open under that whole solid mess of stars, or under a moon big as half the sky. Sun comes up and you roll onto your back to see the last star go. I'd smell the fire smoke in my clothes, and I'd know that if I was brave enough and quick enough, I could get the fire to warm me again in a few minutes and get me some hot coffee. So up on my feet, hopping one foot to another to get my pants on, and I see Benny down at the edge of the lake with his fish pole whipping back and forward and then the whir of the reel and the splash of his bait far out. Golden trout for breakfast, tender out of the fry pan, and flapjacks. And through all that, even an hour later when I was scrubbing the pan clean with sand, we hadn't said a word. No need. I could see him—tall man, thin as string, with a straight long nose and dark cheeks and eyes like they were my own, always off on the mountains, then glancing back to me for the contact, for the whatever. He could move. He could do a job for you. No shit. Didn't ask. Didn't take. Helped you out. I miss that man like I miss nothing else. God in Heaven. And there was plenty more of him, anywhere you looked."

He drooped back in his chair, let his head hang forward, mouth open, eyes closed, as if he were passing away, and a while later, maybe a half hour, Hanna returned. "What you boys up to?" she said, and she paused at Gardelle's shoulder, brought her mouth close to his ear. "You been good?"

Gardelle dipped away. "Shit, Hanna, let a man's time be his own."

She laughed. "Go on. I'll leave you. Bye, Blue." She took her packages into the pantry.

"I have to go," I said, standing up.

Gardelle got himself to his feet, reached for me, pulled me closer, draped his arm around my shoulders. His whole body, head to foot, pressed against mine, and his chin was sharp as it pushed into the base of my neck. "You wait," he whispered, his words and his breath full on the side of my face. "You find yourself someone like you, someone who can help you. We all need help. You find someone you can trust." Then his words stopped, his mouth closed, and those lips, rimmed with tough gray stubble, pushed into my skin, just below my eye, hard. The mark was still visible when I climbed into my truck and checked myself in the mirror.

Rolling off my cold, open bed, I stepped to the window. The moon sent the shadow of my cabin down toward the edge of the river. I couldn't separate the sound of wind from water— both roared, steady, away.

Sam, when he first came to me looking for a job, spoke of the mountains. Before showing him around the place, I made him lunch, and we ate in the dim air of my cabin. He held his sandwich in his full, small hand. His head dipped as he looked out the window and up the slopes toward granite, and then his eyes came to me and he smiled, nodded, ready to settle in and get started.

I thought then, or I knew, that I would stand at sunset at the edge of a tiny, high valley, and watch for the final white to turn to black. I'd see something move across that line of light, approaching, and then I'd hear boots scraping on rock and a pack rattling. When I called out a greeting, Sam's voice would mix with all the echoes the mountains threw back. Sam would come up quietly then, and we'd both walk down to the campsite by the lake. With our sleeping bags unrolled and padding against the rocks, we could lie there and watch the stars move across the sky. And if we sat up, we could watch the stars' reflection move below us in the lake.

I walked from my cabin. The short grass pricked the soles of my feet, and I moved quickly to the smooth rocks at the edge of the river. My skin, my legs, back, arms, chest, tightened in the damp air that settled above the icy water.

What could I have said? "That Indian is gone. It's me. It's Blue. That's all. Derek got away with something crazy. My fault? Maybe. But bad things happen, and then you work at setting things right. I'll make sure Sam is healed properly. I'll make sure the work gets done—myself. No one else needs to bother with it. That's the whole story."

Gilbert would've backed into the center of the empty dance floor, spun, held his arms out. And then he was away, nothing of his chant left to foul the music. A thousand miles toward the ocean, the rocky edge.

I stood as naked as Gilbert had stood in the motel room. A step forward, and my feet were washed in the river. I scooped water and smoothed it over my skin, watched reflections of moon grow as beads took shape and descended. I was as smooth as Gilbert, but more angular, sharper. And Sam was damaged. I could take care.

David and Jake loaded two horses into the trailer, stacked boxes of food and clothing into Jake's truck, and hefted in a few sacks of grain. At noon, the truck ground into gear, and they passed out through the yard and onto the road. Jake would return alone, later.

I took the afternoon to get the bunkhouse ready for Sam. From what I knew, the bunkhouse could have stood empty for fifty years, empty except for cardboard boxes loaded with the Fishers' Christmas ornaments, barrels stuffed with stiff canvas camping gear, and a few wobbly chairs. I filled a corner of the granary with most of the stuff, rescued three of the chairs with glue and some screws, and swept. Knots stood up like tiny buttes on the eroded pine floorboards.

Next, I went to the prefab cottage overlooking the river, up past the main house. The Fishers had built the cottage for Mrs. Fisher's ailing mother, but the woman had died in an apartment in San Antonio before she'd had a chance to settle in to the cottage, sit on its back deck, drink gin-and-tonics, and listen to the river. I lifted a bed and bureau into my truck and took them to the bunkhouse, filled the bureau with Sam's clean clothes, placed his books and maps and a lantern on top, and tightened sheets over the mattress.

Sitting on the bed, I reached for the dusty curtains and pushed them aside. The view opened past my cabin, across the river, and above the cottonwoods to the slopes of Whiskey Mountain. If Sam were still laid up in the bunkhouse through winter, he'd have a clear view of bighorn sheep grazing, the herd taking refuge from the deep snow in the crags and fissures of the high peaks.

Later, in the kitchen of my darkened cabin, I laid out carrots, potatoes, celery, tomatoes, onions, and chunks of beef for a stew. As I got a rhythm going with the knife, I looked out the window and watched the steady glow of the lantern in the bunkhouse, watched for the wisps of smoke from the trial fire I'd started in the ancient woodstove. The stars wavered in the heat rising from the stovepipe at the far end of the roof.

There must have been a time when the two long bunkhouse walls had been lined with beds, each with a wooden chest for storing clothes, a time when the antler pegs between the windows had hooked hats, slickers, and chaps. The woodstove centered in the far wall would have killed the chill as summer passed to fall and would have roared with a hot fire all winter. A murmur of voices as the men undressed in the lantern shadows. The peace toward dawn as the breeze shifted and the windmill blades swung slowly around, as the fire snapped and hissed. I couldn't be sure of when the men had scattered out into town, each to his own cabin or trailer, his own television and frozen food and privacy.

A few evenings later, after Sam's stitches were removed, I brought him back from the hospital. Drugged, he settled into a pillow against the truck door, slept as we crossed the reservation from Lander and followed the river.

In the bunkhouse, I pulled back the covers and lowered Sam onto the open sheet. With the lantern lit and adjusted, Sam's face came clear. He relaxed a little, his eyes remained closed, his breathing steady. I tried to figure how to make him comfortable. His clothes had twisted around his limbs. He lay slightly over on his side, bent at the waist, as if his wound had contracted him. I perched on the edge of a chair and worked at his shirt buttons—one, two, down his chest—opening to skin so pale it seemed almost blue. As I neared his waist, he grasped my wrist and followed my hand's movements.

His bandage came loose, caught by his waistband. A dark purple line ran down across his abdomen and ended where the hair had begun to grow back above the scoop of his navel. With his hand still on my wrist, I laid my palm out flat on the scar, allowed my fingers to settle, prickled by the cut hairs. Something churned beneath the surface, as if his guts were working hard. As my hand pressed, I felt the uneven tension of the skin.

"No," he said, and he lifted my hand. His eyes slitted open, roved slowly, and closed again. "You're cold."

I left. A half hour later, holding a tray, I got myself back in through the bunkhouse door without spilling anything from the bowl of stew or the full glass of milk. Sam's shirt hung from a hook above the bed. His shoulder tented the blankets and hid his face. I sat on the chair beside the bed and balanced the tray on my legs. "Sam, I have some dinner for you."

He settled onto his back, and his eyes came open. "I could eat," he said, nodding.

I helped him shimmy upright against the headboard and

placed the tray on his lap. The sheet slipped down his chest, and he tucked it in around his hips. "Seems like I'm hungry," he said as he took the spoon, dug out a square chunk of potato, and shoveled it into his mouth. His neck strained. He fingered the edge of the bowl. "You made this?" he said, and his eyes drifted closed.

"Yes."

"It's good. Better than Jell-O."

With each bite he took, his neck craned forward, his torso stayed rigid, and his breathing came high and shallow. He kept his gut as loose and still as possible. As he swallowed a sip of milk, a flush colored his collarbones and shoulders. Red, jagged splotches stood out against the white. The remnants of his bruises emerged like greenish thumbprints along his chin, neck, chest.

"Are you all right?" I said. "What about those pain pills you took for the ride home? You were out cold."

"Oh, the pills still got me." He dropped the spoon into the bowl from a height, pushed the tray a few inches down his legs. "I think I won't eat any more right now." His squinted eyes scanned the room slowly, landed on the bureau across the bed from me. His hand rose and shifted a map to look at the one beneath. "My maps," he said, "and my books."

He took a map and held it close to examine it, lowered it to his lap, and let his head loll back. He didn't move, remained still, except for his eyes, which came open several times and roved the ceiling, the patterns of lantern light. I took the tray and put it on the floor, out of the way, and he crossed his arms over his belly. After a few minutes, he lifted his head, faced me, and, holding his eyes open, said, "You'll help me lie back down?"

Before dawn, I left a breakfast of an apple, bread, cereal, a glass of juice, on the chair next to Sam's bed. When I returned a few hours later, he had gotten himself upright against pillows, the food was gone, the dishes jumbled on the tray, and he looked up from a book. "Oh, Blue," he said, and a slow grin came to his lips. "Where you been?" He seemed stronger. His color had come back, and his eyes were well focused.

"I've been working with Jake."

"Yeah? What at?"

"Getting equipment ready for haying. It's a good year. Near time for the first cutting."

He reached a hand out, parted the curtains, looked outside for a moment before letting the curtains fall closed. "How many guys you need for cutting?" He slid the book onto the bureau top and inched himself up straighter against the headboard.

"Three. I need three men for haying."

"You and Jake and David?"

"David's at the cow camp."

"David?" His shoulders twitched back into the pillow, but his faint smile remained. "When?"

"A few days ago. I had to get someone up there."

He looked out the window again, in silence for half a minute, then turned back toward me. "Hot outside?"

"Hot and dry."

"Dry heat. Yup. You know, when I was a kid, we had a trailer out in an open spot in the cornfields. The air was wet and green as the corn. You were always in the shade of the air and the stalks. I'd sleep on the roof to get a taste of breeze and see some lights or trees way out somewhere. I like to get up high." His weight shifted forward, and the sheet slid down to his waist. He straightened his arms, trying to lift himself. "Hey, give me a hand, will you? I need to use the john."

"Sorry." Standing over him, I took his shirt off the hook and helped him on with it. His forehead pressed into my upper arm as I reached around him. A shiver rose up his spine, the muscles of his back fluttered, and his head snapped away from me. He hissed. Pulling his shirt all the way on, up to the neck, I took his shoulders and tried to help him settle back. He fought slightly against me, I could feel the resistance, and he said, "I'm fine, Blue." His head tilted back and he gave me a brief, darkened stare. "Let go." I released him, and he loosened, settled back.

"Of course you're fine. Let me help you."

He shook his head as he buttoned the shirt, slid his feet to the floor, fastened the top snap of his jeans. His hand gripped the headboard as he stood and slipped his feet into his boots, no socks. "Now," he said, releasing his hold on the bed and steadying himself. With his fists on his hips, his body hunched forward off vertical, eyes on me strong, and his odd pale smile returning, he said, "Now you can help me."

He accepted the link of my arm through his, and, with his weight balanced against my side, we took slow, short steps. Outside, his free hand rose to shade his eyes against the sun. "Nice," he said, and we made our gradual way across the yard to my cabin.

Inside, I took him to the bathroom door, and he said, "Leave me, okay?" I handed him a towel and walked back through the bedroom to wait in the living room. The tub faucet squealed—unexpected. Leaning against the back of the couch, I heard the water run and then the splashes as Sam lowered himself into the tub. A half hour passed, and then the water began to suck loudly down the drain. I stood up and paced the room, stopped to listen. First a sound like a fist dropped onto an empty metal box, and then a gasp like air torn from a pressurized seal.

I said "Sam" as I approached the closed door. A high, open, momentary groan. "What is it, Sam?"

He mumbled something when I knocked on the door, so I turned the knob and stepped in. He lay inside the tub, twisted on his side, his torso draped out over the edge. He stretched an arm across the floor toward his jeans, looked up at me, squinted a flash of smile—embarrassment or pain. He exhaled a spurt of air and said, "I fell." His head sank.

"Here," I said, "we've got to get you on your feet." With

great force and little help from him, I propped him upright in the tub and leaned him against the back wall.

He couldn't straighten—he bent at the waist with his center pulled into shadow. I held his pants toward him, saw it was useless. He faltered. I lifted him bodily out of the tub and set him down on the toilet, where he leaned forward, his shoulders twitching. "We've got to get you back in bed," I said. He sat up slightly when I slid my arms under his legs and torso, and he kept his face out of sight, turned away, as I carried him to my bed. I ran to the bunkhouse, returned, helped him sit upright long enough to swallow a few of his pain pills, and then he lowered onto his side and curled up. The blanket fell away, and I tried to secure it over him again, tucking it under his hip and shoulder. He brushed it away, saying, "It burns." His breath hissed. Ribs on his back like veins of a leaf. A few black moles near the bumps of his spine. Muscle spasms slowing.

"Blue," he said, "the full pain is back."

I couldn't give him any more pills—he'd already had too many. Leaning forward, I laid my hand out flat beside him on the bed. My hand, steady and splayed, seemed dark red from sun, and Sam was bloodless white. "I wish I could do something," I said. "I don't know what to do."

"It's okay." As if feeling for his own heat, he rested his hand on his forehead. "It's getting kind of hazy now." He rolled slowly onto his back and flopped a forearm across his eyes. "I don't know if I told you," he started, his voice thick, "but it was like Derek was bound to put his fist right through me."

"I know."

A breeze moved the curtains, the room momentarily brightened, and tiny bumps rose on Sam's skin. Nothing between him and the air. His jaw lost tension and his breathing slowed. Nothing to protect him. I heard something from outside, a grumble and a shock, a slam. Then the quick pounding of a fist. Sam's hips twisted toward me.

The front door opened, and I rose to my feet, tried to draw the blanket over Sam, but he brushed it off and rolled onto his belly, cradled his head in the crook of his elbow. I stepped from the room, glanced back to see a foot rise, wiggle in the air, and fall again to the mattress.

Jake stood at the open door. "Don't want to bother you, Blue," he said, "but I could use an extra pair of hands right now, if you don't mind. I finished my lunch, and I'm back into the gears, up to my elbows."

"I'm coming."

"Are you doing something?" He looked at the bare kitchen table, looked past me through the bedroom door. "Is that Sam?"

"Yeah. He's kind of passed out. Drugged for the pain."

"You're nursing him? He's got you running?"

"I'm taking good care, like I'd do for anyone."

"Sure." He shrugged.

I backed him out of the cabin and shut the door behind us. We went to work, getting the baler running smooth. As the sun blazed hotter, Jake leaned in the shadow of the machine and watched me. "I thought you'd got the bunkhouse ready for Sam," he said.

"I did."

"I didn't think I'd see him in your cabin."

"He hurt himself again, when he was in the john. I couldn't move him."

"Seems like he'd be light enough. But, whatever. You know, I'd say you're not his mother. I'd think the bunkhouse would be fine for him."

"Jake, he just now fell and hurt himself again. Okay?"

"Okay. But I think it would seem clear enough to anyone that you'd got the bunkhouse cleaned up real nice, and that Sam could be comfortable there no matter how hurt he was, anywhere this side of dead." He came into the sun and took up a wrench and started where he'd left off. "So I'll help you carry him when we finish here, if you want."

"Whatever Sam wants."

∎ ∎ ∎

As evening approached, dark clouds rose from up the valley. I found Sam in deep sleep, wrapped in the blanket. For dinner, I heated up some of the stew, sat beside the bed, and ate as I waited for him to rouse. He rolled toward me and his eyes opened. The room had grown dark. I switched on a light, and his eyes shut again. Holding up a spoonful of stew from my bowl, I said, "Are you hungry?"

He grunted and waved me off. When I finished eating, I put the bowl on the floor, and the spoon clinked. Sam's eyes opened, landed on me, closed. He yawned, ran his fingers over his lips. "I was off guard, you know, or I would have done all right," he said, curling tighter in the blanket, looking off at the darkened bedroom door. "Derek kept saying 'squaw,' like that Indian was there with us. I wasn't hearing too good. He got me in the face a few times right at the start. I wasn't laying a hand on him—not enough to hurt him. I wasn't even seeing things clear." He rolled away and pulled the blanket up so it cut across his face, muffled him.

"When my middle gave out and I couldn't stand any longer, I looked up at his face and his hands, and he was tight and angry, and I thought he would come down on me and make an end to it. Derek's ugly when he's mad—not something you'd want to look at. But he was gone, and suddenly I couldn't see anything but black, and then I kind of missed him, like I was afraid I wouldn't ever see anything again. You know he hurt me?"

I rubbed his shoulder. "Sam, you can go to sleep."

"Something touched my face and stroked my cheek. Something softer than Mother's hand—bigger and stronger. That long black hair. Do you think I saw him? He put his hand on my cheek."

I got up, walked around the room. I imagined an echo to Sam's voice coming from far beyond us, but outside the window there was nothing. Sam shifted under the blanket, his voice a whisper now, unintelligible.

If Gilbert approached from the road, circled the cabin, stood in the bright light from the window, he would hold his palms out flat toward me, his eyes squinting with his smile. He'd enter the room, brush past me. I'd smell his sweat, nervous from long miles on narrow mountain roads. He'd sit on the edge of the bed, his hand on the center of Sam's chest, his hand on Sam's throat, on his forehead. He'd touch his lips to Sam's ear, hold himself there, leaning forward, and speak.

I returned to the chair and sat down, leaned closer, and said, "You're safe, Sam. You're all right."

He sat up, winced. "Did you see him, Blue?"

I shook my head. He watched me. Gradually, his head also began to shake, to mirror me. Then he ran his fingers up into his hair, grabbed a handful, and forced his head back, sighed. He looked at me, and he seemed awake, fully, his eyes clear. "You hired me," he said, straight out.

"I did."

"And I still have my job?"

"Yes."

"I'll be better soon, you know. I'm a good worker, aren't I? I'll be fine in no time."

"I'm sure of it."

"We made a deal?"

"Yes."

"Shake my hand. Shake on our deal, Blue." His hand lifted, came at me, and I took it. He leaned forward into the clasp, put some strength into it, and a shiver rose from his gut, out his arm, into my hand. "Ouch." He laughed. Releasing me, he settled back onto the bed and rolled into the blanket. "Could you please turn out the light? Thanks."

I left the room. The rain had begun. It roared on the roof, as loud as it would roar on the roof of the cabin at the cow camp. David would be sitting at the table, in the faint light of the smoking kerosene lamp—would he know to trim the wick? With the steady, freshening rush of the rain above him, he would smile at the thought of his morning ride.

There would have been fresh coyote tracks in the mud by the pond. His horse would have come down from the aspens when she heard him. He thinks sometimes that she likes to ride more than he does. He got her brushed and saddled quick, and then decided to go up over the ridge past the corral, and not over past the spring, which is more gradual. The going was rough, with round crumbly stones and short grass and some big animal holes, so they sort of picked their way around the dangerous spots. But neither of them had much of an eye for the ground, because the sky, at that point, had gone the cold white it gets just before it turns blue. Over the pines that hang in the bowl below the edge of the ridge, a few clouds began to come out of the white into pink. The clouds seemed to be falling fast at them from the sky, growing suddenly bigger with the color. As they passed through the bowl, everything started to move—the pines swayed above them, the shrubs shook a little, and a gray jay dove from somewhere, crossed over them, and cried out just as they reached the lip of the ridge. With the jay's call the wind hit them, the wind full of the smells of wet soil and tundra. The sky seemed to swing up from the east and fall solid blue behind the cliffs and snowfields rising above them, straight ahead, the Ramshorn, so huge and sharp that they might have hesitated a moment before continuing, as if that mass of rock were dangerous.

Sam slept through the rain.

Early in the morning, I left Sam asleep and drove to town. The motel neon still glowed in the cold before the first sun. I parked down the street from the cafe, tightened my jacket against the chill, and slumped into the seat, leaning against the door. Nothing moved. The sky was bare. Tall cottonwoods hung darkness over a line of tourist cabins. Within five minutes, the green bulbs of the cafe sign began to flash and a few vehicles pulled up to the curb in front. I stepped down the sidewalk and in through the door.

Mimi paced behind the counter with a pot of coffee. She

92

filled a mug, slid it to me as I sat down, and said, "Morning, dear. Hungry?"

"I could use something."

"That's why we're here. You should remember that more often." She dropped a menu in front of me and tapped it with a pen. "We've added low-cal specials for wheezing tourists. Order four or five of them—that should keep you going till lunch." She moved on to take an order at the far end of the counter—Chad and Willie from the telephone exchange.

The room was harsh with heat and light and the radio playing a rock song, something about love letters. The door opened and a few more people came in, stopping on their way to work—to teach at the school, to type something at the town hall, to sell bait and tackle. The tourists would return in an hour or two from their dawn excursions along the Wind or up Horse Creek as far as Wiggin's Fork. Mimi took my order and then wandered out from behind the counter, taking more orders during the lulls in her chatter. Straight ahead, in the chrome behind the stacks of glasses and plates, I could see the distorted, shrunken reflection of each person in the room, see their coffee mugs rise and lower as they talked. Jean was going to re-roof her guest cabin before her hated in-laws arrived for their annual visit. Eddy wanted to trade in his jeep for a new half-ton. Flan might have to go all the way to Salt Lake City to have her blood treated.

As my food arrived—sausage and scrambled eggs and a waffle—Jake came in, slapped me on the back in silent greeting, and sat in the far corner. I poured syrup on my waffle and dragged a piece of sausage through the overflow. Some of Albert's hands came in and joined Jake. They talked about getting together for elk hunting up in the Bridger-Teton. Who had a license? Who had a decent tarp? Could Jake get hold of that great mule of Larry's?

Then Albert was sitting beside me at the counter. I dropped my fork and shook his hand.

"Morning, Blue," he said.

"Albert. Let me buy you breakfast."

"No, no. Just coffee. I ate already. I'm here to chase my guys out." He shook his head toward the far corner. "We've got a big day. If they don't feel me waiting, they're liable to stay here until there ain't a doughnut left. Bruce is bringing a backhoe up from Riverton. Can't waste time."

"No. Those things cost."

"Yeah, but we'll be done with it today, if I get these guys started on time. Hey, you got any need for it?"

"Not that I can think."

He stopped, gripped his large hand on my knee, and jostled me. Looking right at me, he said, "Now, you know, Blue, if you need any assistance, you can give me a call."

"I know."

He smiled, said, "Okay," looked for Mimi, caught her eye and ordered coffee.

After Albert and his guys left, after Jake asked me if there were any special instructions for the day and took off, I ordered more coffee and a grapefruit half, a plate of toast, some apple juice. "Hungry or lazy?" Mimi said.

Sally came in with Braden, her five-year-old, on her hip. He seemed as tall as she was, his legs hanging past her knees. They took the far corner, and after a few minutes, Walt Allen joined them. Sally was going to drop Braden at her mother's for the day, and then Walt would swing by and pick her up and they'd go to Jackson to the dentist. If there was anything seriously wrong with their teeth, they'd plead poverty and promise to pay over time, hoping that after a year or two their debt would be forgotten. They laughed and pretended to pour heaps of sugar into their coffee. Max had gone out of town for a few days, to beg for work in Saratoga. "He doesn't like me to go to the dentist," she said, and Walt nodded slowly. "He always wants me to wait and wait." They finished breakfast quickly.

Sally smiled at me over her son's head as she paid her bill. "What are you doing, Blue?" she said.

"Eating breakfast, Sally."

"Glad you have the time."

"It's early."

"Hell. It's almost seven-thirty. You'll be eating with tourists in a few minutes."

"That's all right."

"I thought you'd be busy. I won't ask, but I think you'll have a tough time haying with only you and Jake. Even a whole pot of coffee won't make up for missing bodies, if that's what you're trying. Jake was talking last night. He could only laugh. He ain't got any magic powers."

I'd had all I needed at the cafe. I stopped over at the merc, loaded some groceries in the truck, and headed out to see how David was doing, trying to think of what to say. The road had dried enough to be passable. I took it slow and watched for breaks in the barbed wire that traced in and out of the narrow valley. An antelope stood still at the edge of a sharp cutbank above the creek, and he took only a few quick bounds as I approached, then paused again, scratched his cheek on a bare branch of sage, and closed his eyes against the low sun. A picket-pin darted across the road in front of me, leapt a patch of grass, and stood up, straight and squat, at the mounded entrance to its den.

The engine idled with an easy rumble as I paused, rolled the window down, pushed my face out into the shade of the first pines, and looked away beneath the low ceiling of branches to the ripples of the creek. That might have been the spot Sam had meant when he'd spoken of sitting beside cold water. I let up on the clutch, slipped my foot off the brake pedal, and allowed the truck to continue its pull up the gentle incline without much pressure on the gas.

Ahead, the aspens around the pond rose above the red road, and then I passed the circle of water that lay still and dark beneath the deep sky. The hollow opened out in front of me. The cabin's green roof and the tin finger of the chimney pushed up over the willows that jammed the marshy acres below the meadow, the acres that narrowed down and drained away in the first fast stretch of the creek. I stopped, stepped out with the sack of food, left the truck behind, and walked down along the final curve of the road. Nothing moved. No one stepped out onto the porch, waved, or stood waiting. David had probably gotten up and headed out. Just past the broad, rocky end of the road, the corral stood empty, although the horse, my favorite, Starwood, could have been out of sight behind the tack shed or anywhere in the surrounding meadows and slopes. I could wait a while for David or just leave the groceries on the table and drive home. But I wanted to talk to him, to get some sort of idea started.

Sam had sat up in bed as I came from the bathroom that morning, on my way out. "I'm thinking," he'd said, "that it can't take forever. The doctors tell me it's a month or so till I'm real again. What do you think?" He looked at me and smiled a little. "Do you think it can take that long for me to be back doing stuff?"

"They know more than me, Sam."

He asked again about the cow camp. I told him that soon as he was ready, he'd have what he was promised, what we'd agreed to. How soon? I tried not to picture him sitting in that beautiful, dark cabin at the cow camp, sweeping up ashes beneath the door of the woodstove, pushing open the window to watch more clearly the passage of a cow moose and calf, an odd, dangerous pair, through the upper reaches of the meadow, then into the aspens and up the ridge.

I stepped across the springy porch boards. The knobs wobbled in my grip, squealed as it turned, and there, inside, across the room on the bed in a bright square of light, David forced himself up onto his elbows. His red hair clung to his forehead, and his chest, splattered with large freckles, expanded and contracted across the tight push of his ribs. He coughed and shook his head hard, blinking and squinting, then swung his feet to the floor and pulled himself upright, slumping there naked except for a corner of sheet. I turned around and set to unpacking the groceries, lining up the cans on the open shelves, and said, "How are things going, David? Working out all right?"

I heard his pants zip as he stumbled against the table. "Fine, Blue. I was just getting ready to get up. No problems."

I turned around to face him. He tried to button his shirt with one hand as he reached for his socks with the other. "I'm sorry," I said. "Take your time." I pulled a chair up to the table and waited for him to finish dressing. The room had a musty, sweaty smell I hadn't noticed before, as if the windows hadn't been opened yet for the summer. A moth beat at a window pane with a dull hum. I pushed an empty can and a spoon out of the way and leaned my elbows on the table. "Do you like it up here?" I said, and I caught the bright willows out the window behind his bed.

"Blue," he said. He stopped, fingers in the loops of his boot, and looked up. He seemed unsteady, as if he were going to fall, his knee up against his chest, his eyes small above the wide-open black circles of his nostrils. "Sure." As he started to teeter, he forced his foot into the boot, and then he took a seat across from me. Pushing more trash into the center of the table, he leaned forward with his head down and traced a finger up the tines of a fork. "I don't mind it."

He stood abruptly, snatched up the empty can and a plate, and started shifting things around on the counter, in the dishpan. He brought back a plate with a few slices of bread on it and placed it in an open space on the table. "Let me get some jam," he said, returning to the counter. Then he sat down and spread some thick purple grape onto a slice and took a bite. He slid the plate an inch toward me and said, "Help yourself." His eyes shifted around the table, and he quickly pushed the dishes into a tighter cluster. With a slow breath, finally pausing long enough to look at me for a few seconds, he said, "How're things down home?"

"Going fine."

"Seen Betty?"

"I saw Betty at the merc, getting some pellets for her water softener. She seemed fine."

"Good. That's good. And Sam? You seen Sam?"

"Oh, sure."

"How's the kid doing? Must be better by now, almost."

"It hasn't been too long yet. He's not all that well."

"But he's healing, right? When's he taking over up here?"

"I don't know, David."

"But Sam was gonna do it, huh? It ain't too hard. He'd have to be better soon." He ate another piece of bread in three bites and paused to catch his breath. Smiling for a moment, he fingered the knife blade, then wiped his sticky fingers on his pants and sighed, a forceless sound I hadn't heard from him before.

"Are you all right up here?" I said quickly.

His tongue shifted in his mouth, and his eyes tightened as he swallowed. "Don't think I'm some nut case," he said quietly, "but I'm not sure I like it too much up here. It's been, what, a week or so, and I don't think I've got more than an hour or two of real sleep in the dark." He twisted sideways in his seat and turned his head to look out the window. His face went red enough to drown his freckles. "It's like I hear footsteps when the wind blows."

"That's all right," I said. "David. Dave." Of course he was unused to solitude, unused to being baked in the wide-open sunlight all day, listening to his own voice if he wanted company. I could help him clear out of there, leave the place clean. David would be home. It wasn't as if someone *had* to be up there twenty-four hours, even though someone had lived there every summer for fifty years or more. I'd assumed that David had already claimed it as his own.

"You can come back down," I said, and his face relaxed slightly. "I'll ride lines for you today. Now. And I can keep on riding lines till we get Sam going. You clean the place up a bit. We'll head home in a few hours." He shook his head hard again, a few strands of hair flopping loosely, and started right in at clearing off the table.

■   ■   ■

I found Starwood in the shade beside the tack shed, saddled her, and rode up the shoulders of the mountains. Two miles, three, moving quickly, nothing alive in sight, silence all around the rocks Starwood kicked underfoot. We came out on the old trail I'd always followed during my summer at the cow camp. The trail was sometimes just an indentation in the short grass, no more than a shift of light and shadow, and sometimes it eroded into a jagged ditch for a few yards. Below the trail, over the edge of the ridge, a hollow faced north enough to remain moist through the dry summer months. Heavy green bushes clung to the steep sides. In the center, a small area of thick, matted grass, the long blades bunched up and pushed over. In against the bushes, three heifers slept, their legs pulled up under their bulk, and four calves stood on the grass, their black coats whorled with white. The darkness of the forms huddled there, the flash of the orange tag on each ear—Fisher Ranch. They all looked well—no worms, no disease, injury. The heifers raised their heads and brought their eyes open, the calves turned, and they all watched me where I paused. My shadow reached nearly all the way down among them.

They had slept there through much of the night, out of the wind, soft in the padding of the grass, had wandered in the dull light before dawn to graze and find water. The calves had filled on milk. Then they'd all returned, stayed close, breathed slowly as the sun warmed.

Starwood shook her head and exhaled, blew out dust and spit, inhaled the clean, bright air. Shifting, the calves stood shoulder to shoulder, and one closed its eyes and gave out a cracked bleat. A heifer roused herself to her feet and turned her rump to me, craned her head back around and up to watch me. They all could have scattered. With the sound of crushed branches, they all could have pushed through the bushes and run out into the shorter grass, the area of sparse sage, the calves moving on their stiff legs through the chunks of earth tossed up by their mothers' digging hooves. But nothing moved.

At the slightest squeeze of my thighs, Starwood continued along the line of the ridge, head low. Coming to the crest of the long incline, coming over the final wall that blocked the sky, we faced the Ramshorn. Square and pillared, sharp at the top, it gave down to fields of broken boulder and a skirt of dark evergreens. Directly below us, the earth fell away in a wide valley before taking on the bulk of the mountain. A tangled creek meandered through the valley. Oases of aspen. Fields of blue camas, biscuitroot, sego lily. A pair of antelope ran from below us, leaping through sage and then straight across open fields, pausing only when they were far out on the flats. A gun, held steadily, might still have taken them at that distance. Turning to eye us, they lowered their heads to graze.

Swinging down from Starwood, I dropped the reins at her feet and she took a few steps, started snipping at the grass. On the lip of the ridge, on the lichen surface of a slab of gray rock, I sat and hugged my legs to my chest. The sun, still far toward the eastern horizon, was in my face, brightness making all that land below me hazy, making distances deceptive. Whiskey Mountain, with the town invisible at its foot. The red badlands and buttes toward Crowheart. The flatlands beyond. A strip of black asphalt straight out, dipping through the ripples and gullies and canyons, passing through a town, another, clear out of the state and on to somewhere else.

I hadn't ever gone far, not much out of the state except to some ranches just over the border south in Colorado and west in Idaho, up into Montana every now and then. On the road, there's a group of houses and stores, always a gas station, and then nothing but fences for miles, for hours, with hills and ridges thrown up, rocky on the south side, green with pine on the north side. I'd seen oil wells pumping out there, microwave towers on hilltops, dirt roads winding away and out of sight, the remains of old trucks and cars rolled down to the bottom of steep banks. But always, on the road, all that passes by without its own sound, so quick that you can't make it mean something before something else comes along, all seen while the wind roars around the windows of your truck. And then you've arrived wherever you've headed, the wind is gone and there are voices, a hand to shake, you're invited in for something to eat, and you have the time to look people over, to pick up a book from a tabletop and see if anything is written on the first page, to take a good breath and judge the smell of the place, focus on the walls, all before drifting into the work at hand, knowing something about where you've arrived.

And that place is a home to someone. He takes you back out into the yard, past your truck, down toward his barns, talking all the way, never looking down or ahead to see where to place his feet. His dog barks at his heels and he doesn't flinch. The view around him, no matter how steep and sunlit and alive, is like air— always there, nourishing, sometimes unusually clean and pure, sometimes, for a brief moment, chilling and wonderful. But he's on to opening doors and pointing out the bull you've come to see or the piece of equipment. The way he talks and moves and pauses, the way he gestures back over his shoulder and continues with his speech, slapping you on the back, pushing you on ahead, you know you could never know what he knows, could never live in his place exactly the way he lives in it. Far away, he is, in his home, far out at the end of a road after many miles.

And back at home, in town, my home, when I was young, for many years I was alone with my mother, my father out there on the road, at work on one of his jobs. He never wrote, not once that I can remember, but he telephoned every Saturday to let us know where he was and when he'd be passing back through to stay for a few days. Mother took the call, held the receiver tightly to her ear. "Yes, dear. I'm all right. No, we haven't had any snow yet. Really? Well, you keep your jacket zipped." Then she passed the receiver to me, and I listened carefully for every sound. Music played, something like dance music, and maybe something was dropped or a door slammed, and voices shouting and laughing, passing. Then Dad's voice quickly drowned everything. "Blue? You taking care of your mother?"

When Dad said his good-byes and hung up, I turned toward Mother and we smiled, kept silent. After dark, the curtains drawn, we were alone. This time Dad was working at shale oil on the Western Slope in Colorado, and he'd be back in three weeks. Mother opened her book and read again, running her fingers down each page as her eyes moved, the pages rustling. She recrossed her legs and cupped her chin in one hand, leaned forward over the book, her lips moving as she mouthed a sentence or two. In a few minutes she would put the book aside and get up to start dinner, but for now she seemed as if she would stay in the chair forever, unwilling to let the story pause.

She might have been beautiful—I was too close to her to be sure, too familiar. A few times, when she'd dressed herself up for something special and, coming around a corner, I'd been surprised by the look of her, by the sudden, momentary newness of her curled hair and the deep red of her lips, I'd guessed that, seeing her, men would pause, want to linger. As she pushed past me, looking for her shoes or giving me instructions, her voice and the twitch of her shoulders brought her back, the woman I knew, and without thinking I was answering, following, even the scent of her perfume seeming usual. She would be gone for a few hours to a church function or cocktails, and then she would be back.

She would sit in her chair, get up to fix supper. I switched on a lamp and reached for a book myself. A car passed on the road outside. Frozen rain crackled faintly against the window panes. I leafed through the pages, found my place, and continued. Mother returned. She turned a page. I turned a page.

Where was my father when he'd called? It had all the sounds of a bar, somewhere in a small town on the high desert toward Utah. The building would be low and square, white stucco, dark brown trim around the two large windows and the single door, a flat roof, two bare floodlights focused on the dirt lot where the cars and trucks were parked. Inside, the ceiling lights were covered with red cellophane, and the only clear light came from the illuminated clock behind the bar, the clock face surrounded by a picture of mountain peaks and snow and a section of rushing river. As the song changed on the jukebox, people fell silent in the lull, then talked again with the music. My father had been there maybe every night since he'd been in town. He'd grown used to the strength of the drinks, to the temperature of the beer, the way the bartender slapped change down on the bar. He sipped from his fresh beer and turned to whoever sat beside him—someone he worked with? A man like himself, in town only for the work, temporary, poorly shaven. They talked of the local stuff, the things they had in common—their boss, their paychecks, their breakfast at the cafe. They didn't look past each other much as they talked. People came and went in the dim room. My father ordered another beer, drank it, glanced at the clock, got his coat and left.

He parked in front of his motel. A thin tube of pink neon ran the length of the overhang. Stepping from his truck, he heard the rattle of the ice machine from down by the office. An eighteen-wheeler whined to a stop in the dark lot past a row of bare trees. He unlocked his door and went in. The room had the dense smell of old cigarettes and dirty clothes. The ceiling, heavily textured, sparkled when he switched on the overhead light. Removing the wax paper cover from a glass on the desk, he got himself a drink of water and washed his face. He was too bleary-eyed to read, too wound up to go to sleep. He pried his shoes off and dropped them on the floor, lay back on the bed, looked at the ceiling and imagined the imbedded sparkles were stars, imagined that he was outside, that he was where he wanted to be. Night after night.

But whenever he called, he never lingered. He just ran quickly through the details of the weather, heat and cold, the specifics of the job, gave us his love and his usual lines, and said good-bye. He never had difficulty hanging up.

When he came home, what did he think when he stepped through the door? We stood up from wherever we were sitting and greeted him. I shook his hand. Mother hugged him—they held each other for a few long seconds—and then backed away. He stood there looking at us, up and down, a plain smile on his face, and then brushed past us, stopped at the center of the room, and turned slowly. "Yes, yes," he said. "Fine." He seemed happy to be there, was never unpleasant, did more than his share of chores and fixed whatever was broken, whatever I hadn't already taken care of. We went for a hike, or we went hunting. He took Mother out to dinner. At night, when I was supposed to be asleep, I heard the dull, steady drone of their voices as they talked in their room, a soothing, calm sound. And then in a few days, never more than a week, he left with the same smile on his face, the same look around the living room and over us, over Mother and me. What did he think when he left us?

I couldn't see how he could have been unhappy when he left us, not with the smile on his face, the hug and handshake before he drove off. He had no fear of being away.

So I thought that someone might wait for him in his motel room, sitting on the edge of the bed. Or a knock might come on the door and he'd rouse himself, watch himself move in the mirror, unlock the door and open it. Would they speak? As my father unbuttoned his shirt, would he turn away, reach for the light and switch it off? Would the color of the walls and the pattern of the curtains and the feel of the sheets take on for my father the name of the person he lay beside, take on the feeling of love or passion or whatever, so that the room became somehow an important place for him, and he remembered it for days and years afterward, thinking of that person and the room and the act of love in one thought, one picture, so that it meant home to him, home as deeply for him as his home in the mountains with Mother and me? More deeply? Maybe there are people like that, maybe my father was like that, all those years on the road. Still like that. No word from him now in over a year, no sight of him since he left me five years ago.

Starwood kicked at some stones, and I got to my feet. Up on her back, I turned her in a tight circle and we faced west, off past the Ramshorn. In the distance, stone masses rose like some sort of temple—the Pinnacles above Brooks Lake? The distance distorted the shape. I would have known those rocks, had always known them, when I stood at their base and leaned my weight against their solid coolness.

I gave Starwood a tap with my heels and snapped at the reins. We wheeled around and with great speed passed along the lip of the valley, moved without trouble across the flat rocks and stunted grass. Then, down over the edge, away from the Ramshorn and the valley, a last look at the stone mass against cloudless sky, I guided Starwood, she guided herself, through scattered, gnarled pines. A bull, my bull, Christoff, bolted from behind a gray log and paced us. His thick shoulders, slim rump, square head. With a sharp turn he kicked up his hind legs and ran back uphill without effort.

Somewhere west, maybe a thousand miles already, all the way to the edge of the ocean, where rivers gave out and sediment settled, Gilbert traveled. Fast along a road, his hand coming up off the steering wheel and waving loosely in the air. With no thought of where he'd been the day before, or a month before, or even over the last mile, he kept his eyes ahead, looking toward where he wanted to get, soon, out along a road.

After sunset, he drove from wooded hills into fields of young wheat, descended farther to scrub, toward dunes, all vague in the small glow of his headlights. A town came up, flashing lights on the two motels, seaside names, vacancies, and he stopped beneath the brightest sign, walked into the office, took a room. At dinner, later in the bar, he talked to whoever would stand still long enough to listen. He rolled his beer mug against a young man's, touched knuckles with the boy, and he was safe when the boy didn't pull away, didn't flinch.

In the motel room, the only light came from the neon outside, falling in a tall line through the split in the drapes. Gilbert saw nothing but his own skin in that light, then the skin of the boy. He spoke softly, telling stories, letting his hair fall away from his face. Reaching up, the boy took Gilbert's hair in his fist, opened his fingers and ran them like a comb through the warm slickness. Gilbert could have been anywhere, deep inside his stories, far away, deep inside his body, soft and sad and reaching, now, taking, hushed and sure.

Continuing down the mountain, a few miles above the cow camp, through a broad field, with Starwood in a braked trot, I followed a trail thick with wildflowers. I pulled Starwood to a walk. My summer at the cow camp, following this trail, wondering if it had once been a road, so high up, strange, I saw green glass in the dirt, light reflecting up through the grass. Then, as now, I turned

105

off the trail and circled out into the field. What had looked like humps of grass fifty yards out there became a foundation of stones, the half-buried black square of a woodstove, and the end of a log spiked with two long nails. How many heavy winters had it taken to stamp it out? How many years had it stood empty? I had asked Gardelle about it, but he knew of no one who'd lived that high. The snows would have blocked the windows and door, even blocked the chimney sometimes. A summer cabin? Line cabin? Who? I had swung down off my horse and kicked at the ground, unearthed more nails and a chip of white porcelain, utensils, a complete cast-iron skillet. Someone's home, abandoned? If the person had stayed through the winter, many winters, in spring he'd have stood beside his cabin, as I did, and looked up across slopes of flowers straight to the Ramshorn, so close and sharp that he could see water running on its face. People live where they want to live.

Starwood cantered. We entered woods. The dry scent of pine. Ducking to avoid low branches, I glanced toward light and color. A meadow, tiny purple elephants' heads on their green stalks, a single unconcerned calf, mother nearby, the sound of her low call.

David was waiting. He'd carried his stuff up to my truck and loaded it in the back. I unsaddled Starwood, gave her some oats, and brushed her down. She wandered toward water.

"I appreciate it, Blue," David said as we got in the truck and I turned the key in the ignition. "I'll work whatever you want. Sam'll take the cow camp, won't he?"

"I'll work something out."

"Shit. I'm no fool, you know. But I knew I was gonna start missing Betty and things."

The cow camp disappeared from the rearview as I let the truck accelerate. Less than a mile and then, straight ahead, woods closed in as the walls of the valley narrowed for a stretch. There, trapped between the slopes, my truck's roar echoed in through the open windows, and I skidded to a stop. Another abandoned homestead. David got out to open the wire gate—always a relief to have someone else take care of it. He unhooked the loop and the gate lost its tension, falling into a tangle of posts and wire that he dragged off to the side. I coasted through, fifty yards, and stopped to wait.

To the right of the road, under the trees beside the creek, the old Anderson cabin stood with its log walls fallen in on each other like a pile of broken fans. To the left of the road, and so close that I could almost stretch out my hand and touch, two cement pillars and a construction of halved logs framed an opening dug back into the slope, an old garage and storeroom, the ceiling hanging with roots, the dark floor filled with a foot of crumbled dirt. The cement pillars, with colorful rocks pressed into their faces, had always seemed close to something I imagined on an ancient road across the wilds. A man would lean back in a chair against one of those pillars, and as a car approached he'd tip forward, remove his hat, run his hand over his thin hair. The storefront would seem welcoming—screen door propped by a round rock, white soft-drink letters on a red circle, sundries. I'd pause, fill the truck with gas, the bell ringing out the flow, buy a bottle of something cold, a stick of dried beef, a roll, an apple. The voice of the man, unrushed, would follow my movements through his store, tell me of all the land available around these parts, of the game waiting to be taken, the rich pastures and the sturdy men, the women.

David rested his elbows in through his window, held his chin in his palms. "Shit, what a mess," he said as he looked past me at the dark opening. "I want my own bed."

Years ago, at the back of that ruined garage, behind a wall of well-anchored boards, I found barrels and pipes, a few brown glass bottles—a still. "Sure," Gardelle said, "Joe Anderson would brew some and take it down to town on weekends, Saturdays. That's when we'd see him. Ran some cattle up there. There's a couple of old places in that valley. Let me think. I must've known all those people once."

Besides the cow camp and the Anderson place and the ruin in the high meadow, there was one more place I could think of, one more ruin. Up the ridge, south toward the Wind River, in a stand of cottonwoods long dead, I remembered finding a root cellar, its door half covered in old mud, and a strangely intact roof lying close to the ground, the walls crumbled straight away below it. That made a total of four places somewhere out from the spine of the creek. Maybe they had all been occupied at one time, before even Gardelle would have known of it, and on summer evenings when the breeze stayed warm, the people would have wandered along the trails, met by lantern light, and shared some brew and a look at the stars.

David wanted to be let off at his house, a few miles west toward Togwotee. On the way through town, we stopped at the post office. I waited in the truck as he went in and emerged with our mail rolled in our copies of the thin county gazette. By the time I got back to the ranch, it was early afternoon. Lulled by the closed space of the warm cab, I switched off the ignition. Ahead of me, my cabin's windows reflected sky. I'd left breakfast and lunch in the refrigerator for Sam, and by now he'd have eaten his fill and left the dishes in the kitchen or beside the bed.

Before I could step from the truck, Jake caught me. Someone had phoned—there was a fence broken at Red Willow, a heifer loose on the road. He climbed into the truck, I turned around, and we headed back out through the gate.

We returned at nightfall. Jake stepped down and walked to his own truck, drove away. I parked by the barn, took out the key and stuffed it in my pocket, scooped my mail from the floor and leafed through it in the glow of the dome light.

A postcard from the Fishers—they'd be back in ten days—could I get someone in to do some light cleaning in the big stone house before they arrived? Maybe that was something I could give Sally or Max to do, after I'd gotten everything else settled right. They'd appreciate it. They'd see us all working. Sam up and moving under his own power.

A letter without return address, sent to me, in this town, in Wyoming, no box number or zip code. In a town this size, after living in it all your life, mail would probably make it to you with just your first name scrawled across the front. I ripped the envelope open, pulled out the folded paper—three sheets—and when I saw the Dear Blue and the tiny, careful writing peeking over from the top of the first page, I snapped the letter open and held it close.

From behind me, a vehicle approached. I folded the letter quickly, slipped it into the envelope, rolled it and the rest of the mail into the newspaper, and got myself out of the truck. As I slammed the door, I squinted into the glare of the headlights. The vehicle stopped and someone stepped out. I turned and hurried toward the lit windows of my cabin, feeling as if something were aimed at my back.

"Blue," Derek said. "Stop."

I kept walking and entered my cabin with footsteps close behind. Off through the bedroom door, Sam lay on my bed, the blanket pushed off. He tried to sit up, but he fell back with his arms thrown out on the sheet. He made no attempt to cover himself.

Then Derek came up on me. I saw the knife he pulled and thought it was a joke, no reason for it. Maybe he wanted to get past me to Sam, to hurt him again. His knife caught me on the lower back—enough pain that I wanted to be done with it—a hot line in the flesh above my belt. I got after him, kicked at his balance, knocked him down and away.

"Leave it, Derek."

Fallen against the edge of a table, he seemed large and uneven, dulled. His eyebrow slowly split, and the blood swelled, started to flow when he poked at it with his fingers. Then it spread down and filled the white of his eye.

I got him to his feet and held his arms behind him to keep him from starting again. Outside, across the yard, I hoisted him into his truck. From the rack in the back window I took his rifle and emptied the chamber. Derek struggled and clawed at my shoulder and neck, and I pushed him over on the seat, held him down with my weight as I searched the glovebox, the floor, behind the seat, underneath, looking for bullets. I found one yellow box, let Derek up, slammed the door against him, and threw the box far out into the dark field toward the river. He twisted his key, the engine came up, lights on, and I jumped back as the wheels turned sharply over, spitting gravel.

Sam stood at the bedroom door, a sheet for a cape. I crossed to the dark bunkhouse, scooped up his things, threw them into the back of my truck. I wrapped Sam in a blanket, wadded up his clothes and held them under my arm, supported him across the yard, into my truck, and drove. He touched my cut, and I pushed his hand away.

A few hours later, on my way back into town from the higher country, I stopped at Sam's trailer, hooked his jeep to my tow hitch, and took a winding route around town, down to the ranch, left the jeep in the back end of the stuffed, dusty storage barn.

I sat in the gray room off the sheriff's office. Danny—big, careful, a star in metal-working shop in school—came in with two Styrofoam cups of coffee, handed one to me, sat in the other wooden chair, and leaned back against the wall. Taking a few sips of the hot coffee, steam rising across his face, he watched me over the rim. The early sun angled at him through the window, and his eyes squinted closed. He slowly rotated his cup between his palms.

"Blue," he said, "thanks for coming in," and he stood up, drew the shade, and took a notepad from the table. He stood over me for a second, fumbling for a pen in his shirt pocket, saying, "We have to follow up on this kind of report. You can't know how much I'd rather go fishing."

Settling back onto his chair, he wrote a few lines on the pad, kept his eyes lowered as he spoke. "I'm going to ask you a few questions. I've known you most of my life—I trust you to tell the truth. Derek told us a story. Now, you've never done me harm or anyone harm that I can think of." He looked up. "Just a few questions. Then we'll be done with this, at least as far as you're concerned. Okay, man?"

I nodded and he began, his eyes back on the notepad.

"What's your ranchhand's name?"

"Which one?"

"The guy who Derek hurt at the bar—allegedly." He gave a short laugh.

"Sam."

"Yes. Isn't he still hospitalized? Shouldn't he be?"

"He was released."

"Okay. Where was he last night?"

"In my cabin."

"Okay. Did Derek come to your cabin last night?"

"Yes."

"Did he seem to just want to talk, like a social call? I mean, you've known him forever, right?"

"He had a knife out."

"Knife. Okay. *His* knife? He didn't pick it up somewhere in your cabin or take it from you after some sort of exchange had started?"

"No. He came in the door, took out his knife, maybe from his pocket or from a sheath, and was on me and cut me."

"May I see the injury?"

I stood up, turned around, raised my shirt, and heard Danny slide his chair closer, then back against the wall. I sat down.

"You had someone look at that?"

"It's all right."

"Okay. Did you do anything to defend yourself?"

"Yes. I got the knife away from him and gave him a few good knocks to keep him off me. Then I got him in his truck and he drove away."

"That's all?"

"Yes."

"What were you doing when Derek arrived?"

"I'd just walked in. I'd been down at Red Willow with Jake."

"And Sam?"

"He was asleep."

"Where?"

"In my bedroom. He'd been staying in the bunkhouse, but he reinjured himself, so he stayed in my cabin where I could watch him closer. You know what Derek did to him."

"Alleged. But I know, yes. So, where were you when Derek came in? Did you go to answer the door?"

"No. He busted in. I was a few feet into the living room."

"You weren't in your bedroom?"

"No."

"Were you fully dressed?"

"Yes."

"Okay. What was Sam wearing?"

"I don't know. He was in bed. Maybe he had on a T-shirt or something."

"That's it? I mean, that's the whole story? Anything else?"

"Nothing. What did Derek say?"

"Oh, you know Derek. Anyway, I guess that's all I need from you now. I might need to see you again if Derek pushes this thing—I'll do my best to talk him out of it, buddy, but it might not be a bad idea for you to press charges against him. I mean, that cut of yours is a good piece of evidence."

"No charges."

"Right—best to leave this sort of thing alone. If we can nail him with assault, maybe even attempted murder, against your ranchhand, we might be able to put some fear into him or get him locked up. You think Sam's feeling good enough to testify anytime soon?"

"Sam's gone."

"Gone where?"

"I don't know. He loaded up his jeep and took off last night, after I put Derek out. I think Derek scared him. He might be back when he's better and Derek's in jail."

"Shit. You sure he left town? He's not staying at his own place?"

"No. I checked his trailer. No sign of him."

"Shit. Can you reach him?"

"I don't know where he went."

THREE

I had known Gilbert for only a few hours, less than twenty-four, almost a month ago now, but his voice remained clear in my ears. I laid his letters out on the bed, the first and the two that followed. Postmarked in Idaho, Nevada, Utah, circling out there through the desert. Maybe he wasn't driving straight for anywhere. All those words written so carefully. As he composed, did he perch on the tailgate of his car, hunch forward at a desk in a motel room, sit along a trail in the shade of a rock wall? All I had were his words. He wrote nothing about me. Just his life.

When I was still a young boy, my mother moved us off the reservation to the edge of town, out where the only thing beyond us was dry buffalo grass full of tin cans and bedsprings and socks dried in stiff clumps. Walking into the long, early-morning shadows, I looked across the fields to the line of mountains that ran toward our old place. Stickers poked through my soles—I never learned the magic that protects your soles if you're Indian. On open ground, I faced away from the sun and shifted my little hips. I did a snake dance on ten-foot legs.

The air was clean and empty. I could hear a car coming up the road from miles away, see the silver gleams across the brown flat fields and wonder who it might be. For a few months it was a federal worker with a white shirt, yellowed mother-of-pearl buttons, and a tie so tacky he should have been hung by it, choked blue. He smelled as if he'd just eaten a short stack of pancakes with an ice cream scoop of whipped butter and a lake of blueberry syrup. He said, "Morning," as if we hadn't figured that out yet. He said, "Just want to make sure you all are eating well and so forth."

Mother waited at the back door. She smelled like corn. Like beans. She would watch me approach, then back away into shadow, and enter sunlight again at the kitchen table. She'd sit there, quiet, unmoved, as if her hair wouldn't go gray.

She painted her lips. I took the red, painted my own, and stood beside her in front of the mirror to make sure we looked alike. She said, "You're mine, Gilbert."

I said, "We could be the same person."

She laughed. "You think so? I think maybe you have a lot of your father in you. But you have me too. My color."

"And Father? Tell me again."

"Your father is a beautiful man."

"A beautiful man."

"With yellow hair."

"Yellow."

"And blue eyes."

"Blue."

"And he loved your mother."

"Loved you."

"And I love my baby."

"Love me."

"And you'll be the best of your mother and the best of your father, so nothing can hurt you. Nothing in this world."

"Nothing."

■ ■ ■

Through dry mornings, we ate with the window open. A fly buzzed around the food or landed on the edge of the orange juice pitcher, if we had orange juice, and the warming breeze brought in shreds of cottonwood fluff, the song of a bird, or the sound of a car from far down the road. The cars turned off the state route, took the curve fast past the yellow warning markers, and came straight and humming along the road as if there were nothing but morning and horizon ahead, nothing but sun always rising and hills like temples to be skirted.

For hours, I'd stand in the shade beside the house and listen for the whine of tires on that gray asphalt. In the next car would be a lady, maybe one of my mother's employers. She'd have feet that could take a shoe with a heel and eyebrows so perfect they'd seem painted. I drew pages full of eyebrows. She'd drift to a stop in front of the house, and the grass would bunch against the car door. I'd lean in at the window from the passenger side and inhale the scent of her powder. She'd turn to me.

"Aren't you a beautiful boy," she'd say. "You come with me. You'll be mine."

People took our picture. Traffic flowed through town all summer, heading up into the mountains, over toward the national parks. The people wore plaid shorts. Mother and I had matching ponytails, a spot of turquoise on a wrist or finger. We held tightly to each other's hand as a man backed us up against a storefront. He ran his hand over my hair, shook my shoulder, and said, "Ain't you cute as the devil."

Mother decided to take me to church. "A good balance for what you are, what me and your father are." The night's cold moisture evaporated around us as we walked through the stark summer morning, down to the state route, then straight toward the big square shadows of the buildings. Flies fought in the air over the trash bin beside the A & W. A truck passed, rumbling slowly, the only vehicle on the road this early, waiting to rev out into the vacant miles beyond town. I looked back. A few round clouds sat on the spine of the mountains. Cottonwoods shimmered along the river.

We sat at the back of the long, narrow room and pulled our shirts out from our damp skin. There was no clean light—our hands, laps, the necks of the family sitting in front of us, everything, was colored through pictures in the windows. A white man in a silver dress held his arms out toward the people, his fingers pulled into fists, and he spoke in a deep, tight voice, not letting a sound miss our ears.

". . . the wicked bend their bow, they make ready their arrow upon the string, that they may privily shoot at the upright in heart."

In the building behind the church, I sat at the end of a table and listened to the woman with the gold cross and the stiff, copper hair tell us a story about fire raining on a plain and burning away cities and people and plants. I thought I smelled sage burning. If my mother were turned to salt, would she be a stack of the pink mineral blocks the ranchers put out for their herds? Maybe she would be white and pure.

The woman bent at my shoulder to hand me paper and crayons. She smelled of flowers and cigarettes.

My grandmother's house on the reservation was a whitewashed square at the edge of a gully. Beyond the bare dirt that surrounded the house, prickly pear, sage, and short grass grew on clumps of their own refuse.

I'd sit by the back door and watch for Uncle Gordon. Granite spires rose around a fissure in the face of the mountains. I took a scrap of paper and drew petroglyphs for the walls of that high gate.

Copulating waterbugs. Strings of stars tangled. Figures frozen in dance, in flight.

My grandmother had dark teeth. She took me to where I

would sleep during my visit, pulling me past walls hung with heavy blankets. Spirits watched me from the pottery designs and the bunches of herbs hanging from the ceiling. My room had no windows and smelled of tanned hides. I could reach out in the dark and stroke a deer's back or run my fingers through a bird's slick feathers. The animals waited with me. They heard what I heard, the sounds focused in the complete blackness.

It wasn't my language the adults spoke, the calm, slow expressions, Gran almost in a whisper, punctuated now and then by a clucking laugh or a light slap on her thigh, and Uncle Gordon talking as if he were about to cry, unable to say anything harsh. I imagined his lips moving. He would close his eyes as he spoke, as if his voice came from his sleep. The edges of his body—the shoulders solid, and his limbs loose and gangly and soft. His voice fell into the rhythm of footsteps.

He followed the tracks of an antelope through a stand of aspen, across rocky barren stretches, around the edge of a pond. When he finally approached the antelope, it watched his zigzag from cover to cover, and it stood its ground, waiting, curious. He stopped close and set his arrow, keeping eye contact. He said, "Please. I won't hurt you," just before he killed it.

Nothing moved in the house. I tried to sleep, but the sound of my own breathing made me kick my legs, back and forth, beneath the blankets. The dead air against my face forced me down into my own warmth, away from the silence.

I imagined my uncle standing outside the house, the sun hazy on his arms, his long fingers, calves. He grew smaller in the fast-moving shadows of clouds. I tried to keep him close to me so that I could see the rough skin on his elbows or his profile if he glanced to the side. Long strands of hair fell between his shoulder blades.

He walks toward me, and I wait in the shade beside the house, looking out into the glare where he moves. With the sun behind him I can't see his expression, just the mass of his body, so much larger than mine, like an idle space out in the rush of

119

rising heat. He enters the shadow of the house, stands above me, and his face makes my breathing fast.

Our clothes lay in a heap among the roots of a tree. We slid down over the carpet of pine needles and entered the water. Steam rose around us. Uncle Gordon's prick submerged and floated out from his body.

We sat on the bottom, on the rusted, slick rocks, at the edge of the warm spring, only our faces in the air. I rolled onto my side, a casual move. Uncle Gordon shifted into my embrace. We rarely talked, just fell to it. Now I was almost as tall as he was, and I could hold him under water, throw his weight over.

We spread out on a slope of granite, crumbling black lichen, and water ran off us, pooled under us. The breeze traced along our exposed spines, our necks, between our legs. He flopped his hand onto my back and turned his face toward me. Bits of pebble and lichen clung to his cheek. With his eyes closed, he said, "You should live here. On the reservation. It's the only place."

"I'm not all Indian."

"Of course you are. Every bit I've touched is pure Indian, and I've touched every bit."

"I think about others sometimes. White boys."

"That's not right. You can think of me. You can think of other Indians. That's the only way. Look at what's happened to your mother."

"She's fine. She loved my father."

"Do you love him?"

"I love what I know of him."

"What do you know?"

"He's beautiful. He loved my mother. He was from across the ocean. He gave me my life."

"What life is that?"

"My *life*. My breathing."

"But he's not in you. I'm in you. Your mother's in you.

Gran. We can give you the life of our people. You're berdache. That's the only way. With us."

"White boys."

"They're not for you."

"They were for my mother."

"Not for you."

Ray. I gave him a square of hard cornbread at lunch. He took it without looking up and ate it in three bites. I would have laid my hand out flat on his forehead and pushed his hair up out of his face. I would have picked the crud from the corners of his eyes.

My friend Louise was big at a young age. Her breasts moved like dangerous waves inside her clothing. We sat in the fields beyond my house and picked stickers from our socks. "All you have to do is take what you want," she said. "No one is going to put up a fight."

Louise was feeling ballsy. She picked me up in her Dart, red interior, Saturday night, and we headed out along the dark roads, the lights of town always off to the side, obscured, fenceposts flashing past in the headlights. We passed the dump road and pulled onto the shoulder. She shut off the engine, and we sat in darkness, listening to the car settle and pop, smelling the sage and the last of the exhaust fumes. "I can hardly stand it," she said, passing the schnapps. "The air is so warm, it's like it's part of your skin. It's got me all tight. I've got to heat up or cool off, fast. I'm in trouble. Help me fix my lipstick."

I held the lighter while she looked at herself in her pocket mirror. Her lips took the greasy red. Then she reached over and placed a red dot on my upper lip, on my lower lip. A final swig of schnapps.

We started across the ditch, through the lines of barbed
wire, into the fields of short grass, the scattered humps of sage,
the invisible cactus.

"You sure this is right?" I said.

"Never fails. Every Saturday night, all summer. You must
know that. They'll all be stoked. I can't believe you haven't been
out here before."

We walked in silence, came to the top of a broad, steady
slope. The land dropped away in a shallow plain, the horizon a
line of distant hills, flattened by the moonlight. At the center, a
small flame burned.

As we continued, in step, our arms swinging and almost
touching, the flame grew, became a bonfire of crackling dry
brush. When we could just begin to see the boys' faces clearly,
we knelt behind a low sage.

Bodies moved around the fire, stepped to the cooler, bent at
the radio to increase the volume, bring up the bass. Ray, I was
sure, in a stiff, off-balance swagger, passed across the fire. He
held his arms over his head, his beer bottle glowed through with
red firelight, and then he spun around and shouted, howled, out
into the darkness that the fire blinded them all against. His
voice was familiar to me, but the howl, taken up now by the
other boys, had an alien intensity, something they hadn't shown
me, hadn't invited me into. I opened my mouth and tried to
imagine the sound rising from my lungs, but all I felt was the
dust and smoke blowing through my throat.

"This is it," Louise said, heaving herself up into a squatting
position. "See that?" A boy had broken out from the circle of fire
and wandered off to the left. "Good luck," she said, and she
kissed me on the mouth quickly, stood up, and headed off, skirt-
ing the fire, in pursuit. The taste of liquor stung my lips. She
faded, was lost, and then the close, huge noise of the bonfire
faced me.

I felt heavy on the ground, unable to focus, as if her kiss
had hammered my drunkenness straight between my eyes.
Forcing myself up, grinding earth into my palms, I squatted

there, watching. Another boy broke out and stumbled off to the right. On my feet, I moved quickly, without thought, pursuing, and the steps seemed natural. The moon opened the ground out before me, and I ran, long and wild strides, a hundred yards, and then I slowed, moved up, silently, to the boy, his legs spread in a rocky stance, far out from the music and the light. Another step and I reached around his waist from behind him, pulled his body against mine, ran my lips up his neck.

He arched back into my advance, his hands suddenly on me as he lurched around to face me, pulling my hair out from its ponytail, pulling me down to the ground with him, speaking in urgent commands, but I couldn't be sure of the voice, couldn't pull enough light from the surrounding darkness to recognize the features. He rolled on top of me, his weight and the liquor of his breath falling through me. Pain forced my voice out, but he continued.

Then, for a moment, the touch of flesh, the warm air drifting across us, the rhythm of breathing, my nose pressed into the hollow of his neck, light enough on his face above me that I knew it was Ray, knew suddenly the smell of him, knew he would settle into me, slowly, and we would laugh, and his voice and his skin and his life would be close to me.

A sharp pain in my gut, his fist, my shirt yanked out, and the sound of voices. Not my own voice, not Ray's. He wouldn't stop, kept at me, his hard fists. His mouth was open, strange, an animal choking, eyes rolling into its head.

A burning branch, flashlights, approached with a whoop of voices. I fought to wedge myself out from beneath the weight, but my escape was cut off, my hands caught in his hands, legs tangled with his legs. They surrounded us. The light was full. His face, strong, sharp, pulled up from me, descended again. He shouted into me with the crowd's voices. The voices all aimed at me. And I heard nothing I recognized but the crackling of sage, the rich bones consumed by fire.

■   ■   ■

123

Mother lets her fingers linger on her breast as she watches herself in the mirror. Her skin seems somehow altered. She closes the front of her cotton blouse—she won't look at herself anymore. She paints her lips, names the window, the door, in English, walks out onto the hot surface of the earth, steps up onto the gray asphalt as if it were a path, walks quickly to town. Inside the woman's house, Mother faces her employer with a strong smile, sets to her task, as if it is natural, as if she likes the scented cleaners, as if she appreciates the money, as if she has something to prove. She polishes white porcelain, tries to ignore her reflection looking up at her, as if it is confused with alien images, strange continents, as if she has betrayed her people, won't look up.

Mr. Fisher came over from the main house in the afternoon and fired me. A month since I first saw Gilbert. A month of people asking me questions, stories shifting.

I packed my stuff and loaded it into my truck. Boxes full of clothes and photographs and any number of things that had kept me going over the years alone. Night fell. With the lights shut off in the cabin, I looked out the window at the river and the face of the mountains. That cabin—such a small stack of logs. Years. The dusty smell, clean dirt and wood. The fireplace that had held a steady fire through long evenings.

I climbed into my truck and leaned forward over the steering wheel. The lit windows of the main house—the shadow of the windmill—the dark shape of my cabin indistinct. I'd been settled. If I turned onto the road and drove flat out, away from town, onto the plains, I'd drift into someplace strange where no one knew me. Dawn would come up on land that seemed like another world.

Climbing out of the truck, I kicked the door closed and crossed the yard toward the main house. I knocked on the back door. No answer. At the front door, I let the heavy knocker drop a few times against the wood before pounding with my fist.

Nothing. Stepping off the stoop into the wet grass, I moved from window to window, looking in wherever I could. No sign of anyone, no sound. At the back door again, I let myself in. I stood at the center of the living room. Bright table lamps and floor lamps were scattered all over, glowing through their big barrel shades. Straight over in the corner, I sifted through the stacks of photo albums. A single couple posed against hundreds of backgrounds, smiling or not, aging, cross-eyed or rumpled, well traveled. I left fingerprints on the slick surfaces, held the albums directly beneath a lamp, saw the shadow of my own reflection looking up at me. There had to be thoughts behind their tiny, faded faces. My fingernail ran across the foreheads—with a little more pressure, I could have scraped away the color and left white paper, something to write on.

I drove out beneath the main gate with my boxes piled in the back of the truck. The mountains rose around the town and held everything in a tight pocket. Streetlights brought my face into the windshield, into the side windows, brightened me in the rearview mirror. Coming parallel to the bar, I slowed to a stop, looked across the street and in through the broad front window and the neon signs. There was movement in there. I parked the truck and walked across the street. The dull thump of music leaked out through the walls. I opened the door and stepped inside.

At the piano at the far back of the room, Clarence was the only face I could hold clear as I looked around the crowd, up and down—his round pink face, greased black hair, jagged teeth shining as he smiled toward the couples, turned back to the job at hand, back to pounding out a song that threw bodies together. I watched my own feet, edged the dance floor, and came up against the end of the bar. Hands held onto glasses and bottles, a woman circulated a rag.

"Blue," someone said to me, close to me, and I looked up and David sat on the next stool, holding his jaw in his hands. His red sideburns bushed around his fingers. He smiled at me, shook his head, glanced next to him at Jake, and then they both smiled and shook their heads. Gripping the edge of the bar, I leaned back to the full extension of my arms and tried to keep both David and Jake in the dead center of my focus. "What are you up to, Blue?" David said. "What are you looking for on a Saturday night? In a bar?"

"Are you looking to find us and put us to work?" Jake said.

They leaned together and said something I couldn't hear, drank from their beers and talked, looked back between them into the crowd. Jake shouted at a tourist girl dancing with her father or grandfather, and she flashed her face toward him, her puckered smile constant behind her whipping mass of sleek brown hair.

Pulling myself upright, I leaned on my elbows, looked down at the blackened wood grain. I couldn't make out a single word anyone said—just a babble that fought with the music, played with it. I didn't move.

A month ago I might have sat there, at the end of the bar, and those people who were happy and surprised to see me would have passed by, paused for a bit of conversation, offered me a drink. "I tell you, Blue, if I can get that property up toward Union Pass, I'll slap up one of those kit cabins before the first snowfall and be home free. I could ski right off the back stoop."

"You get that property," I would've said, "and you let me know. I'll give you a hand building that cabin. Nothing I'd like more than to spend a winter day skiing the meadows toward the pass, looking clear over to the Tetons."

Or a woman would lean on my shoulder. "I can't be sure of him, Blue. You watch him and tell me what you think, honey. You think he might be dangerous?"

"I don't know," I would've said. "You can't tell much about a man by just watching him. Gotta see how he reacts. Throw a snake at him. Or grab him around the waist."

I would've given the slap on the back or the fingers laid gently on a forearm, the casual contact that flickered throughout the crowd as if nothing were happening. That whole life went through my head as if I'd lived it. Or could live it. I knew it. A month ago, I would've sat at the bar as Clarence played the piano, and I would've recognized almost every person dancing.

It would have happened like this— The song somehow makes me think of hot soup bubbling in a pot, pepper swirling in dark clouds on the surface, a long, slender hand taking the ladle and giving it all a violent stir. I want to dance. No young woman in this town has ever gotten me to my feet, ready to stomp around to the music, so I look for who else might be available—tourists or summer help from the dude ranches.

In a booth across the room I see a girl who seems friendly— she has thick red hair pulled back from her temples, a round face that bunches up against her nose when she smiles. Soon I'm dancing with her. Her eyes are hazel, and I see my reflection lurching around in there. I wish I had a better sense of the music and of where to plant my feet, but whenever I seem likely to just stop dead with frustration or embarrassment, she tugs lightly at my hand, leans into my shoulder, and we're right back to spinning steadily around the floor. She smells like vanilla.

She is from the East, attends a college in Massachusetts, works at the Box D Guest Ranch watching over the French tourists' children, has worked there the last two summers, loves the town, loves the mountains, would like to stay, but what would she do here year-round, how would she live? I have no suggestions. She's lovely. I make her speak French to me, and she laughs as I watch her lips move, fascinated by the rasping flow of her voice. I don't know what she says.

We hike a long mountain trail. She walks far ahead, pauses, turns, and waits for me. She is a dot of sharp color against the evergreens. I step up to her, loop my arm around her waist, and we continue, side by side, our hips jostling together. The rocky path carved into the grass is too narrow for us, so one of us walks on the edge, the other down in the path, shifting advantages, stumbling.

We reach the edge of a creek, too rough to step through. I climb onto a fallen log that spans ten feet above the water. I grasp her wrist and she is up behind me. I'm going to fall, she says. Hold onto my waist and walk fast, I say, starting to move as soon as she grabs hold. Either of us might speak now, but we'd hear only water among boulders. I help her off the far end of the log and we scramble up the bank, duck through barbed wire.

After a while, we rise out of the trees and enter the bright, colorless sunlight. The dry scuffing of feet on dirt—the wind in our ears, in our mouths, in our lungs—below, at the bottom of the sheer drop, the needle points of the pines and the rocky cradle of cold water.

We approach a scar, black at the center, on the mountain wall. I reach back and take her hand, and we step down into the dank opening in the rocks. Climbing over the carcass of a dead tree, sliding down a patch of loose rock, we are in the grip of the mountainside. I stop at the bottom of the opening, take a flashlight from my pack and hand it to her, take one out for myself, and shine the light on a horizontal crevice at my feet. Lowering myself onto my back, I shimmy into the crevice feet-first, leave light dancing in her direction, call to her. She imitates my movements, feels the cold, sharp rock against her back, and begins to work her body along the ground in pursuit. After a few feet of progress, she feels the weight of the earth's surface pressing down against her body. Her breathing goes silent.

I grip her ankle, her thigh, her hand, and we're upright, leaning forward over a curved stretch of rock, our feet on a ledge. My light shines on dull surfaces. Then we are walking freely into the closed echoes of the cavern. She takes long strides, following, and skids, lands with her flashlight under her. She reaches for the light, switches it on, shines it on her palm, and studies the blood flowing from the scraped surface. The light flickers. She shakes it and it goes out.

Across the cavern, I wait in a niche of glowing rock. She approaches me, her footsteps slowed by the carpet of gravel, the petrified bat shit. My light shines on some scratchings on the wall—pairs and dates and obscenities. I crouch on a rock ledge that runs down one side of the niche. Matches scatter the floor. Wax drippings. Read this, I say, tracing a finger across the wall. She leans into the niche and squints at the words. John and Jan. Dirk and Betsy. Tom and Pauline. She leans in farther and continues reciting names until she can't pull any more from the scarred rock. Then she scans the wall for the perfect empty space.

Sit down, I say, and she squeezes in beside me, her body against my arm, thigh, calf. I switch off my light and darkness falls, buried in rock. Nothing remains but animal heat. She leans her head on my shoulder, places her hand on my thigh, a pure touch that closes me with her in the darkness, in the heavy mountainside, stationary, with no air moving through, no water flowing away. Out there, above us, daylight is strong. No clouds could have come up so quickly.

We could take a house in town—I know the one—pale green siding, a glass-enclosed porch that faces across fields toward the Ramshorn, lilacs beside the driveway. We would open all the windows to clear out the smell of air freshener, take the covers from the bed and drape them over the lawn furniture, dig our fingers into the garden soil and pull out weeds by their wet roots. Our children follow us around the yard, watching us closely, each move we make—we sit on the front step and watch cars pass, we twine our fingers and let our thoughts drift in the heat. Slowly, our children wander near, sit at our feet, lean back on elbows, face the street—our son with his bristle of red hair, our daughter with her dense mass of black, both with wide-open blue eyes. A truck pulls to a stop and from the cab step a man, a woman, two small children. They cross the lawn in a tight little group, hands held. My family rises from the step and the two groups merge with embraces and laughter, and soon we're all eating corn on the cob and black barbecued chicken, tossing a spongy ball, setting all the children down in their sleeping bags on the porch in time for the arrival of the baby-sitter. We drive to the bar, four blocks away. The crowd is thick, and as we dance, hour after hour, we're pulled apart, carried off by new partners, old friends or youngsters who can't stop moving, and then we're back together, drinking from each other's drinks.

When we return home, slow along the dark, gravel streets, weaving and laughing, our children are asleep, the baby-sitter snoring on the sofa, the television mumbling through a grainy romance movie. We all whisper. Our friends carry their children to their truck, close themselves in, creep forward, turn at the corner, and head for any one of the darkened houses scattered beneath streetlights. We would watch until their lights settled out of sight.

I lay aside the flashlight, step out into the cavern, the echoes of my movements like a hundred other men circling. I step, blind, and turn back toward the place where she sits. Come here, I say. There's a rustle and jumble of sound like rock crumbling, rock ground underfoot and chipped overhead, and then just her breathing beside me.

People will like her. I could hold her. Her arms like soft branches. Her hips like bundles. What do I do? As I take hold of her, I can't tell which way she's turned. Her hair, which should be dusty with rock and the trail, sharp with the scent of pines we've forced ourselves among, is clean as white soap, an empty smell. If only I could see her. I taste blood as her scraped palm brushes across my lips. She cups her hand there, presses at my mouth, and I can't speak.

For a month my ranchhand has been at the cow camp, out there, up there, in the high-altitude light, that light barely filtered, burning. He waits for me to arrive, pause, speak to him. He is starkly lit, no shadows.

This woman has tangled her arms around me, and I kiss her. Her body against mine is all soft loops I can't discover. Losing balance, we fall to the floor of the cavern. Our limbs knot on the gravel—echoes. Her hand forces down between us and takes hold of me. I don't breathe. She stops. Black air around us, a sealed bag, no breeze or life.

My ranchhand, out there, lies on the grass beside the cabin. If I were to stand above him, look down at him, far away from the sound of engines, if I were to speak to him where no one could hear, no one would be unhappy. No one has ever forced me to speak. If things get dangerous, stay quiet and do your job. My job.

"Hey," I said. "David. Jake."

They turned toward me, looking bored. "Blue," David said. "You're still here?"

"Don't you have something to do?" Jake said. "Some work somewhere? You shouldn't be wasting your time with us lowlifers."

"Why don't you go roust up something more interesting?" David said. He jerked his thumb toward the door. "Why don't you leave us alone?"

"What am I doing to you?" I said.

"You ain't doing *nothing* to *me*," Jake said, and he leaned so far away on his stool that he lost balance and teetered, and as David got him steady they both laughed and slapped each other. "God fucking damn, Blue," Jake said, catching his breath, "you're fired, ain't you? We don't even have to look at you anymore. No way we have to *listen* to you. You've lost it. You've got it all wrong."

"You tell me, Jake," I said, and I got to my feet, "tell me what I did."

They stood up and backed away a step. "Come on, Blue," David said. "Just leave it alone."

I lurched around the corner of the bar and grabbed them both by the arm, pulled them until they bumped against me, their faces hard, so close that I could barely focus. "You assholes," I said. "How am I supposed to live?"

They drove their shoulders into my chest, and I was down on the floor with them on top of me. A knee to the gut robbed my air and I thrashed with them with my mouth bloody and locked, my lungs burning, trying to start breathing so I could say something, ask something.

Someone pulled them off me, and with a roar I sucked in air, rolled onto my side, held my knees until the burning subsided. I was at the bottom of a hole, the rim, far up, lined with faces looking down.

"Why don't you head out, Blue?" Albert said. "This fight's over."

"Dear," Mrs. Talbot said. "Honey. Whatever your trouble is, why don't you take it somewhere else?"

Across the rocks, into woods again, we found the line of fence, caught the trail that paralleled it, and headed downhill. The wire strung taut from post to post, unbroken. The woods opened—a heifer wandered a few slow steps away from our passage—closed in again. Aspen came into view, we rushed beneath the pale leaves, and then I pulled Starwood up short, used the end of momentum to land myself on the ground. The shock sent pain up my spine. Taking the reins, I led Starwood forward. The grove was narrow, and within a short minute we came to the far edge and stopped.

The sun had just begun to warm. The cow camp—the cabin, from above, with its roof as green as the meadow. The spring rose from the slope below me, flowed through a fist of young willows, then straight across the grass, past the cabin, into the larger willows and the tangle of the marsh. My truck sat at the end of the road, beside the corral and the tack shed.

From down toward the pond, Sam walked beside the tall willows, rounded the edge of the marsh. Shirtless, his white body was bright against the leaves. His hair was shiny wet. He reached the cabin, and with one hand on his hip, the other on the railing, he took a slow step up onto the porch. Pausing, shading his eyes, he scanned the surrounding slopes. He didn't look high enough to catch me watching. Then he stepped inside, out of sight. No sound but Starwood's deep, tired exhalations and my own breath catching, releasing.

Nothing moved now but the sparkle of water in the channel. The water flowed past the cabin, through the marsh, toward town, picking up soil, coloring red. What seemed like years before, Sam had said that during a flood in the river near his father's place, he'd seen a body, a man, float past in the branches of a tree.

The branches swung up, and the man hung over the water, the rain washing his skin clean of the churned-up flow. Then something snagged, the tree shuddered, and slowly it swung over, taking the man under. It loosened, moved again, downstream, and the man came up, an arm flopped, hung limp. Leaves covered his naked body, shifted, clung, washed away, under water.

Difficult to breathe. As I inhaled, something seemed to bump in my chest like a chunk of wood swirled in a bucket of water.

Starting down the slope toward the corral, I led Starwood, her weight jolting with each step as she held herself from lurching forward, from crushing me. We reached the circle of wooden fence, overhung by the aspens that continued on around to the pond. I dropped the reins and Starwood waited for me to remove the saddle and halter, brush her down, pour out a coffee can full of oats rich with molasses.

Flapping their wings, rustling the leaves around them, three silent magpies perched in an aspen. Starwood wandered away along the road—her hooves scraped rock and thumped. I made my way toward the cabin, across the porch, and as I opened the door the rusted hinges squealed.

At the far end of the room, Sam sat on the bed, leaning back against the headboard, wrapped in a heavy, gray blanket. "Blue," he said, his face blank, and he turned just slightly toward me, eyes hard over and still. He couldn't expect much from me— maybe I'd brought a box of groceries to leave off, having already finished riding lines despite the early hour. But I didn't move, didn't offer my usual quick greeting and excuse to be going. He strained to focus. "Hey." Shrugging off the blanket, he landed his feet on the floor beyond the bed and pulled on his jeans. Hunched forward, he hurried through the dim room. His hand hovered in front of his scar. Up close to me, suddenly, his breath was like wet soil, his gray eyes off my eyes, on my cheek. I raised my hand, ran my fingers over my skin, over the crusted blood and stubble.

"What happened?" His voice, a soft whine, and his scent. He took hold of my arm. "What can I do, Blue?"

I shook free of him, pushed past and left him behind me, and faced the room. There were dishes stacked on the open shelves above the dry sink—books and maps sorted into piles on the bureau—jacket hung on a nail—the metal bucket filled with small, split logs for the stove. A month without any duty but to keep himself fed with the food I provided, to gain strength and keep warm, without distraction. I rode the lines, I drove the road. Now he wanted to help me.

"When?" I said, and I spun around, found him directly against me, the door closed. I could feel the raw strain in my voice. "When are you going to do your job?"

"My job?" He took a step back, and his arms linked loosely across his stomach. "I'm getting stronger."

"You can lift a saddle, can't you?"

"Maybe." He glanced up at me, held his eyes there a second and then backed away another step. With his fingers spread and drawing over his skin, toward his waist, he said, "No, I don't think I'm ready yet."

"When?"

"A few days? I know I feel better. I know—"

"Why the hell does it take so long? Why can't you saddle a fucking horse and ride? You *have* to do your job! I can't keep doing it!"

I shook, felt a sleepless night and all the pain in my bones harden, crumble, sting my eyes. I turned around, looked across the bed, out the window, into the green wall of the marsh.

"Don't you know," I said, my voice cut to a whisper, "that someone came up here? That someone saw you? You were lying in the grass. Don't you have a mind to protect yourself? You didn't even move. A truck came up, stopped, turned around and left, and you didn't even move. You had nothing to do but take care of yourself. Can't you hear a truck? If it had been me—" But if it *had* been me, he wouldn't have moved. I would have parked, watched him for a minute, hurried across the grass with the groceries, and if he'd opened his eyes I would have tossed him a greeting too soft to be heard before catching Starwood, saddling her, riding away. No time to think. If I'd paused, I might never have gotten myself moving again, might've lost hold of what I had to do. "It's a mess." Taking slow steps, I stopped only when my knees hit the bed. "Mr. Fisher has been back for two weeks. He came up here and saw you, after I'd told him you were gone. He said we ain't running a charity. If I can't fire and hire to keep things going, then he'll get someone who can. I've got years with him, and not once did he question me. Jake and David must've said something. So that's it."

He was behind me. His hand brushed my shirt above the remnant of Derek's cut and pushed at my shoulder, pulled me around, got me seated. With my boots off, my feet were free and cold, and then the sheets and blankets covered me to the neck, the pillow puffed around the weight of my head. I heard Sam shuffle, shift things. Then the door shut, followed by silence.

My summer in the cow camp, five years ago, my first summer alone, I would sleep until first light, rise in the chill, pull on clothes stiff from the cold, and get a fire going in the stove. Then, outside, my feet left silver prints on the wet grass as I crossed the meadow, pissed at the edge of the woods. The birds that flew among the trees and marsh had been singing since well before any hint of dawn. My horse grazed at the upper edge of the meadow, her brown form dull against the evergreen trunks and the floor of dead needles. She snipped grass, white flowers, took a step.

Then to the wooden box over the water. Lifting the lid, I reached into the wire mesh down in the cold flow, in among the cans and jars and sealed plastic bags, took out a small tin can of orange juice, a jar of apricot jam, some butter.

No telephone. No contact. I'd stocked the place with food for weeks. There was noise enough—the bullfrogs and the creak of the saddle, heavy breath of the horse on an incline, and the fire popping in the stove, the hiss of a lantern—through days and nights alone.

Someone arrived—a truck, the engine echoing first from far down the valley, then the strain of unsure brakes as it descended into the hollow. I stepped out onto the porch. That would have been Mr. Fisher climbing from the red truck, leaning into the bed to pull out the packages. Approaching across the grass, he laughed, held the food out toward me, dropped it into my arms and kept on past me, in through the door. "Coffee," he said. "Damn. This is the real thing."

He stood in the center of the cabin, his arms crossed, and turned around slowly. "This is what I'd have if I could," he said. "You've got yourself set up like a professional, Blue. I don't know what kind of idiot I am to let you have all the fun. It's like I owed you something—a big favor. But I don't owe you. I'm just busy. And you're lucky. Damn, do you know how lucky you are?"

"Yes, sir."

He laughed at me as I turned and set to putting away the food he'd brought, dropped the kettle on the stove, stoked the fire, went to put the perishables into the cold box. "Yes," he said when we sat at the table and drank from tin cups of hot coffee, "you've got yourself set up like a real adult. Like a man who knows how to take care of himself. Glad to have you on, Blue. Glad to know you don't need someone to clean up after you."

Then he was gone. I rinsed the cups, saddled the horse, rode uphill. The small cabin, tight and well-ordered, left behind for the day, returned to at dusk.

It wasn't something I had to think about, keeping things in order. Mother and I, in our cabin in town, had always neatened things in silence, once a week sweeping and leaving the windows wide open, even in winter, to clean the air. With her gone, I'd continued, everything scrubbed, shaken out, fresh sheets on her bed as if my father would return to use it. He was the only person who'd have reason to pull back the flowered spread. I had my own room, my own single bed with gold eagles woven into the spread. Irish

136

setters on the red curtains. A black silhouette of a moose on the lamp shade, a silhouette I'd thought for years was a clump of ferns until I'd finally seen it right—in a blink it froze and looked at me, and I knew the scent of it and the great size, the width of the antlers, the blindness that would keep it frozen, watching, until an unfamiliar smell or a noise sent it crashing away, trampling.

My mother's dresses shifted on their hangers when I pulled open the closet door and ran the vacuum down among her shoes. With the windows open, her curtains puffing and snapping, the dry dusty earth smell passing through, moving the bedroom door, carrying away the scents from the cluster of glass bottles on her bureau, the Emerald and Lady Belle and Rose, I caught myself hunched and eyes on the floor, glancing at the mirror as I rounded the foot of her bed. The vacuum's roar shut off. The mattress, old and worn down, gave into the box spring as I lowered myself onto the edge, heard the springs grind, felt that the whole thing might rip out from under me, but I grabbed fistfuls of bed and held myself there, face square in the mirror above the glass bottles, the scents of the perfumes gone with the flow of fresh air. She would have died there in her bed.

She kept her light on late into each night. From my window in the next room, I could see her light shining out onto the fat pine by the fence. She was reading. The light on the pine flickered. The serious books were on the shelves in the living room, her name written on the first page of each, but she had her new thin books to interest her, and she'd buy them by the sackful at the church Opportunity Sale, twenty-five cents a shot. Paperbacks, Westerns, family stories, young people against forbidding parents, travel. Late at night, working her way steadily page by page, dozing. Many times I'd seen her when I wandered in the darkness outside. In the lit square of her window, she lay with a book still open on her belly, her eyes closed, head fallen back into the pillows.

I might open to a page in a book taken from her bedside table. A car rushes away from the rising sun. Over the soft rolls of the land, islands of trees drift back toward the light, taking with them clusters of white houses. The young boy sleeps as the woman drives, and she flips the rearview mirror toward the ceiling to extinguish the sun's glare in her eyes. They had driven through the night, with towns like stars scattered, stars like clouds of light in the wide-open blackness. She is trying to take her son someplace, fast, take him away from somewhere. With his head on a balled-up jacket, he sleeps against the door, lulled by the car's vibrations. If he were to wake up and see the speed at which she pushes them, he might cry out. She lets up on the gas and eases off the highway at the next exit, stops in front of a restaurant no bigger than a trailer. They go inside, sit at one of the three tables, and she orders for them. It's all that matters. Food for her son.

Or a book with a mountain on the cover. A cold wind rushes snow around the log house. From above, on the roof, sharp sounds like footsteps—the frame is shifting, or a pine cone has fallen, hit, bounced down. She opens the drapes and faces herself in the window's reflection, night streaked with the swirling snow that catches the light, close by, and the glitter of an iced branch. That blast of wind—it's still early in the evening, but she can't go out, can't risk forcing her low-slung red car through the drifts. She unlocks the glass-paned bookcase on top of the mahogany secretary desk. A gift from her father, long ago, the desk was always stuffed with papers when he'd had it, the shelves lined with his law books and almanacs and repair manuals. The bottom left shelf had been saved for three decanters, silver labels hung around each neck on a silver chain—gin, brandy, bourbon. Now the desk clears the ceiling of the close room by only an inch—it takes up most of one of the short walls, seems likely to flip the room toward its weight. And no decanters on the shelves. Opening the lid of the desk, she grasps a letter opener, hefts it, traces the inlaid, jade-colored glass in the handle. The blade is cold when she touches it to her wrist, draws it gently up to the crook of her elbow. Her father, at the desk, as he bent far forward over a sheet of paper, his hand scripting careful letters with a fountain pen, would have reached into the lower left shelf, taken a bottle, refilled his glass—a long swallow. The clocks are all five minutes fast, five minutes slow, dead.

Quietly, I would climb from my window, lower myself to the grass, and, avoiding the line of light from my mother's window, cross the yard to the fence, jump, land on the dirt-and-gravel road. The town was nothing more than a few streets, two dozen blocks, each block with a cabin, a prefab, maybe a corrugated barn or garage, a sunflower windmill, a fenced-off section for a horse, mule, dogs. A few minutes and I was past the streetlights and into the Hayes Ranch, the fields that bordered the whole town along the northern edge. I ducked through barbed wire, listened for water in the irrigation ditch. Against the stars, the low badlands that snaked around the town stood out, their peaks and pillars and buttes. Horse Creek, wide and steady, gave out its little noise as I approached, paralleled it for a mile, paused. Across the water, up a ridge, the road from town passed on its way toward the forest, with turnoffs every few miles for a vacation home, a campground, a ranch access road leading to a corral, watering station, or maybe a cow camp far up. With the moon full, the Ramshorn might be clear—pale and distant and far above it all. I could sit on bare, plowed soil, or if it was hay season I could nestle in grass and watch the massive peak beyond the close ridges. In those fields, during the day, I'd seen twenty crows standing like black stumps— there couldn't be crows that large—and then they all took off with one movement and circled up until their squawks were lost in the bright air. I sat where the crows had stood, lay back, counted ten meteors, felt the cold ground, my warm skin. That was all. With my eyes closed, the scents of lichen, pine, snowfield trickle, sage, nest, all the world I'd known, touched, and traced in my mind, it all flowed over me. Sleep. Walk. Edge the creek back toward the streetlights and dark houses. Mother's light was out. Had she looked in on me and found me gone? Had she done anything?

And then, on a certain evening, I sat on the edge of her bed. She handed me her last book to take away with the dishes, asked me to crack the window an inch. "It's cold," I said.

"I want the air."

"It's dusty and windy."

"Fine."

In the kitchen, I filled a glass with cold water, took it to her. With eyes closed, she drank it down in a few long swallows. No makeup, no color painted on her lips or eyelids, just a faint flush on her forehead. She smoothed the covers over her legs, arranged the pillows to keep herself upright, and she wanted me there, on the edge, even if she had nothing to say for half an hour at a time. Over the preceding month, she had spent a few days in her room, in bed, cozy and pale, letting me cook for her, look in on her. She hadn't known I could avoid burning everything or boiling dry. But the meals were fine, and she ate what she could. "You don't have to sneak around," she'd said. "I like to hear you."

"Blue," she said after a long silence. "Let's make a phone call."

Not easy. To find my father, I called information, tracked down the numbers of the motels in the Utah town—there turned out to be only three—called one, not there, called the next, found him, got his direct extension, wrote it down. Mother held the paper, and she folded it, unfolded it.

"He should be asleep by now, if he has any sense," she said. "I'll catch him drowsy so I won't have to be too precise." She smiled at the number, held it closer to her face, took the phone and dialed. Rolling slightly to her side, she settled her cheek into the pillow and pushed the receiver up under her dull black hair.

"Hello—"

Would the lights be on in his room? What voice? He'd been gone for over two months. Each time he'd called, he'd told me a quick joke with a violent punch line, something his new foreman had told him—a long, forced laugh that seemed to fade as if it were swallowed by whatever room he called from—and then he told me to take care, to watch out for Mother.

She listened, her eyes drifting slowly. Then she continued with her voice tight against her lips, soft. "I know, dear. I thought you should know. I have to tell you. I have to leave. Of course, I'm the most comfortable here. Blue doesn't know." Her eyes closed fully. "Blue will take me to Lander tomorrow. Yes. Me, too. A surprise. I made a call today, got the details. There's only so much I can expect. Blue's fine. I'll tell him now. No, I'd rather you didn't—you can talk to him later, if you need to. I'll see you in a few days. Hurry, if you can. Bye."

North into the fields, up onto the crumbling badlands, on my night walks, on a quiet night, no wind, I'd stop and stand still with bits of loose soil rolling away from around my feet. Then the perfect silence, perfect to the point that all I heard was the high thin whine in my ears, the noise that had worried me until I asked others if they also heard it in silence—yes, in deepest silence the mind registers something, maybe itself. And looking back along the ridge toward town, I saw the glow that reached up on the wall of the mountains across the Wind River, saw the windows and a blinking sign or two. A rare car might drift on a road and stop, but usually there was no movement. I could have turned away, always, and kept walking. Take myself away. Mother lay in her bed. If I had kept walking on any particular night, years ago, age nine or ten or eleven, if I had camped high up and never returned, she might have left, might have gotten up one morning after I'd been missing for a month, two months, and driven away on a long, long road to find someone she'd known, a friend whose address she'd once scribbled on the last leaf of an old book. I didn't know that I should have disappeared. I wanted to see her in the morning, wanted to hear her voice, the rhythms so much like my own, the words my words, even my own thoughts sometimes. She picked out the new light on a granite cliff above Whiskey Mountain as spring brought the sun to a fresher angle, talked of the slop of a deep, wet meadow I'd struggled across as if she'd walked there herself. She hadn't. She'd rarely gone into the surrounding mountains, hardly ever lost sight of town. She just listened to me, gave me back my words, and I heard my voice, gentle and clear.

She replaced the receiver in the cradle and settled again on her back, eyes open toward me. "I've been sick, you know," she said, "and I need you to drive me to the hospital tomorrow."

The next morning I got her into the car, and we drove through town, down along the river, past the houses and ranches, past the red cliffs, and out into open country, across the reservation toward Lander. We had just the hour-and-a-half drive with the roar of engine and wind. I kept us at a steady speed, cruising along the curves of the road.

"Why aren't we on our way to somewhere *you* want to go?" I said.

"Oh, this is fine."

"But we could have gone somewhere, sometime. We never really went anywhere you wanted to go."

"I went where I wanted."

"No. If you had a choice, where would you have traveled?"

"I wouldn't have. But let me think—" She rapped her knuckles slowly on the window. "There'd be more water, bigger water—a great lake or an ocean. Someplace where people came and went, always a different crowd, new faces, and no one who thought they knew you more than by name. A place to dance. But I don't want to dance.

"I want to see a flat horizon. That means hundreds of miles from here. Stand out in a field and turn around and see nothing taller than me. Buffalo grass, I think it is, never more than ankle high. No hunk of rock too big to pick up and throw.

"I'll tell you where I'd like to have gone. Someplace where I step out the back door onto a thick, green lawn in bare feet, and the wet is cold on my skin. Early morning, the shadow of the house is long, and I have to take a few steps to get out where the sun is bright. There's heat then on my skin, and enough moisture in the air that I don't feel scratchy and baked. Beds full of flowers—I've got hollyhock and sweet William and trumpet vine. And a tall pink dogwood shading a wooden bench. As I sit with a book and a cup of something cold, a few pink petals fall onto my page and into my drink. From across the green yards, all connected and hidden behind my tall fence, dogs yip and get quiet, lawn sprinklers click through their cycles, children shout and hide, and screen doors slam shut, pulled by springs. Noon comes up and I'm in a clean circle of shade directly beneath the dogwood. I want something to eat. Past the flower beds, the garden pushes against the corner of the fence. I snap off some pea pods, peel them open, and roll the peas into my palm, pop them into my mouth—they're crisp. Warm strawberries that smell sweet and musty. Tomatoes hanging on fuzzy stalks. A cucumber, eggplant, raspberries, spinach leaves. In the kitchen, I run it all under water, fill the sink and swirl it all together, shake it dry and spread it all on the counter. The window frames a wall of green and red and violet, and blue sky above, and the line of the pine board fence running through shrubs and garden and flowers.

"A few rooms is all I want. There'd be a room for you, if you'd like. And your dad—I don't know—he might like it. No. He wants us in the mountains.

"But, I tell you, if I stepped out that front door and looked both ways, there'd be paved roads and curbs. No big piles of dirt washing away. No tobacco-juice mayor. No mule and ax and people who want to help me. I'd have my house. I'd have you. But you wouldn't want to be there. You wouldn't know where you were in a place like that, Blue."

Two days passed and I drove back up the road from Lander, into town, parked in front of our cabin, stepped inside. In the kitchen, reaching up into cabinets, into the refrigerator, I assembled bread, fruit, salami, jam, a water bottle, cup. From the back hall closet and my room I got my pack, knife, sleeping bag, poncho, candle-lantern. On the back stoop, I paused as I latched the door behind me, cupped my face against the glass and looked in. Dark halls, no lights left on. My father wouldn't be through town for two weeks, for the funeral—he'd returned straight to Utah from the hospital in Lander. School wouldn't miss me for a few days—they could have given me my diploma right then—the last five weeks before graduation would be loafing and waiting. I'd already made the funeral arrangements, and I'd be back in time to take care. So I turned around and looked out into the early afternoon, looked straight across post-and-rail, across the sheds and trailers and every name I'd known every year of my life, across hayfields, up along the badlands, and I saw the first green edges where I'd camp, rest, sleep.

· · ·

The stove had heated the room. A muffled clanging of tins. I opened my eyes.

Sam scooped flour, salt, and powdered milk into a large yellow ceramic bowl. He poured water from a height, stirred it in with a wooden spoon. Taking a fist of flour from the largest canister, he sprinkled it on the board, dumped the ball of dough from the bowl, rolled it out with the empty beer bottle. With his knife from its sheath on his hip, he cut the dough into neat squares and dropped them on a baking tin, slid the tin into the oven at the side of the woodstove. Kneeling, he kept the oven door open for a few seconds, watching, before he shut it.

Steam rose from the spout of the dark blue kettle on top of the stove. With a rag, Sam popped the lid, scooped in some coffee grounds, tossed in a chip of eggshell to help settle the black to the bottom. Then he replaced the lid and, after a minute or two, shifted the pot to the edge of the stove.

From a nail on the wall above the dry sink he took down the slab of bacon, opened the netting, brushed at the salted surface of the meat. With a few quick cuts he laid out thick slices on the board. He closed up the slab and hooked it again on its nail, took down the skillet, put it on the stove, careful not to bang it, dropped the bacon in, and waited until it started to spit.

Then, I don't know, Sam got me to the table and sat me down, placed a blanket around my shoulders. A mug of coffee, a can of juice, two buttered biscuits, black on the bottom, and three long slices of bacon.

"The best I could do," he said.

"It looks fine." Taking a bite of biscuit, I chewed slowly, no taste, and washed it down with a swallow of juice.

"My father would talk at the breakfast table sometimes. You want me to talk, Blue?"

I broke each slice of bacon in half and looked at Sam's hands, small, flat on the table, fingers spread, clean. He leaned far forward across the table, got his face down to where he could look me in the eye, and waited. My ribs ached. I ate all I could, and I inched the plate away with his eyes still on me. With patience, he could have sat there for as long as it took for me to say something, to ask for something, but silence wouldn't do for him.

He stood straight up, stacked the dishes. Then, from behind me, he forced a hand under each of my arms, leaned close to my ear, said, "Get up," and heaved. I was on my feet, my weight back against him. "We're going to get you scrubbed and rested."

The surface of the water was warm, held up against the sun, but the water beneath swirled in cold eddies. I stood a foot deep in the pond, arms crossed over my bare chest, facing away from Sam. The thick black muck on the bottom padded my soles. Around the edge of the pond, aspen stood at almost even intervals, leaves shaking above the white trunks. A few more steps, and I was deep enough. Bending my knees, crouching, I submerged, the warm surface water at my neck, my body numbing.

Clean reflections spread in front of me—sky, hills, trees—nothing to disturb them, no breeze, no ripple, until a dull splash from behind me and the slosh of slow wading. As fingers found the top of my head and rested there, ripples swelled past me and muddled the picture. What was it now? What would the picture be if someone watched from the far edge of the pond? A person would see a head on black water and a young man behind whose fingers seemed to keep the head from drifting. Would it mean anything?

There was a time, years ago, when I carried a dozen crates of canned food to Fred Connell's truck. It would've appeared that I'd roused myself from the steps of the mercantile to lend a hand to someone we all knew, someone who himself would have offered a helping hand to anyone if it was needed. I slid the crates into the back of his pickup. "Dudes will eat anything," he said. "They get famished up here in the altitude." Ham-sized cans of beans, pickles, corn. Fred's forearm descended from his rolled sleeve, the skin dark against the faded green plaid, a dusting of bleached hairs that stopped at the wrist. He took my hand, his grip circling my fingers and squeezing them straight together, painful, and he said, "Blue, you come up to the ranch some time and I'll put you on any horse you want. A free ride, Blue, for a good kid. Thank you." Back on the steps, I might have been watching the tourist traffic rumble past, tiny mobile houses roaming the roads. But my mind was up past Wiggin's Fork— Fred Connell stood at the stable door and waited for me to approach. He'd removed his shirt, and those same bleached hairs dusted his collarbones and descended in a narrow line to his navel. I placed my hand on his shoulder and pressed my cheek into the center of that chest. I would have. I saw it clearly. I needed to hear his voice growling from beneath his ribs. I would have heard it if he had stood there, if he had let me, if it had happened, if he had said, "Blue. I don't know. Stay here. Don't move. Like this. Yes, this is right."

Sam had brought a washrag. He let it drop into the water, plucked it up, and, still standing behind me, ran it over my brow, across the back of my neck, and he leaned forward a little to see clearly as he patted at the scrapes and bruises on my face. As he worked, the water felt like nothing on my skin, but when he dropped the rag back into the water, the skin he'd cleaned tingled and felt tight and chilled.

Age sixteen, I walked the streets after dark, on my way out. On a summer evening, kids would gather in small groups, late, and as I passed through backyards, corrals, as I crossed streets in the space between lights, I paused and listened, looked. Five boys stood beneath a streetlight and watched insects swarm around the orange glow, and they laughed each time a larger shape, huge among the little flutters, swooped through—bats. The boys punched at each other with their laughter. "They're fast fuckers." "Big wide-open blind eyes." "Get what they want." These boys, my own age, if they'd seen me standing not fifty yards away, could have called to me to join them, asked me what made me so shy, teased me a little and welcomed me into their games. I could have followed them from light to light. If they caught sight of some girl in a window, I could have recited her name along with them—who couldn't? I never—watching the boys stand, hearing that slap of fist on shoulder, imagining the shock of muscle—never paused long enough for them to call to me, never long enough probably for them to even see me. To anyone, I was out on a walk with nothing on my mind. Those boys, they jostled each other in a small group, and later, maybe on a darkened porch or in the bed of a pickup, they got drunk enough or tired enough to let their arms go loose and soft, settle back, and talk about scents and heat and questions.

"Stand up," Sam said. He reached into the water and took me under the arms, pulled, and I stood as he drew the rag down my spine. Water ran off my fingertips, dropping a half inch to the pond surface, drops with the sound of small rain, no sound at all.

He pulled at my shoulder. I turned to face him. His shirt-tails moved around him in the water, blurred shadows on his pale legs beneath the surface.

"You've got to feel better now," he said. He dabbed at my chest. He lifted the rag from the water and held it above my shoulders, let water fall over me like fingers along my edges and nerves. The pain, each bruise, distinct and clear, was surrounded by cool evaporation, water drawn into air, Sam washing, the breeze shifting.

With my eyes closed, with my feet in the ooze of rotted leaves and grass, bark, fallen animal bone and muscle, all my long limbs and tough weight was clear to me. Water around my legs, water falling now from my head in a cool web, my torso surrounded by breeze like invisible cotton, I saw myself through it, my head lolled back so that my hair brushed at my shoulder blades, my black dense hair, water pooling in the hollows of my eyes, the taste of water working in past my slack lips. The taste of decay in that water. Twigs that had clogged and dried. Leaves that had gone from green to rust. Maybe a taste of me. Blood drawn from a cut and caked black. Blood beneath the surface pooled in a cloud of purple. Old thoughts.

Sam had turned. I heard the water slosh. I saw him step up onto the grass, his shirt dark where it clung to his buttocks, white where it puffed over his back. He took off the shirt, tossed it to the side, and turned back to face me, moving as if I couldn't see him, as if there were nothing open about him at all.

"*What?*" he said, and I closed my eyes for a moment, found my hands rising and looking for somewhere to rest. "You going to stand in there forever? You're clean. Now get some sun on those pale bones."

No clouds yet, with the sun higher toward zenith. At the edge of the pond, I shook my feet clean in the water and stepped out onto the grass. Sam lay face down. Lowering myself beside him, I rested my chin on my crossed arms. Already my back was dry. Stretching my arms up, I dug my fingers into the grass, hardened my toes and forced them down, made myself thinner, more taut, held to the earth, and then relaxed. My arms slid down and rested along my sides. I turned my head toward Sam.

Grass—the thin wet green with parallel veins. A flower like dozens of waxy fingers held up in a bunch. Sam's eyes opened and closed, gray with spokes of black from the pupil. My own reflection was in there, the hairy outline of my head and the hot point of the sun far up, behind. Sam's nose twitched, and his head shifted forward an inch. His tongue tipped out and wet his lips, retreated and left a tired smile.

"Sometimes you have to tell someone what you're thinking," he said, and then he kept talking, his mouth low to the ground, close.

In Ohio, the fields were cut from thick tracts of forest. Sam was fourteen then and lived with his family in an apartment tacked onto the back end of a barn. The roar of rain pelting the roof of the hollow barn would overwhelm the apartment, drown the radio and the voices. Spilling from the roof onto the dirt lot, the rainwater dug a trench beneath the eaves, and then flowed away toward fences and fields and the manager's house, carrying bits of straw and manure.

Before dawn, no lights brightened the apartment windows. Sam's sister, Beth, was asleep—her chores could wait for daylight. Sam waded through mud, avoiding work for a half hour as he found his way to the fenceline, followed the posts through darkness, and approached the musty edge of the woods. Water dripped from the leaves, and Sam held his face up and let drops strike his closed eyes and his cheeks. He tasted the water that gathered at the corners of his mouth—it seemed pure except for a hint of salt, Sam's body.

Sam's father would rise after Sam had already mucked out the stalls, measured and poured the grain and fluffed a few leaves of hay in each manger, brushed and watered the horses. The cleaner Sam kept the barn, the fresher the air seemed in the apartment. The manager, alone in the two-story house, never spoke to Sam, hardly seemed to notice him from his perch at the back window or his makeshift office in the barn, never smiled as Sam made his way through the yard, to and from school, never mentioned to Sam anything about how he might improve. Sam took his orders directly from his father, and no one, not his father or the manager, ever saw him with a rake in his hand or hauling a bucket. Everyone slept as he worked. His father only checked after the work was completed.

Sam's father said one evening, leaning in Sam's bedroom door, that he was through doing another man's work—they would be leaving soon. He wanted to get west, where the air was so dry and pure that nothing would rot. Air held up on piles of red rock and granite. There would be plenty of land that no one else would want. There would be a job that would be more than just acting out another man's desires.

Sam expected the trip to take weeks. Miles west, hauling their new trailer, they'd drive up over a final ridge, and the setting sun would blind them, cause them all to close their eyes hard and then try to refocus. The red of the wasting sunset would color a wide-open stretch of land, the rest of the country left a thousand feet below. They'd park the trailer at the center. At night, rainfall would tap evenly on the roof, pool briefly where it drained to the ground, and then trickle away toward a gully, a creek bed, enter a river, go far away. Stepping from the trailer, Sam would walk for miles with nothing to block his view.

On the road, Sam crouched in the back of the pickup and looked forward through the cab window, out through the windshield, and watched the gray rush of interstate as they dipped across the Mississippi and started to ascend. The white dashes flowed into a single line, a thick rope to pull them along.

But the truck threw a rod—ruined. They got someone to tow the trailer to a lot on the fringe of a huge farm. In exchange for odd jobs around the farm, Sam's father was given free rent on the lot. They hooked up the electricity. Sam's parents talked about saving enough money to buy a new engine for the truck, or a new truck altogether. Sam and Beth walked to town and enrolled in school.

Winter came, a humid summer, and then another winter.

Sam listened to the rush of water in the river. He wondered where the first drops had fallen and accumulated and started to flow.

Sam looked out from the bedroom window. Stars wavered in the hot air, moisture rose from the massed corn. Settling back onto the sheets, he tried to stop breathing, to stop thinking, to sink. Blood pulsed at his wrists and across his belly. His pores were tiny lakes.

A curtain hung across the doorway and blocked the light from the living room, where his parents would eventually fall asleep on the couch. His father was talking. The guests might have left already, but he hadn't heard the screen door slam or a motor rev up. The voice went on. "It gets dark as muddy shit. You have to cool off when the heat gets bad." Another man spoke, two women laughed, and the stereo came on, droning steadily.

Out in the lot somewhere, Beth slept in a pup tent. Some nights, when the air became too stagnant, she left Sam alone in their bedroom, took a sheet and a pillow, went outside, and zipped herself away from the mosquitoes. On those nights, Sam slept without pajamas.

Someone flipped the curtain open, light hit the wall above his head, and Sam grabbed the top sheet, pulled it to his neck, curled himself away from whoever.

"What do we have here?" It was Jack's voice. "Somebody get this kid a beer."

"If he wants to join us, I don't give a shit," Sam's father said, his voice moving away through the trailer.

"I'll check." Jack's weight lowered onto the edge of the bed. "Do you want anything? A beer would feel good—make you hazy." His hand rested on Sam's neck. "I bet it's hard," Jack whispered. Sam didn't move. The hand rubbed his shoulder, then two hands circled his neck, slowly caressed up behind his ears, slid along his arms, increased pressure as they worked his tightening muscles. Sam might have been locked in sleep, forced into the barest intake of oxygen, trying to retract his nerves far below the surface of his skin. He felt his lungs burn. The hands worked in unison down his back, pulling the sheet with them, to his buttocks, then retreated, took hold of his hips, massaged. Sam gasped. He heard the sound he made—a cracked squeak. Jack left him, cut the light with a snap of the curtain, and said, "Some other time," his voice back in with the others.

Sam stood at the center of the bedroom. People shifted and muttered in the living room. After a half hour he heard, "Good boy, Sam," as if in the darkness Sam were visible, illuminated. He reached out and shifted the curtain in the doorway, let a sliver of light cut from his solar plexus to the space between his planted feet. As he swayed, he watched the light on his skin, almost felt it trace the length of his prick and nuzzle his balls, loose in the dead air.

Sam slid on a pair of shorts, a T-shirt, and sneakers. He pushed at the window screen, and it fell to the dirt outside with

151

a blunt rattle. Hoisting himself up and out, he landed beside the screen and quickly replaced it. As if the sun had just set, the trailer's metal wall radiated heat, but it was late into the night.

When his eyes began to take in the darkness, he saw the pup tent a few yards out, against the corn. Beth could talk to him, tell him a story. Squatting at the tent door, he gradually raised the zipper, keeping its action muffled in his fists. "Beth," he whispered, and ducked his head in. His hand slid forward across the tent floor, caught the pillow and the wadded sheet—empty.

He walked around to the end of the trailer, climbed up the skinny ladder, and looked out over the roof. Lights shone, far off—blue lights on poles, one for each farmhouse, something to define the huge flat black of the fields, and at the edge of the world the town gave its light straight up, streetlights and porchlights reflecting off pavement, walkways, and stones painted white. Maybe Beth was in there somewhere, in the town. She'd wandered off. She didn't like to be alone.

She might sit among the darkened houses, in the darker night beneath an elm, and hear a dog bark, a door open and someone yell, close by and cut off. From far across the fields, if the wind was right, would come the pulsing whine of night traffic on the interstate, the huge trucks hauling desks, stoves, lettuce, a soothing drone that gives way too quickly to the buzz of insects. The boy beside her would run a finger across her knuckles, and they'd lean their thin shoulders together. When the boy tried to kiss her, he'd grab a mouthful of her collar as she turned away. Could he buy her a Coke, the boy would ask. She'd laugh and say she had to go. Everything's closed.

She glanced back once as she turned a corner, out of sight, and then she moved quickly to the edge of town, the grove of old shade trees. Running along the country road, she laced among the potholes as if she could see them, past a half mile of soybeans, a half mile of wheat, a mile of corn, and then the trailer was at her hip and she stopped. This late, the lights were all off. Who would have known if she had stayed out for another hour? The boy had flattened her rumpled collar between his palms. She took weightless steps through the lot. Her mother and father would wonder about such a young and handsome boy. They might be angry. She zipped herself away and slept.

Another year passed. Sam walked miles on roads that rarely saw traffic—a tractor or truck at certain times, harvest or planting or someone lost. If it started to rain, mud would splatter his legs brown long before he could get anywhere close to home. The moon lit high tiers of cloud, the only real distance he could see. The land was tight around him—it surged for a stretch, then rolled over on itself in a soft, ranging trough.

As he walked, Sam looked up at sky, down at what might be the horizon around him, all blurring and stirred together. Someone might come across him at any moment. The approach from farther than a hundred yards was swallowed in corn. He would probably recognize almost any of the locals. What would they be doing out there? Aunts, tiny cousins, flat-voiced grandfathers—they'd all lived so long on this land that they all had the same shrouded eyes and straight, abrupt nose. They shifted among each other.

Sam stepped into the trailer—home.

Wanda and Jack, standing at the kitchen counter, chopped stalks of broccoli into bite-size pieces and dropped them into a bowl. Sam's father knelt in front of the open refrigerator, shifting containers back and forth, and came up with some sour cream. He opened it, stuck his nose over the edge, and inhaled. "Hunger," he said, dumping the cream into a mixing bowl. "I ain't eaten for days—I *feel* like it."

Ripping open a packet of soup mix, Wanda shouldered Sam's father aside, emptied the powder into the cream, and started to stir. "We have eats, gentlemen." Taking a scoop of the brown dip with her finger, she painted it across Jack's neck.

Jack wiped off the dip with a piece of broccoli and ate it. He chewed quickly and swallowed as he took up another stalk.

Paul came out of the bedroom and asked for a smoke. They all started searching pockets, tabletops, until Wanda pulled a cigarette out of her purse, placed it between her lips, lit it, and took a few long draws before handing it over. Then they switched off the kitchen light, sat on the couch or on the floor around it, and ate seriously for a few minutes before passing around a bottle of whiskey.

"I'm better. I'm fine," Sam's mother said as she emerged from the bathroom, and she sat on the floor and slumped back against the wall at the end of the couch. Her face was tough and red. She'd combed her short bangs up off her forehead and secured them with a half-dozen bobby pins. As her eyes closed, she refused the food and bottle that Paul passed her way. "You know, I could kill all you guys," she said. "I swear I could run you all flat over. I can see it happening. Then I'd go over to *your* houses and lie around on *your* furniture. I swear. On God's earth, there's nothing finer than you lovely people."

"Honey," Sam's father said, "why don't you brush your teeth? You'll feel a lot better. Go on."

She didn't move.

"Why don't you brush your teeth and go to bed?"

Her eyes slitted open. "Spearmint toothpaste won't help me. I know it won't."

"Wash your face, then."

"I just washed it."

"Use cold water. And *drink* some water. And brush your teeth."

Her eyes closed again. "Sweetheart—don't say anything else."

Paul looked around at each face—no one moved. He reached an arm smoothly over the back of the sofa and pressed a button on the stereo. With a plastic slap, a record fell onto the platter and started to revolve. The music, a hair too loud, forced its way through a hiss of scratches. Four more records were stacked above and waiting to fall. "I don't see why you can't get yourself some fresh music," Paul said, taking the bottle from Sam's father.

Wanda looked at her feet, raised them into the air a few inches, and clicked her heels together. Jack unfastened a shirt button and pushed his hand into the gap, raised it up beneath the cloth, and seemed to rub his chest gently. He looked up at Sam, who leaned against the wall beside the front door, held Sam's eyes for a few seconds, and then lowered his gaze to Sam's chest and held it there.

Sam twisted against the wall, turned around, stepped over to his mother and crouched beside her. Her head was flopped back against the wall, and the tissue beneath the skin of her neck shifted up and down as if she were swallowing repeatedly. Sam held his hand close above her forehead and felt the heat rising from her damp face. "Mom," he said, pressing a finger into her shoulder, "why don't we go for a walk outside? You could use some fresh air, huh?"

Her eyes dropped open and her head fell toward him. She looked at his outstretched finger buried in her shoulder. "Why can't the men in this family leave me alone?" she said. "Why are you always picking at what's good for me?"

"I thought you'd want air."

"Don't think about me. Don't be stupid. There's a God-fucking world full of stuff to think about. I'm not it." She leaned away from him.

"He's a terribly concerned young man, isn't he?" Wanda said to Sam's father. "He's certainly a much more attractive personality than you could ever hope to be." She snapped her fingers toward Sam. "What are you doing here, Sam, with these primitives?"

"He likes us all right," Sam's father said. "He tries to make us proud. Not an ounce of trouble. Never knocked anyone up, you can be sure of that. You ever seen him have fun?" He grabbed the bottle from Paul and held it out toward Sam. "Get away from your mother, Sam. She's feeling a little sentimental tonight. Why don't you have a drink with us?"

Taking the bottle, Sam slid back against the wall beside his mother. Everyone watched him. He took a swallow. It tasted good, so he took another. His eyes watered.

"He's not much up to anything," Jack laughed. "He's still sort of pulpy. Do you think he shaves?"

"Oh, dear, he has to," Wanda said. "I'm sure he's got hormones."

"Jesus," Paul said, "I hope I don't catch them. I'm too tired to go out prowling."

"So's Sam, I guess," Sam's father said. "You think he's shy or just scared?"

Sam's mother roused herself and clamped an arm around Sam's shoulder. "It's like this, Samuel," she said. "You get out there and do it once and then it's easy. Your father won't tell you this. Maybe you don't want to stir up any trouble. That's the right attitude—stay away from trouble. So what are you supposed to do? You could follow Beth and see if she'll introduce you to one of her friends. But you're shy. Okay. You know, there used to be a way for a guy to get himself some experience—"

"God," Wanda shouted, "I swear she's going to tell the poor boy to use a *hooker*." She got up, stepped over a few legs, and stood above Sam. "Paul, turn up the stereo." The music strained the speakers. "Give him to me," Wanda said. She pulled Sam up from under his mother's arm. Jack switched off a light, the corners of the room blackened, and dim shadows bunched on the wall above Sam's mother. Wanda led Sam to an open space beside the front door and turned him to face her.

They'd do this sometimes—talk about him, watch him. They all seemed to want him to take some action, probably something they could laugh at. He could ignore it—they hadn't touched him. But now Wanda took both his hands in hers and held them up in the gap between their bodies.

Beneath her mass of wavy, reddish hair, Wanda was short and thin and almost frail. Her eyes, a pale, unclouded blue, were steady behind her pointed nose. Lifting one hand and then the other, she started Sam rocking with the music. Suddenly she fell limp against Sam's chest, he caught her, and she regained her balance and held close to him, laughed gently. With her arms looped around his waist, she rocked him.

Sam saw his parents watching, his father with a flat smile and his mother with a grimace. Paul laughed loudly and took a long swig from the bottle, put it down, and started snapping his fingers as his eyes fluttered closed.

Wanda pushed the top of her head against Sam's nose. Her hair smelled like smoke. "This is dancing," she said. He had the feeling that she might want to climb up and hang from his neck. Closing his eyes, he tried to hear the music above the confusion of the body against him. He found the beat, planted a foot with the drums, made a small turn, taking Wanda with him, and left his back to the room. Through the screen door ahead of him, the blank night stretched away.

Fertile land. And town after town. Each town with the same people. How many picnics could there possibly be? Family gatherings—three or four or five generations, and stories that reached back another fifty or a hundred years. Sam had seen a backyard full of redheads, a baseball diamond crawling with heavy brunettes. In three years in this town, he'd heard stories about voyages west across the Atlantic, covered wagons and steam locomotives, a spring wedding beside a creek before the church was built, sod-roofed cabins and finally the first brick house, death by blizzard, a love lost to the flu epidemic, forty-three grandchildren and one great on the way.

Wanda slid her hands into Sam's back pockets and wiggled her fingers. "Don't you listen to anything any of these low-balls have to say. There's no rush. You're doing fine." Her body tightened against him. He felt the sharp edges of her hip bones and the shifting flesh of her chest. "One, two. One, two."

Maybe tonight, in the calm air, he would hear the sound of the interstate. It droned like voices or music, but it was simpler, more direct. Not much difference between the whine of the various engines as people traveled from one far place to another. They all kept going, rarely pausing. Who would break down and accept it as final?

Insects, again—a roar. At twilight, huge flocks of dark birds would fly over the fields, snatching the insects from the sky, and circle, shift in one big fast-moving clot, and land in the branches of a huge old cottonwood, partially green among the splay of bare limbs, far out in the lost center of the farm. Each night, a storm of chatter, a pulse of settling wings, the tiny claws seizing hold on wood. Sam could stand beneath the tree at night and listen. Faint, hard-edged calls, clicks, a few whistles like sighs, descended on him. A breeze would blow through, a gust of wind, and the tree would seem to expand slightly, to rise up and spread out and catch its balance. Black pairs suspended on the network of branches, differences indistinguishable in the darkness—even in daylight, the female just faintly less black than her glossy mate. They all huddled together, pulling in tiny lungfuls of air, sleeping half-alert for any change, for a snap, something crawling.

Beneath low clouds, the town glowed, two miles away. In there, somewhere, Sam's sister laughed with someone her own age, a boy, any one of the number she knew.

Over the past year, Sam had listened to his parents, hoping for a change. Night after night they sat in the trailer and talked about heat and cold, told each other and their friends how to earn more money or improve appearances. Sam's father was settled—his job kept him tinkering for most of the day and then left him alone. With no grandparents alive to go visit, nothing essential that couldn't be picked up in town, they had gone as far as they would.

The music crashed through the room. Sam kept his limited movements on the beat.

Jack would be watching him. Lounging on the couch next to Sam's father, Jack would raise his head toward the ceiling, seem to lose focus, but always his eyes would be on the boy. Jack—tall and plain, his hair buzzed short above the collar, a single small blossom tattoo on the inside of his left forearm. Those petals spread in a tight, contained cluster, a spot of color on the long length of exposed skin. Jack, night after night, settled into his seat, taking his part. Through the past year, Jack had moved close to Sam when they were alone, out of sight for a minute. "I bet it's hard," he'd say, and Sam would hold still. At some point, some day, Jack might finally figure something else to say. He might catch Sam with a few new sentences that startled them into something.

Fingers reached into Sam's hair. He struggled to exhale.

Wanda was kissing him. With a flinch, he shook her loose and stepped back. His chin was wet. Her nose and mouth were flushed blotchy red. She let a half-smile tilt her lips, and she reached for him again. He felt the hardness in his crotch, felt his scalp burn with heat. He wanted to duck. "Shit—shit—shit," he said, his arms folding up over his head. "Don't—" With two lurching steps, he tried to get past her to the door.

Grabbing his arm as he passed, she spun him around and held him steady. "Oh, baby, it's fine. You're a very sweet boy." As she tried to run her hand through his hair, he jerked his head away. "Now, Sam—"

The music had stopped. Paul was asleep. Sam's father sat forward and glared. "Goddamn it, Sam. You act like an idiot. You could've really hurt the woman. Tell Wanda you're sorry."

"I'm not."

"Fuck. Say you're sorry."

Sam stared back at his father.

"I'm tired of your holy-shit attitude, Sam." He made to get up from the couch, trying to shift his weight forward.

Sam didn't move.

From the floor, his mother said, "Now, dear, I don't think Sam has ever seemed—"

"The fuck he hasn't. He's too good. Too fucking good for any of the boys in this town. You think he'd ever have a friend? He's too good for the people of this whole *state*, this whole fucking state."

Sam freed himself from Wanda's grip and stepped back against the door. "I'm not too good."

Jack stood up and looked down at Sam's father. "What's with you? Why don't you leave him alone?"

"He could've hurt her."

"He didn't do anything to her." Jack looked directly at Sam and seemed to struggle against a smile. "He's not *ever* going to do anything to her."

Sam got himself outside and ran to the center of the black road, looked in each direction. Nothing moved.

He wandered back into the lot, slowly around the trailer, and climbed the ladder to the roof, crouched at the edge above the door. The air hung over the fields like a sheet of steamed skin. The smell of harsh fertilizer in the air tightened his chest, and he tried not to inhale too deeply.

After a long stretch of time, during which the stereo was turned up again, the bass vibrating through Sam's haunches, the door swung open and slapped against the side of the trailer. Wanda stepped out. She paused, held her hair up from the back of her neck, let it fall, and tucked her blouse into her jeans. She turned back toward the light. Her eyes were murky. "People," she said, not loud enough for anyone inside to hear, "I'm going home." She ran a finger around her lips and rested it on the tip of her chin. "Jesus Mary. I've got traffic school at eight fucking a.m. Thank you very much." Waving slowly over her head, she wandered to her car at the edge of the road. The engine idled for a few minutes before the lights came on, and then she crept forward, flattened a few stalks of corn, and found the center of the pavement. For a full half hour, the red dots of her taillights and the glow of her headlights drifted over the roads as she made false turns, trying to find her way back into town.

The door swung open again, a hand held it from striking the trailer wall, and then Jack pursued his own shadow toward the corn. He stood at the edge of the first row, leaned forward, and seemed to peer into the darkness. He might have been

talking—his head tipped back and forth, nodded for emphasis—
but Sam couldn't hear the voice.

Sam crawled back over to the ladder, landed on the ground,
and he was level with Jack, who still motioned toward nothing
at the edge of the lot. Sliding along the trailer wall, Sam paused
at the edge of the door, glanced inside for a second, and saw no
one upright or alert. He stepped straight out to Jack, came up
beside him, looked up at Jack's bleak eyes.

Jack's mouth was caught open in silent midsentence. His eyes
went hard over toward the trailer, then squarely back on Sam.

Pushing through the first row of corn, through the second,
deeper, Sam pulled Jack behind him through the slash and rustle
of the leaves. Light was left behind, sound, the dull music,
buried. The sharp leaves cut Sam's arms, opened a line of warm
blood across his temple, and Jack kept pace, no resistance. Then
Sam caught his balance as he forced through a final row, sensed
a void, stopped abruptly. Jack bumped against him and remained
there. A few feet ahead, water rushed in an irrigation ditch, a
bass gurgle with a hint of chill.

Sam released Jack's wrist and took a step forward, stripped
off his clothes. As he looked down, his body was almost invisible, his limbs shifting from black to dank gray as he stared, and
he felt the air drawing moisture from his skin.

Sam could sense no movement from Jack, but he heard
breathing, a slow sucking at the air, a pause, a deep exhalation.
He heard a steady thump like a fist slammed. Jack didn't
move. Maybe he waited to gather enough hints of light and
sound to see Sam, or to sense him, to create in that darkness
the young man he had contemplated in a hundred different
situations—Sam as he might raise a glass of clear alcohol to his
lips and take a swallow, Sam as he might roll up his sleeve and
pinch his own bicep, Sam as he might purse his lips to spit. It
could have been anything in Jack's mind, but Sam knew it was
focused on him.

■   ■   ■

161

Settling, they slid from the edge of the ditch, down into the flow of the water, against the slick mud. Sam twisted his legs around Jack's, tangled his arms around Jack's neck, and they rolled, bucked, lifted into the current. The water moved them together a few inches before a leg caught against the bottom, a shoulder hit, and they slowed, rebounded, moved again. Sam could have held on, without air, through the entire length of the gradual decline of the irrigation ditch, giving out eventually to the final reach of moisture, miles away across the fields, lost among rows and roots to the south. If he'd opened his mouth and inhaled—he *wanted* to open his mouth—he would have taken into his lungs the water that carried them.

They found their clothes and got dressed.

"We're finished here, Sam," Jack said. "Let's go." He took a step into darkness and waited for Sam to follow.

"I can't find my shoes." Sam crouched on the ground. Thistles scratched at his hands, and then the soil chilled him. He sat down, stretched his legs out straight, groped around him, and fell back flat. He couldn't be sure if he heard the insects—maybe just a bit of static like a rustling breeze, the ongoing passage of water through the ditch. "I want to stay here."

"No. My car's at your father's trailer. If we don't get back—"

"I want you to take me to your house."

"I can't."

"Well, come get me tomorrow and take me driving somewhere."

"I don't think so."

"Then we'll walk somewhere. We could walk somewhere *now*. I'll go with you and we'll take a hike."

"Not now."

"Tomorrow, then."

"Not ever. You changed things, Sam."

"No. I just pushed things."

"Whatever. But now they stay like this."

"Come sit down, Jack."

"I can't. I have to hurry."

"I'll follow you."

"Don't, Sam. No coming to my house. No walks. Nothing more than this."

Sam ran along the edge of the irrigation ditch. He ran toward the river, following the ditch as it plunged under dirt roads, across fallow fields, between walls of corn.

At the juncture where the ditch drew water from the river, Sam rested beneath crowded trees and looked across the huge, flowing space before him. On the surface of the water, an occasional gray crest flashed. Gnats swept along the bank in dense clouds, searching for something, never venturing into the cooler flow of air above the river. They swarmed around Sam—he felt them on the whites of his eyes, in the hollows of his ears, brushing at the bubbles of spittle at the corners of his mouth—he couldn't part his lips or breathe—then they were gone.

Taking off his sneakers, he held to a clump of roots and stepped into the edge of the river. If he stepped again, if he walked down the slope, how long before it bottomed out? The scoured channel would have a gentle floor down deep. If Sam were to sink, muted in fast water, he would still be within a breath of the meeting of air and earth. The horizon cut as close as the next cottonwood windbreak, the next wall of growth, the next town in its branching dome. People moved all over that land, seeing and losing sight, coming across each other unawares, carrying away with them the things they saw.

Hours until sunrise, Sam ran upriver along the bank. Night went on ahead of him for half a world. He ran straight into it.

Sam remembered a weight of blankets on him—the dark warmth he exhaled surrounded his body. No light entered his tightly shut eyes. From somewhere outside, he heard his parents' voices. They muttered, set fast to each other. Forcing his palms against his ears, he heard the pressure of his flesh rustling his eardrums, felt the jitter of his pulse. He let a groan rumble through his throat—the sound, immersed in his small body, seemed immediately familiar, the only sound he could understand, as it flexed his limbs, heated him across the back of the neck, the center of his chest, his tailbone. A lone sound that couldn't escape the heat of his blood rushing through. He tried again to hear voices from outside. What were they saying?

Ahead, lights arced over the river—a steel girder bridge and a rush of traffic. Sam stopped at the edge of the last field before the wide cut of the concrete interstate. Cars and semis whined past at odd intervals, sometimes solitary, sometimes grouped in a noisy blur of white lights, red lights, strings of tiny orange lights high up around the edges of the trailers. Inside the cabs, behind the windshields that scattered the insects, nothing was visible. Speed. An ability to keep going.

Sam waited for a gap in the flow, and then he ran across two lanes, through the grassy dip, across the next two lanes, and turned west. When he approached the cluster of lights of the rest area, he cut out into the field, turned down the line of a row, and ran beneath the flutter of gold tassels. He came even with the lights, turned toward them, forced his way forward across the rows, and emerged into an opening where he was brightly lit, stark. Someone stepped from the shadow of the small brick building across the lawn.

On the first night—a young man with round black-rimmed glasses and a bony chest.

On other nights—a tall, gray man whose cap hid the focus of his eyes, whose blue T-shirt couldn't contain the bulk of his arms or the hair that tufted at his neck—or a man who had to pop his knuckles before his hands were pliable enough to caress—or a shivering man who admitted to having left three children sleeping in the back of his long tan station wagon—and more than once, a familiar face, and Sam and the man would duck away from each other, as if out of sight.

On a final night—Sam knelt on the damp ground, in the

shadow of close rows. Overhead, the air was bright from the tall orange lamps not a hundred yards away. He unbuttoned a man's cuffs, reached for the collar and worked his way down, opening skin dark with soft hair and the blank eyes of the nipples. He smelled a scent that made him close his eyes, a scent of soap or beer or some musty unlaundered patch of cloth, made him pull the man down onto him without thought for the man's face, his name, only knowing that this was the closest he had come through a dozen men since that first night, close to something he wanted. The man fought. He tore at Sam's clothes, hissed, "We have to go—" He bit at Sam's arms, at the flesh at his waist, held him in a ball on his lap and bit at his lips until they both tasted blood, a tiny bitter flow, and in less than a minute the man was standing up, buttoning his shirt, saying something over and over to Sam, who lay at his feet, eyes wide and chest streaked with dirt, and Sam heard, finally, the man's words, "We have to go. Hurry. Don't stop until you're safe—" The man stood up, pulled a comb from his pocket and flashed it across his scalp, and then he grabbed Sam under the arms, lifted him to his feet, and left him, running down the row for a few strides, then crashing through to the side.

Sam looked up and saw red light in the air, heard a car door slam, people running, and a shouted order to stop.

Sam returned home, fast across the fields, and found his sister crouched at the edge of light from the trailer, a boy crouched beside her, their shoulders pressed together, and their faces close behind the fall of her hair. Sam ran up to her, grabbed her to her feet, pulled her a few steps from the boy. "What are you doing, Beth?" he said. "Why are you so close?"

"Sam." She laughed and tried to pull away. "I like him."

"No. Why so close to the trailer?"

"Oh. It's nothing. They've met him." She returned to the boy, touched a finger to his chin and raised him to his feet, linked her arms around his waist. They both looked at Sam, kissed, looked again. "Eric, this is my brother, Sam. Sam, this is Eric, my friend. Daddy likes Eric. Do you like Eric?"

Sam tried to pull his sister aside. "Beth, you've got to go off somewhere. Take him. Go."

She pulled him, pinned him between her body and Eric. "Sam, stop it. There's nothing—I'm old enough." Pressing forward against Sam's chest, with her chin on his shoulder, she met Eric's lips at Sam's ear. "They were asking for you, Sam. Jack said he'd seen you someplace. Do you like the way Eric feels against you? I like the way he feels. Jack was tripping. He was choked up. 'Put an end to that. Put an end to that.' That's what Jack said at least a hundred times. Daddy wasn't even blinking. What if a boy like Eric held you? He's held me. Just him and me. You could get to know a boy like him. It would be nice. Sam? Nice to have him over and over. You like how he feels? I love him. Sam?"

Sam sat at a long table. Tubes of fluorescent light hung close overhead. He tossed a knife from one hand to the other and gripped it hard. The blade clanked on the table when he slid it toward the pile of knives he'd already completed that evening.

At the far end of the room, a man in goggles held a blade to a sharpening stone. Water spit on the floor.

Sam grabbed the edges of his box of raw forms and shook it, and the slivers of sharp metal all screeched and shifted and crossed over each other, exposing new edges down into the depth. Sliding his stool away from the table, he walked to the door, pulled it open a few inches, and held his face to the crack. Snow lay in stirred-up ridges across the fields, the whiteness as visible as daylight, and rose into sky somewhere before the nearest tree or fence or building.

At home, it would be hot in the trailer, the windows all closed, drapes all drawn. For the first time since leaving home almost nine months before, Sam pictured the room, a wood-paneled box with an aluminum door, plush red carpet, a black pot half full of spaghetti on the floor beside the extended hide-a-bed. On the bed he saw his parents, Mother with her breasts soft toward her sides as his father rolled onto her. He hunched across her hips, and his hands held her forearms still. She winced. He kept going, closing his eyes, catching his breath, then looked straight down at her as if he couldn't ever stop. He must've thought that nothing mattered, that anyone could pull back a curtain and see.

A few more months and Sam stepped away from the knife factory, outside to the edge of the parking lot, down the road. There weren't many houses, each set at the back of a deep, unmowed yard, with split-rail or chain-link fences running from mailbox to driveway to hydrant. The houses were packed densely at the center of town, dwindling to nothing but stars and dark earth in the open country.

Sam's father hit Jack. Jack's eyes pooled with blood.

Sam headed up into South Dakota, on into North Dakota, where the ground was so high and bare that the earth seemed to end all around, falling away to nothing before life could take a good hold. Sam had bought an old jeep, and in the back he kept his books, maps, and clothes. Roads, gravel and occasionally paved, dipped through the river valley and wandered along fencelines and ditches, passed a gaunt metal windmill and its round water tank, reached a dead end at a rock outcropping, or merged into a state route and continued toward a crossroads where a town might huddle. Winter ice cracked and bunched in jagged slabs on the river. With spring, a hawk tipped her wings and was carried east, looking for prey deep in prairie grass.

"What do you have for me, in the way of work?" Sam said.

A man, who'd stood backlit in his door, deep in across the porch, finally switched on the porch light. "I'll give you food and a bed for a week's work on irrigation. I suppose you can use a shovel to dig a hole?"

Sam slept on a mattress on the mud-room floor. After nine o'clock each evening, with the sky still light with sunset, and true darkness over an hour away, the house was silent. The wind shifted the door in its jam. A scent of diesel from the tractor parked in the yard. A scent of cold moisture settling.

A waitress brought Sam a plate of hash browns, a Salisbury steak in gravy, and a glass of strawberry milk. Sliding into the seat across from him, she started to flip through her order pad, touched her pen to her tongue, seemed to add and figure a variety of bills. Sam was the only customer that late and that far into nowhere. "If you want," she said, slipping the pad into her apron pocket, "I'll put you in touch with a guy who could use a hand for a while. Do you want that, son? He might need you for a week or maybe for a year. You don't want to get rich and die around here, do you?"

A couple gave Sam a room at the top of the attic stairs. Through a door beside the closet, he could step with a flashlight and sit on a caned rocker among busted trunks. In the house beneath him, the husband raised his voice above a whisper only when he sang along with his revival records, late into each Saturday night. Running a finger through the curving channels of his ear, Sam extracted a layer of grain dust and wiped it on his pant leg. The grain elevators rose outside like soft-edged skyscrapers cut loose from some distant city. The weight of the full elevators, the thick columns of grain, pressed into the ground like rock, like monuments. Sam thought of leaning back against the white outside curve of a full elevator, imagined that all the grain behind him had been dumped into a long string of railroad cars, pulled away along the descent of the river, processed into flour, and served at a million meals around a million tables—a man would tap his fingertips on the tabletop, and his wife would reach for a woven basket full of sliced white and slide it across to him. In the empty elevators— always more numerous than the full—Sam would close the door behind him and step out into the middle of the tall hollow nothing, shout his own name and hear it swallowed up. He tipped forward on the rocker, reached for the flashlight and switched it off. No light entered the attic from anywhere in the house. The wife whistled. Water ran for a half minute, followed by a constant silence. Did the husband nuzzle his wife? Did he mount her softened, pale body as she turned her head to the side, her gray hair loose across her face? Tomorrow a train would pull through and empty another elevator. There would be an early breakfast of waffles and sausage. Some maple syrup might drip from the spout of the squat, pewter pitcher, leaving a trail of sweet, quickly hardening drops across the beige tablecloth.

Sam drifted west. Almost every scrap of land had been cultivated.

He took a room with a man and wife who, at each meal, said a long grace, listing their house and cars, their pets, the weather. He worked fifteen-hour days laying fence, dividing country that looked no different on one side or the other—no farmhouses, no trees, just the giant stripes, gold and wet black, of ripening winter wheat and fallow ground. He stood serving punch at someone's family picnic, and a woman pushed her angry, flushed daughter toward him and said, "For God's sake, Iris, *help* the boy."

Sam sat at a bar and traced the blistered varnish. He'd left his last job a hundred miles behind, with no new job yet in sight.

Country music rattled the speaker of a radio propped against the cash register. The bartender leaned at the end of the bar, staring at a magazine. Sam said something, but the man just leaned closer to the magazine and scratched his gray chin. So Sam watched himself and the empty bar in the mirror, straight ahead.

Two guys came in and took stools at the bar. One let his head drop back and shouted, "Ernest, move it, old man. Me and Tommy are thirsty."

Ernest turned a page of his magazine and then stretched his sweater pockets with his buried fists. "Good night, boys," he said.

"Ernest, Ernest," Tommy said. "We really are thirsty. No shit. We was going to the basketball game, but it's a forty-seven-mile drive tonight to see them kids dribble on their own feet. Fuck that. Turn the game on the radio, will ya? And some beers? For me and Frank? Your friends?"

Ernest slid his magazine into the trash, served Tommy and Frank some beers, and turned up the music without changing the station. The guys drank and ordered again. Frank lunged halfway across the bar, reaching for the radio, before a glance from Ernest put him back on his stool. They were all that was happening in the bar, those two guys. Sam watched them in the mirror, Tommy fidgeting inside his shirt a size too full, Frank buffing his teeth with the tip of a finger between swallows of beer. They ordered shots.

Tommy was slightly red in the face, from outdoor work or from the heat of the room. His hands were clean. Frank had a face like stiff cloth, bumpy and slow to move. Frank grabbed his own nose hard and shook it, released it, and it flushed red, a dull jut. He stretched his mouth, gaped it, closed his eyes.

Sam had seen guys like them in town after town—they sat in bars, waited in trucks, stacked charcoal in a grill. They might lie on the bank of a creek, damp soil against their backs, and never wonder about anything but what they could see in front of them—the far bank of the creek and a green edge of wheat, a fifty-yard stretch of flowing water that drained the land somewhere slightly uphill and flowed on down toward something else. Rainless puffs of cloud. The bitter green brambles. They had a world of things they knew well.

It was guys like this that Sam had met without thought and found himself talking to over a beer or at a breakfast counter. They wouldn't force talk, wouldn't flinch at a few minutes of silence, might go on and on about a coyote they'd leveled dead center in their scope. To drink until bleary, wander out into a field, lie down beneath a sky full of summer stars—that was all they might want. From the miles around would come the sound of a windmill rumbling to a stop as the breeze died, the sound of a car pausing as

170

a driver climbed out to open a gate, the scents of exhaust, of soggy ground beside a watering trough, of perfume strained through sheer curtains. The things they wanted were close by—they only had to wait and everything would pass.

Maybe Sam and Tommy, on that night or on one to follow, would drive out on a road and enter across a porch and turn on a light, push laundry off a sofa. They'd talk and finally kill the light. Tommy's forehead was dotted with pale freckles. He didn't even seem to breathe.

Maybe rain brought up deep beds of flowers and the lilacs got heavy around there. Maybe the cottonwoods shook clouds of seeds into the air. That town wasn't large, but maybe the houses had been built when a porch wrapped halfway around and rooms were hidden on floor after floor.

Tommy and Frank would drive off, two friends together in a car or pickup, to sleep in their own beds. Their rooms would be humid with the smell of their sweat. And the next day, next night, weeks and months, they'd be with each other or apart—probably born together in that town, probably never more than a hundred miles apart in their whole lives, hating each other sometimes, stirred up and turning in on themselves. Maybe they'd drag Sam in sooner or later. Given time. An hour, a day, a year or longer.

Sam walked away from the blinking sign above the bar door. The storefronts were each lit from deep within by single bulbs—blue shadows blocked the panes of glass. No cars along the curb.

Trees started where the houses began, and a few streetlights glowed and flickered up in the mesh of bare branches spiked with buds. A half block ahead, moving through the sphere of the second streetlight, Tommy and Frank kept a steady pace.

On each front porch, a yellow bug light hung in a glass globe. Two blocks, and the sidewalk ended. Sam came out from the cover of the bare branches and stopped.

Ahead, a barbed-wire fence ran along the edge of a ditch,

protecting a black field. A final streetlight hung on a wooden pole another quarter mile out along the road, and after a few short minutes Tommy and Frank passed through that patch of light, the last light before the stars took over.

There was no sense of shifting weather in the air. The stars were steady around the streetlight, clear to the horizon, and the cool evening was dry, liable to stay dry.

Sam turned around then, back to his jeep to drive on through.

Sam had spread my shirt over my back, which warmed me, but even in the full sun my legs were chilled, laid out bare on the ground. Winter reaches deep at this elevation, and even in June I could sense the snow not long departed—cool grass and cold roots. I had turned my face away from Sam, covered my eyes with a draped hand, and listened as much to him as to the beat of blood in my ear, my ear pressed to the earth. They went on, the voice and the blood, and I saw only the darkness of my palm and a few shards of harsh sun in the splits between my fingers.

At some point, in an Eastern town, I stood beneath my bedroom window and looked up through the crystals on the panes. The window was open a crack, and freezing air fell through my pajamas. I reached up and tugged the window shut. At the baseboard, I pushed the knob on the grate, and heat rushed out. I stayed there, bent forward. Brilliant light fell from the window. From beyond my closed door, I heard something boiling on the stove, a voice on the radio telling stories.

"You'll want milk in that?" my mother said.

"We could head out, all of us together." My father's voice was muffled, from another room. Then he was clear and close. "There's a world out there."

■   ■   ■

My parents ran through the house. Late, after dark, they were laughing. I stood in my doorway and watched their shadows slide across the walls, out of sight, flashing past. The front door opened, slammed shut, and then the only sound was my mother laughing, catching her breath. I stepped forward, slowly down the hall. She opened the living room drapes, stood at the window. "Come inside," she said, leaning her forehead to the glass. "Come inside."

Out in the snow, deep drifts toward the edge of the woods, lit by the floodlights, my father spun himself, leapt and fell, buried in white, burst to his feet and ran. He wore boots. He wore a cap and a scarf. His bare body was pink against the white. How could he be so strong against the snow? The house seemed hot and close. He jumped, his body in the air, legs skewed. He was cut off beyond glass. Powerful, he touched ground and disappeared into the woods.

In a Wyoming mountain town, we settled into our cabin. I looked for where the stacks of logs were spiked together at the corners, kicked at the base of the broad chimney of gray river rock. My mother carried me to my room while my father continued unloading the truck. My red curtains already hung in the window, open to the sunset and the steep wall of the Wind River Range. I watched the final light catch the highest peaks. Canyons and cliffs traced the mountains. Wind would fall from the peaks to riverbottom, to town. What lived out there? I tried to think of what the animals might look like. Long claws. Blunt teeth for grinding seeds. An arched back with dark stripes. Whatever. They all found shelter somewhere, they all curled in on their own warmth, high up and far away, burrowed into the steep earth. Maybe all the people in town knew the animals and would never be surprised, but who else could ever know them? Would anyone I'd ever known, my grandma or the postman or the children I'd watched sailing bits of stick and leaves in the pond, would any of them ever know how to find me?

"Honey, I'll get work," my father said.

"You'll check the lumber mill?" my mother said. "You'll check the ranches? What do you know about any of this?"

"I could run a hundred miles straight out into nothing, out there. You'd be waiting here. I'd see smoke above the chimney."

My mother never let me sleep in her bed with her, even when the heaviest winds seemed like they'd knock the cabin flat. The empty half of her bed was for my father.

My father told me of the height of the oil rigs, the lights strung on metal up into the sky, the twenty-four-hour roar and the shouting men and the hope that they'd find something rich. He told me of his eighteen-wheeler, the smell of diesel, a stop for hash browns smothered in ketchup—"You'd like them, Blue," he said, "so hot and greasy, and then the rumbling of that big engine to help you digest." I knew he'd come back sometime, and then he'd leave again.

"You be in your bed, and I'll be in mine," my mother said. "What if he surprises us? What if he arrives in the middle of the night? He needs to know that we're where we're supposed to be."

I followed my mother through town, along the banks of Horse Creek. We could see into people's backyards, all the laundry flapping, buckets knocked over on their sides. We ducked and scrambled under the two-lane bridge, and then we were walking on a mowed lawn among tourist cabins, then scrub and willows again. Fences leaned down toward us from the top of the bank.

The creek entered the river, and we turned along the flow. Someone squatted on the steps of a trailer, brushing a fat, barking dog. Behind a metal building, a pile of engines and wheels spilled almost to the water. I wanted to reach for the smooth glaze of a spark plug or the knob of a gearshift, but we didn't pause. As we edged the chain-link fence behind the lumber mill, men in orange hard hats drove around on little yellow vehicles, and woodsmoke drifted from the top of a huge, rusty tipi capped with mesh. At the next bridge, we crossed over the river and continued along the south bank. The town was gone, and now we saw only a tall house with huge windows or a horse trailer alone in a field.

We came up against Jakey's Fork, too wide to cross where it entered the river. Standing in the shade of tall trees, shrubs and fallen logs all around, we looked out into the water as it continued east toward the plains. The roar that surrounded us made us shiver. My mother tested her foot at the edge of the Fork, as if she would walk right through. Looking at the dry boulders that rose out of reach, she teetered forward. I took her hand, and we started up along the Fork, quickly into sage and open sky.

It seemed to take hours to trace that Fork up the foothills. The sun beat down from directly above. We would lose sight of the heights ahead, blocked by a ridge with a fuzz of dry grass, rough rocks, a few bushy pines, and then the mountains would rise again, closer. Beside the water, where the ground was damp beneath the humps of green grass, my mother let me walk ahead.

The pines grew tall, closing in over the banks. There were birds in the trees and in the air. We climbed over a fence, and I saw large animal prints in the mud and piles of their shit in pellets. Jakey's Fork cut so deep and fast that I could no longer see the colored rocks on the bottom—just black water pulling through the reflected sky and trees and my own head leaning over the edge.

I knew I was close to where the water came from the mountain—I could hear it, a constant surge that worked through the breeze, wanted to break on me. I ran. Walls of rock came up above the trees, and then the trees cleared and I faced a gate in the cliff, chipped and broken on its face, smooth and rusted inside where the water flowed. I was as far as I could go, stepping up to the rock, holding on and hanging myself out around the edge to see deep in. Falling in giant steps, water roared itself into mist. Tiny plants flowered on the rock. I couldn't see. A chunk of sky came down into the rock, the water came out of that space in there, but it all ended too soon, cut off. No way to climb up through the water, to see what tunnels and canyons grew farther in, out of sight. The walls could rise forever, swallow that sky.

I heard a cry, like the voice of a ghost or an Indian, and it came around me like the mist and the roar and the cold shadow of the rock. I felt afraid, and I turned.

Far out in the light, in the trees and meadow beside the bright surface of the Fork, my mother watched me. Her red jacket and blue jeans, her black hair. She waved her arms above her head. Now, cupping her hands around her mouth, her voice was her own as she called my name. If she would wait there, calling my name so that I could hear it, I could take some time to look again, to find a path that made its way farther in, over the top.

My father took me up onto the slopes of Whiskey Mountain, carried me on his shoulders. I held onto his thick, short hair, high above the stones and sagebrush and crusted snow. As we ducked beneath the splayed branches of a pine on the ridge, the needles traced across my forehead, and I smelled the frozen pitch. We walked out in the sun, beside the trees, uphill.

I knew then, having awakened to the mountains outside my window for almost three years now, that the ridge would continue across the face and edge a steep canyon. Then it would end in the middle of a stand of blackened tree stumps, dark fallen logs.

My father stumbled, almost went down on his knees, and as he lurched forward, trying to regain his balance, he swung me down from his shoulders, caught me against his hip, and held me tight. "You all right, son?" I nodded, my face pressed into his cheek. "Good boy."

He smelled of his shaving lotions and creams—lime and sharp soap. I would sit on the edge of the bathtub and watch him shave. With a washrag he cleared a circle of steam from the mirror and smiled at me in the reflection. He opened bottles, shook cans, ran water, and swirled things in the basin. He drew a blade across his face, opened a streak of skin in the foam. His large hands, heavy fingers, balanced the blade's handle, moved it quickly, without danger, drew no blood as he pushed his nose to one side and the other, stretched his mouth open, tightened his lips. That was something to learn. His bare back above the towel he'd tucked around his waist—his muscles shifted as he raised his arms, moved his hands, bent forward and cupped hot water to his chin.

From between two pines a bighorn ram sprang, a block of thick muscle and extreme weight of horns and the black eyes that didn't seem to see us, that stayed on his path uphill. His sharp split hooves stabbed into the snow, kicked high, his white rump flashed, the white sack of his testicles hovered beneath the lunge of his body, his dash up the ridge. My father didn't break his stride—he kept moving right into the snow the ram had stirred. What if it turned and came back at us? I grabbed handfuls of my father's coat and buried an eye in his scarf. He moved silently. His breath left my face damp. I still saw the ram, bounding far ahead of us. He was alone up there, but who was to say that he wasn't hurrying to the herd, that we wouldn't suddenly find ourselves surrounded, dozens of rams, each a few hundred pounds of ready muscle and those ornate sharp horns poised. "Stop," I said. "Why don't you stop?"

"I want to see where that beauty is going. Have you ever seen anything built like that? My god, what an animal. What could harm it? If it was healthy, only man could catch it and kill it."

The sun was hot—a cloudless summer afternoon. A boy walked ahead, and I followed. With the town far below us, we traced the ridge and came to the burn, passed straight up among the scorched black and dry gray trees and stumps. Flowers and thick grass and brambles on the downside of boulders made the footing slick and unpredictable. We reached the top of the slope, spiked with tall dead trees without limbs, and then we headed down the backside of the slope, in toward the higher peaks. We had only lunch and water in our packs, but we'd been hiking for hours, moving on as if we wouldn't have to return before dark. Town was hidden now.

Dusty woods. We walked in the shadow of a cliff and came out at the end of a narrow lake. Water stretched ahead of us between steep valley walls. We sat where the rock sloped gently into the water and ate lunch—oranges and chocolate and large hard rolls and jam. We mixed powdered lemonade in our canteens and slept in the sun.

I'd started wandering into the canyons, years ago, toward the peaks, and I thought of little else. Climb up on the face of the mountain wall, up where the valley and river were tiny, where the plains toward Crowheart were pink mottled distance, and then step back, out of sight for a few hours. The rock was warm in the sun. The smell was tart and new, like my own sweat.

The boy woke up and rolled onto his side, toward me. "You know, Blue," he said. "We should keep going. Hike on in to the Divide. I know we could—survive. I have matches. Do you have a jacket? We might find something, buddy. Do you know they never found old Fitchen's body? He was in there, way back on the peaks where only the rams can get footing, and he must've fallen or something. It wouldn't take much. A busted leg and you'd never see town again. Maybe we could find his body, huh, Blue? Couldn't be much left—it's been years—just bones and clothes. He probably made one little mistake, one bad step and that was the end of him. Think of that, Blue, lying there alone, if you'd just wounded yourself and couldn't move, if you hadn't got killed outright, just lying there waiting to die. What would you want? Maybe you'd want a drink of water, or a flashlight to shine at night, or something else."

He leaned forward and pressed his lips to my cheek, his eyes straining to stay on mine. Our smooth faces. As he leaned away, the dull point of his nose traced across my cheek. I smelled the sticky orange from lunch. I couldn't think of a reaction—it seemed right to continue breathing steadily, to wait for whatever would come next, something I imagined to be more forceful. We lay side by side.

But he rolled away, onto his back, and stretched his arms above his head, seeming to shake himself fully awake. Sitting up, he hugged his knees and said, "You think Fitchen killed anything before he died? Think of dying with your prize trophy right next to you. It would start to rot while you held on to living for a few days, and maybe you'd have to watch some birds ruin the hide. The big curl horns would be wrecked by now from lying out in the sun and snow—not good for much more than tacking onto a barn door. Wasted. But maybe we could find his rifle. I know that gun. It could kill anything—a straight, long shot. I could use that rifle. It'd help me start to think about how to line things up."

The boy packed his things and headed toward the trail. "Come on, Blue. Let's get back. We got miles."

I listened until his footsteps were silent. I waited. Couldn't get up and follow for a moment, for a few minutes of nothing but the squawk of a gray jay scanning the rock around me for a scrap. Nothing left. No crusts of bread. No globs of red strawberry. He wouldn't want the few spots of orange peel we'd let roll out of reach. Nothing to eat. Night would come. In town, people would draw their shades.

I could, I thought, die in these mountains. I could hike farther in and lie down and wait. During the day, the hot sun would bake me on a face of rock. My fingertips would inch across crumbling patches of lichen, trace the raised patterns—orange and black dust would cloud my fingerprints. At night, as air fell across glaciers, through my lungs, I wouldn't hug myself for warmth, wouldn't burn sticks and branches. My body would gradually lose heat. I'd lean against the smooth trunk of an aspen and feel no degree separating skin and bark. It would be easy, at some point in the future when I could lie back and remember clearly my life woven with someone else's, easy to give myself to dust and settle into the soil, my bones carried off and gnawed.

I got to my feet, grabbed my pack, and hurried toward the trail, down over the lip. I saw the boy far ahead of me already, moving among the trees below. He seemed to be in a rush, his strides long and unchecked. I wouldn't catch up until we came out onto the ridge, suspended above town.

If I stopped, would he come back for me? You could wait forever, alone and fading in those steep, stark, granite mountains, listen to wind cut through branches, a sound like your own open-mouthed breathing, with a view of silver cliffs like giant wings frozen in sunset, and no one destined to arrive, to rub your shoulder, sit beside you. I descended toward town. Dinner would be waiting.

My father sat beside me as I drove my mother's pickup—it was mine now—up the face of the badlands to the cemetery on the bench above town. Among the sage and short grass, a square of chain-link fence surrounded a green lawn. I parked near the gate and we got out and leaned shoulder to shoulder against the hood, our arms crossed limply over our stomachs. Town was laid out below us, large and clear enough that I could read some of the motel signs, see the brown box of our cabin, but it all seemed pale, sunken below the mountains that rose all around. In front of us the wall of the Wind Rivers, the glaciers and cliffs buttressed by Whiskey Mountain, and behind us the Absarokas, huge carved masses scattered into the distance above parched ridges. Horse-tail clouds streaked the sky. The sun was a small hot dot.

"You tell me what you want now, son," my father said. "You tell me what I can do for you."

"How long will you stay?"

"I've got to get back to Utah. I thought I'd leave tomorrow."

"One night? They must need you bad."

"No. No one needs me. But I don't like to leave something unfinished. Once I get started—" He turned and looked at me. His pale eyes lost focus, wandered to each side. "Why don't you tighten your tie," he said. "And here"—he handed me his comb—"straighten your hair. You have to look good."

"I know, Dad."

"You can't go around looking like you don't care. Show your emotion in the strength of your grip. Hold on just long enough to let them know you'd rather not let go. Here." He stood away from the truck and offered his hand. "Take my hand and hold it."

I took his hand and squeezed it hard, looked over his shoulder at our cabin in the town below.

"Look at me," he said.

"I don't want anything. You go on back to Utah tomorrow. I'm serious. This is my home. I'm fine."

He jangled my hand and tried to bend forward into my line of sight. "This is *our* home, Blue. This is *our* home."

"Okay, Dad."

The hearse pulled up, grinding slowly over the dirt road, followed by a half-dozen cars and a haze of red dust. My father released my hand and we stood apart. Two old men in black suits opened the back of the hearse and pulled the coffin out onto a metal cart. "If you would, gentlemen, please," one of the men said in a small voice, barely audible, his eyes on the coffin and palms turned up.

My father and I took the middle of each side, and the other men took hold—Gardelle, Clarence, Mr. Talbot, and Doug. The watered lawn was soft underfoot—bright green and freshly cut, and the soil dark, almost rich, beneath the blades. We placed the coffin over the hole and the others came up and we all stood together in a bunch, the sun in our eyes. My mother's minister said something, someone turned a crank, and the coffin lowered. I took a handful of dirt and dropped it in and thought that was wrong, that hollow sound, that thump—the dirt should patter in tiny, moist grains.

The hole had been cut square and steep. At the surface, for only an inch, the soil was black and laced with frail white roots. Below, the walls were rusty tan, dry, and embedded with round, gray stones, some as small as a fist, some as big as a pillow. Sediment, laid down over thousands of years. Long before any man, that hilltop had been ocean bottom, and the water of a broad basin sea had risen far above, weighing it all down, soaking it, darkness in the deep salty water. Around the edges of that sea, strange mountains had stood that no one now could recognize. Strange animals. No place out there where you could hear a voice or hold a hand.

As a man pushed the rest of the dirt into the hole, my father and I greeted everyone. They all mumbled softly, and a few people caught the tears that fell when they blinked.

"Dear woman."

"Sorely missed."

My father and I nodded and held onto hands. And then quickly, although people barely seemed to move, everyone left and we were alone.

"Tell me why you brought us here," I said.

"Because it's beautiful. What could be more beautiful?"

"Why did you leave us here?"

"I didn't leave you."

"You left us."

"Because it's beautiful, Blue."

"Do you love these mountains?"

"Yes."

"As much as I do?"

"No. These are your mountains. Maybe that's why I brought you here."

"How could you have known?"

"I couldn't have. You just see what happens."

"Did you love my mother?"

"Yes. I loved her."

The sun fell among the highest branches of an aspen—streaks of warmth and blotches of shade. Sam had stopped talking. My body fell silent, and I listened to the stuttering buzz of an insect from somewhere up the slope, the faint rumble of running water like wet stones rolled together. Only the hollow of my stomach still amplified my heartbeat, tapping like a fingernail on the rim of a metal bowl. As I listened to that tap, I began to feel the throb of each bruise, the slash of the scar on my back, a cold numbness in my groin.

Trying to move without stiffness, I stood up and put my arms through my shirtsleeves. At the edge of the pond, crouching, I dipped my hands into the water and washed the salt, the flecks of dirt, the grass's itch off my face. A few ripples disturbed the reflection of empty sky and then calmed and flattened. There was nothing but blue laid out on the quiet center of the brown water, but all around the edges it was confused with reeds and soggy mats of roots and the tall lines of aspen. I turned to look for my pants, to head for the spring past the cabin. Sam lay on the grass, face down. Far from Ohio, from where he'd started. His white form was settled, and his face was caught in the crook of his elbow. One of my pant legs, sprawled from the lump where the clothes had been tossed, was caught under Sam's hipbone. I didn't want to yank at it, but I didn't want to walk away half naked. Taking up the waist of my pants, I tried to judge how much cloth was caught under Sam—too much to ease out without force. I looked at his shoulder, tapped it once with a finger.

Sam lay still. I don't think he'd moved since he stopped talking, when his voice had fallen to a tired whisper and I'd struggled to free his story from the jumble of my own thoughts. Wouldn't he just rock slightly to the side and let me free my pant leg? Maybe he needed a stronger jolt. I tapped him again and said, "Sam—can you help me out here? Sam? Will you shift a little?"

Sam rolled suddenly toward me, his weight jerking the waist of my pants out of my grip. His eyes were held wide open, gray, and they worked up from my knees to my face. I looked at his chest printed with red patterns from the pressure of the grass. This is how he would have looked—exposed at a man's feet. I knew that he wouldn't stop staring—I backed away a step. I looked at his hip, at the arch of his foot, the line of his scar faded to a stretched pink. He raised himself onto his elbows, a hand flopped to his chest and scratched, drifted down gradually, then reached for me. He took hold of my ankle, squeezed hard, and I couldn't move without losing balance.

"Come down here, Blue."

He was laid out below me.

"I want you down here, Blue."

His scar was another slash in the pattern from the pressed grass. The scar that had almost killed him, that had brought him into my cabin, into my bed.

I kicked at him. As I lurched back, my leg forced forward against his grip, my foot caught him in the ribs, a solid thump that rolled him away, curled him in on himself with a shout, "Blue," like a surprised child. I hadn't heard a voice like that since violent, wild games as a boy, someone slammed to the ground, the ball stripped clean.

"I'm sorry," I said as I regained my balance and grabbed my pants.

"You kicked me, Blue," he said, quickly, loudly, and rolled onto his back again, rubbing his ribs.

"I'm sorry, Sam. I wanted my pants." I turned around and slipped them on, buttoned them.

Then he was on his feet, behind me. His face pressed between my shoulder blades, his hands came up under my arms and crossed my chest, held me, like no one, like Sam, like I might hold something bulky and unstable, balancing his weight against me, shifting with me. I felt all of him. He was strong. His knee forced against the back of my knee and my legs gave out, I fell, the impact sharp through each bruise and scrape. He had me rolled onto my back, he straddled my hips, unbuttoned my shirt as I grasped his wrists and tried to disrupt his rhythm, but the wind was knocked from me and I struggled to inhale. He pinched at my chest, smoothed his palms over my bruises, shook his wrists free from my grip and cupped my face, turned my head side to side as he looked at me, studied me, squinted. I shut my eyes tight as the pain in my lungs released and I inhaled, tight gasps. His mouth covered my mouth. He stretched out on top of me, his chest on my chest, his thighs pushing my legs apart, a hand running down my side, forcing between us, grabbing me, forcing himself at me.

I was tired. I was bruised. In a few seconds I wouldn't struggle. But with my eyes closed, held tightly, yellow swirls of sickly light clouded the black. I opened my eyes, took hold of Sam's hair and yanked his head up off me, struggled to focus on his close, darting eyes, and said, "Why is this right, Sam? Tell me why this is right."

"Blue." He forced his face back down, pressed his cheek to my cheek, spoke into my ear. "Haven't you listened to anything I said?"

He started again. His hands were balled up in fists of my shirt, holding it off me, pinning it to the ground.

I struggled free and got to my feet. My chest pounded and ached. I tried to close my shirt, but some of the buttons had been torn loose. On the ground at my feet, Sam had rolled onto his back. Dirty with grass, he was flushed red. His eyes squinted far up at me, waiting. As his chest rose and fell, his ribs carved lines along his sides, the thin white skin stretched. The hollow at the base of his neck, the tendons in his wrists, the blunt length of his prick, shook with his heartbeat.

"You've wrecked it," I said, and when I heard my dull, stupid, tired voice, when I saw his young face, I wanted to kick him, hurt him, prevent him from hearing me. I couldn't look at him—turned away from his reaction. "It's my fault," I said.

He was on his feet again. "Blue," he said. "It's okay."

"You don't know anything."

"I know enough. I've known from when I first saw you. It's okay. You can touch me and it's okay."

"Shit. Of course. I know that. But I can't live anywhere."

He was quiet for a minute, and then he exhaled. "There's a whole world," he said. "You can find some other place if this is so bad." His hand found the back of my head. His fingers combed through my hair, down my neck. Then he pressed against me—I could feel him at the back of my knees, against my shoulder blades. He held still, and his face warmed me through my shirt, along my spine.

What would it take to turn around and hold him? Nothing. I looked across the pond, down the road to where the red dirt gave out around a curve. Twenty miles of that rough road separated us from anyone who could care a thing for us. I could turn around and let him get me back down on the soft grass. The ground would cool my bruises. Sam would rub my shoulders. I knew that everything would flow along then, and I wouldn't hurt him. I knew his body. As well as I knew his scar, I had come to know the veins that reached up over his taut shoulders, the white down on his earlobes, the deep, red wrinkles at the back of his knees. Things I'd always known?

But I faced away from him, kept him at my back. He rested a hand on my neck, a hand on my hip. The point of his nose traced a shoulder blade. He stopped again.

I heard the buzz of my brain. The sound of breathing, in my lungs, in my ears, his breathing against me, or we both inhaled at once. He would feel my bones holding me together, my heart droning. He would see a shard of my profile, the limp curve of my hands, relaxed at my sides. He waited for me, in that place, held to me. If anyone were to drive up the road and see—but why would anyone approach? I could be dead. Or gone.

A few clouds had come up, flying quickly overhead, and their shadows chilled us beside the pond before letting in the sun again. The blue sky, tall and clean, seemed to glow all over, from above and below, no hint of smoke or dust—just those skittering white clouds. And the sound of running water—washing into the pond through a tiny, choked delta, bubbling and swirling occasionally on the dank pond surface, spilling across the road and into the marsh, caught in the mass of mud and roots. All through that marshy thicket of tall willows and matted, dark green grass, the water sank deep, gathered in pockets of rotting leaves and petals, moved gradually into veins, rose along branches, gave out into the air through the surfaces of sharp leaves. Or the water found the main channel of the creek and entered the flow, broke out of the slow fringe of the marsh, and ran noisily over rocks, out of the hollow, down the valley. From where we stood, that sound of fast water was a faint hiss, shifting constantly out of earshot with the breeze.

Night would fall. Here, the heat gives up into the thin air quickly, and the stars are dense and steady. Here, the sound of running water in the darkness sets a chill down your limbs, and you cross your arms tightly and hurry toward the lit yellow windows of the cabin. Inside, with the woodstove fired up, the air is close and dry. Sam would sit at the table, finish his plate of stew, reach across and trace with a fingertip the creases on my palm. He would remove his shirt, remove his pants, wander about in the stark lantern light as if I weren't watching. On the edge of the bed, he'd sit, lift a foot and cradle it in his hands, pick at the loose flap of an old blister. I'd settle under the covers. In the morning I would ride lines, reach the crest of the ridge when pale sunlight first strikes the Ramshorn. Again, night would fall. Weeks and months. And then, on some day, without fail, I'd have to drive to town. We'd need supplies—bacon and flour and salt. Someone owns this cow camp—what would he be thinking, Mr. Fisher, what would he want to hear me say?

I know all the windows, all the houses, all the people in that town. In that house, with its lopsided addition and dark trim, John and Jan have put their new baby to bed and are washing the dinner dishes. If I were to knock on the back door, John would open it, drying his hands on a dish towel, and say, "Blue, buddy, what are you doing out there? Come in. Come in." And then Jan's face appears at his shoulder, and she squints out into the darkness and says, "Blue. Blue Parker. Come in. Let me fix you something. You look hungry. Are you hungry?"

In the next house, a square prefab with pale blue vinyl siding, Mable Stowers arranges things on the coffee table—a deck of cards, her knitting, a half-written letter. She tunes in the single Lander radio station, listens to a bar or two of a hard-rock song, and switches back to silence. She knits a few rows, shuffles the cards. "Come in," she says when I knock on the back door. I sit beside her on the frayed sofa. "Robert was a good kid," she says, and she goes to the mantel, takes down a photograph, brings it to me. "Handsome kid," she says. He is dressed in a white uniform. His face is familiar—I remember him from when I was five or six. He had held me high over his head, spun me, threatened to drop me. Terrified, I groped for a hold on him, took handfuls of his long, soft hair, and he cried out and brought me crashing down onto his shoulders. I clung to his neck as he ran across the field toward the river. "You know, Blue, how he died in the war. I get sad for him. All the things he missed." He held me out over the water, dangled me by my ankles, and as the blood rushed to my head and my thoughts pounded and swam, I looked first at the water, at my shadow on the shifting surface and the cold rocks beneath, and then I looked up at him, his large hands where they gripped me, his forearms as they strained to steady my tiny, struggling weight, his lip bright with the wisps of a sad young mustache, something that made me think that he was a man in spite of his shaggy hair, the pimples on his forehead, the high, careless squeal of his laugh. He caught me up, rocked me once in his arms—I smelled his nervous sweat, felt his bony ribs—and then he set me on my feet, beside him.

And the next house, and the next. Betty is ironing a long denim skirt. When she finishes, she wraps the warm cloth around her legs, hums a bit of a country song, pours herself a cup of coffee. Max stands in front of the bathroom mirror, running his hand over his scarred ear. Maybe he could grow his hair out a little longer. But the ear is rugged, almost dangerous. He wets his comb and slicks his hair straight back. Susan has made bread, and she lines up the hard loaves on the counter, lays her palm on the domed surface of each as if blessing it. She cuts a slice from the first loaf and spreads it with butter. It tastes gritty and salty. She takes another bite and washes it down with a glass of diet soda. I wander from house to house, looking in at windows. A few hundred people, and I'm sure I know every face.

On that day when I drive down the long dirt road for supplies, for all the familiar sights, who will look out from doorways, up from a table in the cafe, down the aisle in the merc? How do they know me? How do they know me *now*?

In a house a few miles west from town, David will reach into the refrigerator and bring out some beers and a package of orange cheese. He'll return to the living room, where Jake will be kicked up in the recliner, and drop it all on the coffee table. The sun will be setting behind the ridge outside, and David will stand at the window for a few minutes, shielding his eyes against the glare. Soon only a few high pink clouds will be left, and they'll fade quickly to gray.

"So, what do you think?" Jake says when David turns away from the window.

"I think not much good has come out of this whole mess except that now you and me have maybe got ourselves an opportunity for a promotion." He sits across from Jake and breaks off a chunk of cheese, opens a beer and takes a few swallows. "I've worked for Mr. Fisher for a lot longer than old Blue, and there's no reason why I can't do a good job as foreman. I know everything there is to know about the place. I could run the place in my sleep."

"You think so, David?"

"Oh, sure. I mean, I remember when Blue first came on. He was just serious, he just put his mind to it. That's all. No reason why I can't too."

"You really think you have room in your head for all the details and figuring you'd have to do?"

"Why? You think *you* do? Shit, it all depends on what Mr. Fisher thinks. He knows what he's doing. He'll pick the guy who's sharp and in line. Maybe me. I don't know. Maybe even you, I guess."

Jake cranks the lever on the recliner and sits forward. Taking up a beer, he rolls the can between his palms. "So, where do you think Blue went off to?" he says, and he lifts the can and holds it lightly against his forehead.

"He could be anywhere."

"Do you think we hurt him bad?"

"Don't worry about it, Jake."

"You know, when we were really on him, I thought it was something we were doing that shouldn't ever happen."

"Things change."

"And I thought for sure we'd be in shit with the crowd, but no one even looked at us after they broke us off him."

"Why should they look at us?"

"That Mrs. Talbot patted him on the back when he was on his feet. Then I swear she wiped her hands on her shirt and looked at her palms."

"You dig your own grave."

"Well, I think, David, and you know this better than me, since you knew him from the first day he started working on the ranch and you knew him all his life in this town, I think that he's a good kid, a good guy to work with and to know, and if we'd been any kind of friends we would've helped him to his feet and dusted him off and bought him a drink."

"I don't think he would've stayed."

"Then we could've helped him to the door. Whatever. I mean, isn't that what we owed him? Things happen and things go bad, but we owed him."

"No one owes anyone anything, not when you're talking about pushing things way out of line and way off where they're supposed to be."

"But what? You know him. He's never going to hurt anyone."

"Listen, Jake. You're right. I mean, I've known Blue for a long time. On that first day when he started on the ranch, he was all quiet and intent on anything anyone showed him. He watched everything, didn't miss one scrap or one move, like his life depended on it. And in no time he was everywhere, doing everything, and you could see him sort of flinch if everything wasn't perfect. It was like if he could have run the whole ranch himself, he would've been happy. And you know he never gave us a hard time if we weren't just about perfect like him—he just went about fixing things. That's him all over, from when we all first knew him when he was a kid—a careful kid, working hard, polite and by himself mostly. He had his friends, all the nature types. So what does he do? What has he been thinking, maybe for all the years anyone has known him? Who knows how he might've looked at you? But that's not it— Listen, Jake—he went sour. All that perfect wasn't worth shit. Soon as you start hiding things and lying—"

"You think if he would've told the truth—?"

"Shit, if he'd been honest, he would've left town a long time ago."

And then they'll both go on about their business, David and Jake. At some point one of them might actually take over as foreman, or they might get a job on another ranch or start logging or something, in another town or another state. They meet up with other people from town at a woodcutter's jamboree in Encampment or a stock show in Colorado, and they drink a few beers and talk about what's going on back home—how the basketball team hasn't lost nearly as many games this year as last year and how someone's daughter had to give up her scholarship because she's pregnant. They say how they'd really like to move back to town, move home—they miss the people—but it's hard to make a living in such a small place.

Dale gave up on college in Laramie and came home and worked odd jobs. He drove the potato-chip truck on the route from Jackson clear over to Riverton twice a week, washed dishes at the steak house on weekends, worked the cash register at the merc sometimes, all so he could play coed softball during the summer and two-step at night and bullshit with his old buddies. Any one of those guys might go out to Dale's truck and slit his dog's throat, leave the husky dead in the bed, if they'd let some sort of disagreement fester for too long. Dale rented a place by the river, and a stand of old spruces kept him cool through summer.

Gerry took disability after a log crunched partway up his leg, and now he was settled into a dark little trailer with his wife and two kids and twins due in a month. He won't work. His leg's too beat up for him to be out in the woods logging. He won't leave town and learn a new skill, something where his leg won't matter. So his kids take handout clothes from the church, and his wife tries to get the garden to produce as much edible as possible during the short, fragile growing season. He knows these roads and mountains, knows where he can take an antelope off-season by just rolling down his truck window, taking a deep breath, taking aim. He walks across open ground to the carcass, watches blood drain from the wound, knows it was a clean shot, a meaty little buck. He scans the horizon for a while, thinking of his family and the peaks and woods and dinner, and then draws his knife.

Gardelle would wander from the trail. Ahead, in a round clearing fenced by fallen logs, he drops his pack and takes off his hat to the sun. "This is a place to rest, Blue," he might say, and he lies out among the grass of Parnassus and the white aster. "Let me tell you what it was like at first," he says. "It was rare. No houses along the Wind River—just the broad, clear water, high and sweet. It was roughgoing around the cliffs below Red Willow, and then, you know, the valley opens out a little. I felt swallowed in all the altitude, like I couldn't look far enough up to take it all into my sight. The grass was high as your hips along the water and smelled like you could gather it up and eat it and sleep on it. There was silence. Then you'd hear a bird call, and it was like a voice that echoed at you from all around and from above, and it always sounded raw and young. It was a black raven, or it was a finch, out of sight in brambles. You'd follow the dirt track road and think that you were the first man. The first to notice the reflection of snow far up against the sky, the first to find moose tracks in fresh mud, the first to taste the air, the first man to spot an antelope grazing against a red stub of badlands. That solitude. You'd walk like you'd never stop walking. And then you dig in, like a bear or an Indian in winter. People come around your fire, and you love their stories and the smell of their clothes. When they leave, you look out at their footsteps in the snow and at the white mountains like you're looking at a purity, set high above it all."

Sam leaned against my back, urging his weight forward, and I took a half step to balance myself. He stayed with me.

Mrs. Talbot might draw the curtains in her bedroom and turn toward the small glow of the bedside light. Mr. Talbot lies under the covers and watches her approach. She slips in beside him, reaches across him to extinguish the light, and then falls onto him, her fingers up into his hair. Soon they are into a rhythm and then quiet and drifting toward sleep. She hears the wind shake and settle the house. Beams pop like ghost footfalls overhead. She remembers laying out a table with deviled eggs and homemade dill pickles and three-bean salad, bowls and platters loaded with salami, turkey, dessert. She lifted me and held me on her hip. "Here, Blue," she said. "You take what you want. Anything. What can I get you? Anything you want you can have. You sweet boy. You dear boy. Dessert first? Or a slice of bread? Yes. And some nice cold punch to drink." And then she sees me grown up and alone. Someone pulls some guys off me, and I hold myself and can't breathe. I'm gone.

On the day I return to town, if I go see Mr. Fisher, he'll want to know what I'm planning, what I will say to him. Someone else's truck will be parked outside my cabin. The windmill, the blades shut down to swing powerlessly with the wind, will moan and shift. Mr. Fisher will push past me at the front door to the river-stone mansion, and I'll follow him out onto the square patch of lawn. "Blue, tell me what you're going to do. I knew you had it in you to run this place. You ran it like I'd run it if I had the time, like you wanted to hold on to every detail. But now, Blue, I don't know. How can I trust you? Your mind is on something else. I don't like it. Maybe I can't have you on my property anymore."

His voice, and all the voices, went through my head, and I couldn't turn around and hold Sam. I walked away. Sam called after me. "Blue," he said. "Blue. I want you here with me."

FOUR

Up the slope, on bare feet, I picked my way among sharp fragments of rock, prickly pear, tried to lighten myself, to float and barely touch. Reaching the lip of the hollow, I turned around. Far below, Sam stood beside the pond. I backed away, out of sight. Nothing but mountains and sky and the scattered, fast clouds, with a few hours of daylight left.

I walked along the line of the ridge. Open ground, a stretch of pines, aspen—soft, ruined leaves that kicked up and fell away under foot. Then I entered full sun again, with the cow camp below me.

Sam crouched at the edge of the pond. He seemed to be washing his face with handfuls of water. As he got himself dressed, he slouched forward, working at buttons, and then he stuffed my socks into my boots and carried them with him around the end of the pond, across the road, toward the cabin. He threw the boots far ahead. They were black in the deep meadow. He scooped them up and carried them into the cabin.

As the sun gradually fell, smoke rose from the chimney, a faint haze above the roof. Darkness took hold in the willows. Above that close world, the Wind Rivers grayed toward night, ran east across the reservation, gave into the plains where Gilbert's stories had grown, just a few days' walk away. Now Gilbert circled through the desert—with the car windows lowered and the air rushing his long hair back from his face, he drove through the uninhabited blackness and the stars. He wet his lips, allowed gravity to pull him faster, caught miles in his headlights. Someplace to stop. Unknown till morning.

On a slice of open ground, high on a rib of those Wind Rivers, my mother leaned into my shoulder, held me tight, released me. We watched lights come up in town—we waited far past streetlights and store signs until porchlights and windows began to shine, we waited so long for that bright map to complete itself that our trail down off the ridge became lost in darkness. She sang a slow, deep song, something she'd learned as a child from her mother or grandmother. If I knew the words, the meaning might be clear to me now, but all I remember is the image the song brought—a huge fallen log in night woods, the log lined with dim portals like a ship. Wet ferns among the gray humps of boulders. A silence capped by the clouds of evergreen. I had a flashlight that I shined on the portals—there was a blurred face in each circle, someone long gone that I felt I should have known.

In the moonless black of the cow camp, the cabin windows glowed. I gradually got myself down the slope, across the cold grass, and stopped five yards out from the window. With the strong light and Sam's loose movements, it seemed warm in there. He drank something from a metal cup, wiped his mouth on his shoulder. Taking a kerchief from his back pocket, he covered some slices of bread stacked on a plate at the center of the table. He reached for the lantern and lowered the wick until all that was left was a bare spark. I moved closer and eventually made out blocks of shadow—Sam's shape in the blankets on the bed.

Straight overhead, new stars, whole constellations, emerged from behind the eaves. In across the porch, I stepped through the door and pulled it shut. The warmth shook me, and I struggled to hold myself still. The absence of night sound—the groan of the cooling stove—nothing else to hear.

I stared for a moment to focus the murky room, then walked to the far wall, took my jacket down from a hook and slipped it on, picked up my boots and settled onto a chair at the table. My socks were balled up in the neck of one boot. Dusting the grit from my soles, I pulled on the socks and took a moment to massage my feet, to work at my toes, bending them forward and back, to grind them out of their pain and get them ready for movement. With the boots on, I rested my head on the table, closed my eyes, and laid my immediate trail—northwest from the cow camp, with a spring for water by sunrise. I smelled the bread on the plate, reached under the kerchief and took a slice, rolled it up and ate it in three bites. It was heavy and dry.

"I thought you'd gone crazy, Blue." Sam stood beside the bed. He seemed small and rooted, his shirt hanging in folds around his legs. "Where have you been?"

"Not far. I watched your light. But I need to get going. North past the Ramshorn."

"Now? You're going to leave me here alone?"

"You'll be fine. You can use my truck, if you want." I got to my feet, toward the door. "Your jeep's in the storage barn down on the ranch, if you think you'll need it. Don't worry." I stepped out across the porch, onto the grass.

With the dark body of the Ramshorn above me, I hurried across a broad park. I smelled wet air, heard a gurgle, suddenly splashed right through a shallow creek. I knew when the edge of woods would close over me again, how I'd find my way through to the next drainage, to Burroughs Creek, and the spring.

I could walk a hundred miles north. Up through Five Pockets. Follow the Shoshone River toward pavement. Then there'd be roads forever. Fifty years ago, Gardelle crossed the Absarokas north on foot, but then he caught rides back to town along the circle of dirt track roads. He settled in with Hanna.

Long before sunrise, with the air near freezing and my foot-steps stirring up echoes, I followed the base of a short rise, know-ing that it would lead me across open ground. I'd been drawing in what sounds I could from beyond my own noise, what guid-ance I could from the darkness. Then I glanced up and stopped short—above the ridge the eastern sky had barely silvered, and against that new light stood the blacker shape of an antelope buck, the prongs and bulk, not twenty feet above me. He was still, and I tried to listen.

He would have heard me from far down the valley, each stride crumbling a bit of ground, crushing a stem or leaf. Now he'd hear my silence, my heart pounding. My eyes might be bright stars hovering in my face. He must have known what I was, must have made out my size and speed, the length of my stride. Now that I'd stopped close and faced him, stared up at him, why would he think that I wanted anything but to engage him, to take him down? He should have felt afraid. Or maybe there was no fear involved. I listened. If heat made a sound, I might have heard his heat—a sharp pulse—but beyond that, nothing.

I'd left the nearest human behind. In the cabin, close to Sam, I might've listened as every move I made accumulated and jumbled around the walls until the room filled with my stum-bling, filled with remnants of thoughts. The night was empty. For a hundred miles north, not a single thing that couldn't be identified by sight, sound, or scent.

I could have had only one purpose—to take the antelope—and he waited for me to act, watched to see how I would move, knew perhaps that now, at this moment and at this distance, with his focus unwavering and his great speed, he had nothing to fear. Five minutes, he waited, and then I believe he cocked his head slightly and froze again.

He would have been wandering, knowing where he was heading. There were hundreds of open miles of his world. He could get no footing on the cliffs, but almost everywhere else he had straight shots across the fields, benches, riverbottom, an eye set for any disturbance as he followed grass and water and sage. He might be at the upper reaches of his range now, and over weeks and months he'd swing around to the east fork and wander back down to drier land, into the reservation, where brush fires blackened a horizon full of prairie that was quickly green again, where oil wells rocked through the night, where roads in toward the canyons of the Wind Rivers were dangerous with ruts and rattlesnakes. To him, it was all chill on the wind, water in the creek, sunrise on bare cottonwoods along the Little Wind River, the buildings of Fort Washakie dull blocks, with everyone asleep.

"Let me follow you," I thought. Or maybe we were headed the same direction. Maybe he followed me. "Let's go," I said. "Let's keep moving."

Through a full minute I waited until I wondered if I'd spoken, if he'd heard. But then he took a step forward, head lowered, and a few pebbles broke free and rolled down the slope toward me. His shadow compacted, as if he readied himself to lunge, and I stepped back. "Don't be afraid," I said. He hissed, a harsh sound, tossed the spikes of his horns, and bolted away.

Cold water flowed directly from the ground, from a tangle of rocks and tight vegetation. I leaned far in from my perch, cupped water to my mouth, and drank until I could feel the water's weight in my stomach. Then I fell back on the springy branches and waited for the sun to reach above the treetops on the slope below.

No taste to the spring water—not with the whole massive island of the Ramshorn as a filter. The sharp point of the peak, which I'd passed in darkness, still held sheets of snow, and the cliffs of the ramparts behind me echoed with the drip of icy water in the deeper folds. Somehow, through cracks opened by a million winters, the water found its way down. I tried to separate the strata and imagine the seepage through solid rock. Maybe caverns opened out, and the water pooled in long, suffocated lakes. You'd swim for years through those lakes, never knowing what you might approach. Then the water, no more than a sparkle, escaped and flowed away.

Derek would have to be laid out dead, finally killed by someone. Blood would pool around his heart. Prey escapes along the empty channel of a creek, leaves tracings of footprints, skitters into brush.

Derek's body is stripped and laid out on a metal table under blue tubes of light. Liquids drain away through troughs. He is preserved—the torn flesh around his neck and temples, the battered muscles of his gut. His open eyes are too dry to reflect me leaning over him. My cheek against his cheek—rough. His prick points toward his navel. I pinch it upright, let it fall, leave the room.

Then, in my new place out by the edge of the Hayes Ranch, I'll have bare white walls. My belongings will be stacked in their boxes, stair-stepped like foothills in a corner. Lying on the carpet, wrapped in a blanket, trying to sleep, I hear music from another house. Someone shoots a rifle and glass shatters—an empty bottle—another shot and the bullet sails away into the fields. From around kitchen tables, in settings of couch and chairs, from yard to yard, voices rise. A man kicks at his child. A boy lies in the cab of his father's truck, reaches into his pockets and massages himself, imagines driving through the center of town, noticing no one, while people he knows see him at the wheel.

At a barbecue, the whole carcass of a buffalo, shot somewhere on a ranch in Colorado, has been prepared as roasts and burgers. The crew of the volunteer fire department, shoulder to shoulder, serves corn and beans and cole slaw and meat from behind an endless table. As I hold my plate out and shuffle down the line, they load me up until I'm afraid the gravy will spill onto my wrists. The men's matching T-shirts, white with a red buffalo head, stretch taut across their bellies. Behind me, one of them jokes with a tourist lady—"Never been a fire we couldn't tame, not even the ones we set ourselves."

● ■ ▪

I had thought I could head straight north from the spring. Somewhere, I lost my view, and now I could see no mountains, just woods and a close ridge. The sun finally dulled in the forward edge of the high clouds—the air chilled a degree. I wandered down the slope, forced myself into a quicker pace, concentrated at keeping my ankles from folding. Entering the woods, I hoped to circle east and head north again.

The woods had never been lumbered. Ahead, through the deadened light, the ground was thick with fallen trees—some stark white and elevated, some rotting into the ground. I tried to aim for the lowest obstacles, keeping a focus on a tree or boulder somewhere in the distance, something to keep me in line. I lifted a leg, slung it over a log, pulled the other leg over, and stepped another ten feet before climbing again, ducking under a live tree that leaned into its neighbor, trying to find a larger patch of free ground.

On trees far ahead, I kept seeing blazes—the flash of yellow wood and sap where the bark had been cut away—but they always turned out to be scratchings left by a grizzly, high up on the trunk. No man had left a mark with a hatchet.

A few hours, and the air started to mist. I heard wind move from somewhere uphill, saw it sway the treetops, and then the rain fell in large, cold drops, straight down at me as if that dark ceiling of branches were nothing. Blocked in, I couldn't see enough of the storm to judge it. Maybe just a thunderstorm, quickly gone. Closing my eyes, I let rain hit my face, listened to it stir the woods around me.

I opened my eyes. The woods were gray with falling water, distances closed in. Rain had soaked in past my collar, down my back, drenched my pant legs from the pockets to the boots. Maybe I'd been standing there for half a storm, half a day.

The fallen logs were cold as I slid over them. Lichen stuck to my palms. Then I was on a trail—no question—it was cleanly dug into the black soil, wandering in what seemed to be the right direction, with blazes as clear as squares of yellow paper, neatly cut, thick with crusted pitch.

Downhill, toward the hint of clearing trees, I hurried as if I'd find something. I was out into a steep meadow, the cliffs above me. I had come around and was heading north, as I'd planned, rain blowing hard from low clouds. But the trail ended. I turned and ran back to where it had emerged from the woods, turned again and tried to follow it into the meadow—the trail was buried in grass. Maybe it had been abandoned years ago, only kept clear in the woods by the passage of elk.

Running down across the meadow, into woods again, I tried not to slow as I came against another maze of fallen timber. I stepped over what I could, slipped and caught myself on juts of roots. The dead lower branches of the lodgepoles tore at my jacket, and I started to knock them from the trunks as I forced myself through.

My stomach sucked in against its emptiness. I could have filled a pack with food. That last bread from Sam's table.

My boot came down on a fallen branch, and the branch whipped up and cut at the back of my leg, behind the knee. The pain burned, and I saw blood darken my pants. It felt as if I'd torn a tendon. I kept moving, slower, for hours through the woods, and finally the rain stopped.

Here and there, the clouds were clearing. The trees opened, and I could see a creek ahead, what must have been South Pocket, and knew the cliffs now, recognized their patterns. I wanted to get down to the valley floor, down in the open where the pack trail dug through.

And then, soaked and shivering, I stood at the center of Five Pockets. I faced west—the cliffs, a line of dark clouds, and the sun suspended above—felt the warmth cut through the heavy dampness. Taking off my clothes, every stitch, I wrung them all out and hung them in a tree in full sunlight. My skin was quickly dry. A black line of dirty blood filled the gash at the back of my leg.

The clouds rolled above the cliff but didn't advance. I found a slab of gray rock and lay down, warm in the evening sun, and waited. At some point I sat up and saw the ring of cliffs, the five pockets and their white flow of water, the bowl of pale green grass mottled with stands of tall trees, and the distinct final rays of sun reaching down from the cliff. I heard the water rushing.

I rolled awake on the slab of granite and held my knees to my chest. In that empty night without a moon, I heard the approaching wind shake a stand of trees far away. Before the wind hit me, I braced for it, but I couldn't hold myself tightly enough. The cold spiked beneath my chin and down my spine.

There was no way to tell how many hours had passed or how much heat I'd already lost. The storm clouds had cleared away completely, hadn't returned, and the day's faint warmth had risen straight up into the black bath of stars. On the eastern horizon, there was no hint of a moon, huge and warm, that might loom above the valley. No one would know where to begin searching for me. No one might pass through the valley until hunting season, or maybe not until next summer.

Lying on my back again, I felt where my skin had heated the stone a degree or two. Whatever the measure of heat the rock had drained from me, it wasn't enough. There would be no fading past sleep. My nose was running, my eyes watering, and, as I blinked, the accumulated tears drained toward my ears and pooled in the channels. My heart shook my chest, pulsed out through my feet and hands. I tried to force my muscles to relax, to quiet, but I only tensed harder against gravity, arching myself off the cold stone on the points of my heels and elbows. My leg was gashed. My stomach like a sharp, crumpled can.

My clothes had dried in the wind, but they were stiff with cold. Pulling them from the tree, I struggled into them, drawing my pants gently over my injured leg. I couldn't loosen my cramped muscles or take a real stride. Sitting against the base of a tree, I leaned over my knees, as much out of the wind as possible.

Darkness, without a moon. The hiss of rushing water, pulsing with the shifting wind, the five white waterfall fingers completely unseen. I knew the smell of the air—but even that seemed caught up and frozen in the wind. I could have been anyplace in the world where the Milky Way wove through the constellations. If stars were a map you could fall into—but what's one trail or another?

My father stepped away from us. What did he know of this place? What could he have ever known? He held my mother in an embrace that wouldn't loosen. At the doorway, his full hand cupped the back of her head and pressed her into his shoulder. She was raised onto her toes and seemed weightless. Then he dropped her, all at once, he shrugged free from her with a final pat on the behind and walked across the yard to his truck. We followed him. In his side mirror, he would see us standing at the fence, waving, until he turned the corner far down at the gas station.

On out of town, over Togwotee Pass. Quickly, he climbed another mountain range or descended into a desert. Miles and hours with nothing to do but think of where he'd just been, what he'd just tasted, how long it would be before he saw something like that again. He knew my mother's face—its flat slopes from eyes to cheekbones, its pink edges, sharp nose and lips. When she smiled, her eyebrows lowered—she might have been frowning. She cracked two eggs with snaps of her wrists. She stood at his shoulder, holding a pitcher of milk, and looked past him out the window, followed light or a bird, responded with a start when he called her back—he wanted her seated before he began eating. Across the table from him, she rubbed the backs of her broad hands, twisted her mother's amethyst on her right ring finger.

My father knew that gem. He knew places—towering trees and a gray stone building with tiny panes of leaded glass. I'd seen the old home movies, found in a tin marked with my mother's maiden name, in a box in the storeroom. As I watched the film, I tried to listen for my mother's approach through the smell of burning dust, the heat of the old projector bulb, the whine of the cooling fan. On the flagstone patio beneath the windows, she moved through a crowd. Her lips were dark red against the whiteness of her skin and her thick cap of perfect black hair. Freckles on her shoulders. A faint blue dress that seemed to move even as she stood still—its own breeze. Someone had handed her a glass, and she glanced away as she raised it to her lips, took a quick sip, patted at the corners of her mouth with a fingertip. The young men could all have been him—clean faces, wide-mouthed laughs, small black bow ties above white shirts, white jackets. They swung toward her, or the camera circled, and she reached her arms out to each. They were trying to take her glass from her, and she was dancing among them, although it might have been no more than a turn of her head. The sun bled through the picture, then dulled in an arched doorway where someone who could have been my grandfather chewed on a pipe as he faced a woman who ran a string of lavender beads repeatedly through her fingers. A boy led a horse as huge as a draft horse, a gold Irish hunter, from the face of a tall white stable into a paved courtyard. The horse dwarfed the people who gathered around it. Someone reached a saddle far up onto its back. From across a field, a crowd ran up to a white board fence, through a gate, to the camera. Young women, my mother at the lead, and then the young men were with them. White T-shirts. Slim arms. Men aren't so handsome now. Baggy trousers. They held to my mother. And in there among them, reaching through them all, my father, taking hold of her shoulder from behind, his fingers puckering the cloth of her shirt, his head almost shaved of its dark hair, the strength of his incredible, slender face. She stepped forward, and he went with her, out from the others.

I joined them. At the breakfast table, he watched us both as he ate. He leaned far forward over his plate and raised his food a few inches to his mouth, seemed unable to sit up straight while eating. His hands—they lay limp on the table or grasped a fork or slice of toast—were my hands exactly, only slightly darker with hair and work. He would know my palms, the rise of my knuckles, the pads of my fingertips. And my mother, she had the slight droop of my eyelids, the narrow upper lip. Her neck was thin and tense beneath the weight of her head. His beard, though surely as dark as his hair, had never shown as more than a hint of stubble—his face was smooth—and he must have seen my rougher face and thought of it as he drew his blade across. She smelled of perfume sometimes, but he would think of her slightly more sour scent, a smell of dough. He'd nuzzle into it. Her wrists were round and sturdy. Mine also. He'd embrace her and barely remember anything but what he held. She was a person he'd taken up—however he loved her, he always knew how long he'd been without her. And he couldn't wash his hands without knowing me.

Out into the desert, across the brown land, he drove, one range after another. A million peaks out there—snow and tundra and bristlecone—and they hemmed him in, led him, blocked his path and sent him hours out of his way. Nothing but a world of strange land, where shadows fell at unexpected angles and made him glance at the sun to get his bearings. How long had a creek bed been dry? Had it flowed all spring, or was it the trail of flash floods? What flowers bloomed with rainfall? Was it one lifetime or a hundred since the wall of a canyon broke loose, leaving a cleaner sandstone face?

Eventually, on our hikes when he was home, I led him through these mountains myself. No questions. Nothing to confuse me. Pure memory, as if the fluctuations of this land were as sharp and close as my nerves. If I could see him again, find him out there on one of his jobs, he could tell me where to drive, how to see. Maybe it was easy.

He left town, a last flash of us in his mirror as he turned the corner, passed out from the hold of these mountains and on to some distant town. He pulled in at night, found a motel, a cafe for a quick dinner, and then went to sleep. The first light woke him. Opening the curtains, he faced the eastern horizon, saw the notched ridge and knew that that was the canyon from which he'd driven in darkness, saw the peaks and knew he'd face them daily and would soon know their names. Back at the cafe for breakfast, he sat at the counter and drank from a mug of coffee. The waitress, local, stood in front of him with her order pad flipped open. She pulled the cap off her pen with her teeth, gripped it in her smile, and spoke around it. "What can I get you?"

"What do you suggest?"

"Well, let me tell you, Ronnie makes a good Denver omelet. If that sounds good, you can't go wrong."

The omelet was good, and the next day he was back for breakfast again. By now, he knew the waitress by name—Kate, who was surprised when she'd finally finished high school, who hoped to become partners in the cafe within the year. She ran her finger along the edge of the counter and leaned toward him. "You know how it goes in this town?" she said in a low voice, looking out the window. "If you've got your ass in gear, you can breeze past just about anyone."

Down along the counter he could see Donald and Jimmy, faces already familiar. They nodded toward him and smiled. Donald drove a gravel truck out at the highway construction site, and on some Saturday over the summer he'd invite the whole crew to his house for a barbecue—a keg of beer, and piles of burgers and chicken. And Jimmy, who with his wife Janet ran the little department store, felt it was his duty to try to provide everyone in town with what they needed—the town's best business. And all the others in the cafe, passing on the street, moving about inside their houses, felt the day slowly heat, watched for clouds above the western horizon, exchanged advice and glances, and wondered if it would rain that night, if a storm would rush over and clean the sidewalks and keep everyone inside, huddled and dry, turning out the porchlight, sleeping straight through to morning. They all watched the west at sunset—wet clouds rose and swallowed the sun. The breeze stirred up dust, carried the scent of rain. My father drew the curtains, fluffed the pillows on the bed, and sat back to watch the news on the television. He wondered if he should risk going out into the storm later for a beer, or if he should just stay in and listen to the rain.

The name of the town was spelled out in white rocks on a hillside. Gray houses no larger than trailers sat in the shade of huge, old cottonwoods. The bottomland southwest along the river was deep in hay and alfalfa, and the heavy scent of cut fields blew through on summer nights, heightening every breath and the buzz of insects. The ice cream drive-in, ringed in pink neon, stayed busy toward midnight.

In Colorado or Idaho or wherever, beyond the edge of that town, whatever town, in a spot along the river where you could look back and see the town's glow on the hillsides, I would pull off the main road and peer ahead into the darkness. I'd try to make out the ruts of the dirt road and see if there was a sign posted somewhere along the fence—no ranch name or personal name to tell me right or wrong. I drove along lines that angled among the cultivated fields and stretches of scrub. Rising into the hills, I left behind the last hint of the town. Dipping through gullies and thatches of willow, the road continued for a few more miles, and now and then I caught the darker shadow of peaks far up toward the stars. The earth flowed through my headlights—stiff, dry grass and rocks like rusted melons—and then I caught a light suspended far ahead, and I knew I had taken the correct turn.

Gradually, as I approached, that light began to brighten a side of a house—red door, four-paned windows, the ripple of log-ends linked at the corners. And then the windows lit up, some-one moved behind the glass, the door opened, and Sam stepped onto the stoop. I pulled to a stop at the gate, a few yards from him, and shut off the engine, stepped out.

The light closed the night around us, so that the world might have been no more than that sturdy log house, its stubby spruces, brown fence, and a tight expanse of level ground. But I heard the world beyond, could feel it—the chill of thin air fall-ing from the mountains above us. That would wait until morning—a hike toward the peaks.

Sam held the door for me as I stepped past him into the house. He'd gone ahead and set things up. My lamp on a table beside the couch. The shelves lined with my books. He closed the door and followed me into the center of the room. "You're welcome, Blue," he said, tapping me on the shoulder, and I turned around into his quick, awkward embrace. "Why don't you sit down and rest. That was a long drive, huh? You must be hungry."

I sat on the couch, and he backed away a few steps and leaned against the mantel. He held a glass of whiskey, and he took a sip. He was watching me, smiling, taking his time. His color was back, his movement strong—he crouched in front of the fireplace, reached in and shifted the massive logs, arranged some kindling, and tossed in a match. A tall fire. We may have sat there for hours with neither of us ready to speak—there would be other times, hours or days later, when we could talk.

Gilbert stepped from the kitchen holding a tray loaded with plates and bowls. "What's with you two?" he said. "Make some noise. No one will hear."

Long after first light, the sun finally rose over the lip of Five Pockets. I needed the heat of that full sun to unlock my limbs. I'd been thinking that in order to avoid the old-growth forest that had tangled me up and gashed my leg, I'd follow Horse Creek out of the valley, head up Parque Creek, over the ridge and across the Burroughs Creek drainage. It would be more miles, by far, but the going would be clear and obvious.

It was a cloudless day. As I got myself to my feet and started walking, I tried not to favor my injury. The humps of grass and hidden rocks jolted me left and right. Then I was on the Horse Creek trail, so smooth that I could almost shut my eyes against the glare. I had a few miles to go before I'd start to cut overland. The day would be hot. I had already sweated through my shirt. Flapping my jacket, I caught a hint of coolness, and I smelled the nerves that kept trying to tense me. Dust underfoot.

Five years ago, I'd followed my father down out of that valley. He rode ahead. Thinking that he would wait for me once he noticed I was out of sight, I let him put distance between us. When I arrived at the trailhead, he'd already loaded his borrowed horse into his borrowed trailer. He said, "See you at home," and then pulled away. I loaded my horse in my own trailer and crept down the road so slowly that I can't say why I didn't ruin my engine or brakes. By the time I'd dropped off my horse, cleaned out the trailer, hung my tent over the fence to give it air, and walked into the house, it was nearing ten that night.

Just one light on in the hall. I opened his bedroom door. Squinting into the thin line of light, he sat up in the bed. His face was blotched red from sleep, his hair matted and winged. I'd never seen him alone in that bed—not that I could remember. He was far over to one side. He'd pushed the pillows onto the floor. A single sheet had slid down toward his waist, and his white T-shirt, stained from sweat along the collar and beneath the arms, had twisted around his torso. Maybe he hadn't been asleep—the room was too stuffy. I wanted him to sleep heavily in that bed, to awaken at dawn and hear breakfast cooking. Crossing the room, I opened the window a crack, picked up the pillows and tossed them against the headboard. "Where's the blanket, Dad?"

"I threw it in the closet. It smelled like something." He lay back on the pillow, closed his eyes, and patted the mattress beside his hip. I perched on the edge of the bed, and my weight tipped him against me. If I'd moved suddenly then, I'd have had to hold him to keep him from rolling off. "I waited dinner for a few hours, Blue. I thought you'd want to eat with your old man."

"I got held up."

"Everything all right?"

"Nothing I couldn't handle."

"Good." He raised his hand and held onto my shoulder.

"You start your job in the morning. I told Mr. Fisher you'd be there at seven. Do you need anything?"

"I don't know yet."

"I guess not." He released me, crossed his arms up over his eyes. "Everything will be fine, Blue, don't you think? I don't see why not. You can do whatever you want."

"You think so."

"Sure."

I rose carefully, and he rolled away, cupping his face in the crook of his elbow. "Good night, Dad. You want anything special for breakfast?"

"Nothing special. Thanks. Good night, Blue. You're a good boy. Sleep tight."

As I lay in my bed, hot and uncomfortable and wide awake, I heard him moving about in his room and down the hall. The front door closed, his truck started, and he drove away.

Toward four or five, when the sky started to lighten, my mother would have woken up without an alarm, pulled on her robe, and moved silently to the kitchen. The brightness of the kitchen light would have blocked the last of the night outside the window, the heat of the stove and the boiling water would have forced out the chill. She'd mix some batter or lay out some bacon, then pause for a moment at the table as her tea steeped. She'd hold the radio to her ear, turn it up just enough to hear, listen to a song or two, a newscast, advertisements for auto parts or lawn chairs at some store in Riverton.

In that early hint of light, my father was driving, far away from this town. His headlights still brightened the road, but soon they'd dull, and he'd struggle to draw contours out of the rising gray land. His heater blasted onto the floor of the truck, his feet were tight and damp in his boots, but enough cold leaked into the cab to make him hold his collar closed against his neck. The radio was tuned to a station in a city somewhere along the ocean, and through the static, toward the end of the night-time reception, he heard song after song, some familiar, some fresh and tough. He switched off the radio and leaned forward over the steering wheel. Long lines of fenceposts. Whatever that road was, it kept going.

On the first morning, beyond that far town, I'll rise before dawn. There will be many things to know.

Sam sleeps on the high puff of the old pine bed. The light that leaks from the horizon, that enters the window, brightens him enough that, as I stare, I see his eyes twitch, his mouth open and close. He's dreaming, his old dreams about reaching someplace.

Outside, the night's cold is still damp. Birds have begun to make noise, and they flap among the bushes, beyond the fence. The sky is gray.

This is my first view of the land, slowly coming out of the darkness. The peaks are close and wooded, not bare rock as I'd expected. No monument like the Ramshorn, no glacier face or rosy finch cliffs. There is no scent of sage. No blaze of badland stripes, layers of deposited life. I walk out into the field. There are wildflowers down in among the grass.

The door squeaks on its hinges, the noise flies close to the ground, heavy with dew, and I turn back to see Gilbert step out from the house. He is dressed in white, fringe at his forearms and waist, and his hair is free on his shoulders. He bends forward, kicks at the ground with his toe, walks a few paces along the front of the house, and kicks again, seems to examine the dust he stirs. He moves around the corner and out of sight. His high chant rises into the air and comes down over me. The house is dark, it is silent and shut tight, but Gilbert's chant seems to come from that dark square. Then he comes around the house, into sight again, moving boldly, almost dancing. Around the corner, hidden, then into view again, circling the house. The dust he stirs falls behind him. He is fluid and clean.

The sky has gone blue. The windows of the house reflect that blue, as if the house is filled with the immense, cloudless dawn. Far up across the fields there are groves of aspen, deer roaming, cairns built along a trail that leads up a ridge and disappears into woods, a trail like the glacier trail. Certainly there must be starker peaks up there, higher, bare rock in the sky, more dangerous and beautiful, to be discovered, to be learned.

Gilbert swings into sight. He chants.

Inside the house, Sam sleeps. With the day still early and cool, I'll wake him and pack a meal and circle out into this land. Take his hand.

No flash of light. No gray line of a road. Nothing but ridges falling to ridges. I moved through a day, far down from Five Pockets, across marshy thickets where my boots nearly filled with black water, into another night, sleeping for an hour or two beside a spring, and through another day. There were no choices to be made—once I left the Horse Creek trail, I just followed the land, watching the peaks shift perspective, until I had the Ramshorn behind me, the spine of the Wind Rivers ahead. The cut of White Pass was a marker above the place where the cow camp hollowed.

Time changes. The sun moves past noon. Sam might have already moved on. I kept walking, with that lip of the little valley just a few miles ahead. And weeks and months, maybe years ahead, we'd settle in.

A few hours after I left the cow camp in darkness, back when I was starting on my hike north toward Five Pockets, Sam awoke early and got to work around the cabin. He swept the floor, emptied the ashes from the stove, washed the bowls and tins he'd used to make breakfast for me the day before—bacon and biscuits. From the cold box, he took a can of orange juice, and he sat drinking it on the porch, watching the hills and the sky. He saw nothing move but the thickening clouds, a gray jay hopping along the edge of the road, the aspen leaves vibrating even when the breeze calmed for a moment. He identified each sound—

there was nothing he hadn't heard during his days alone. No voices. No footsteps. No words. He heard the bullfrogs groan, the water run.

From his maps he knew the shape of this corner of the Absarokas, but he hadn't yet been out riding the lines. Starwood was grazing at the edge of the willows. He put her in the corral, fed her a can of oats, brushed her. With a bucket, he put a few inches of water in the watering trough. In the tack shed, he ran a cloth over the saddle, eyeballed the stirrups—they were set for me, a few inches too long for him. He must have thought of me adjusting that saddle, hefting it onto Starwood. He must have seen me, many times, ride out of the hollow. He shortened the stirrups and returned to the cabin.

Leaning back in a chair against the wall, he sat on the porch, let his eyes close if they wanted. A heifer lowed, far away, calling her calf. To the north, the sky had gone dark, and Sam could see distant streaks of rain. Every now and then the storm edged over the cow camp and spit for a while. Sam went inside and came back out with a sweater and his lunch. When it started to rain in heavy lines, he ran to the tack shed, grabbed a tarp, and hurried to secure it over my boxes in the back of my truck. From the porch again, he watched pools collect in the creases of the tarp.

Inside the cabin, in the dim, cool light, Sam wrapped himself in a blanket and sat up on the bed. The rain roared steadily on the roof, the sound so hard and driven that it seemed to lower the ceiling over him, tighten the walls, shut out all sounds of life, even his own breathing. The west window panes flowed with water. A lantern wouldn't have opened the half light. Lying flat on his stomach, with his head at the foot of the bed, he looked out through the north window—he could see only the base of the slope I'd disappeared over, and the rest was cut off by the porch roof. He settled down, tried to doze, to hear beyond the rain.

By the time Mr. Fisher drove into the hollow, the clouds had shifted north again. Sam stood at the edge of the porch, reaching a hand into the damp air. Mr. Fisher parked beside my truck and looked it over, checked under the tarp, and when he looked up, Sam was gone, out of sight in the darkness behind the open door. Mr. Fisher crossed the heavy grass and stood in the doorway. On a chair at the foot of the bed, Sam worked at pulling on thick, wool socks and his boots.

"Sam, how are you feeling?"

"I'm okay."

"You mind if I sit down?"

"No, sir."

He closed the door and sat at the table. "How about fixing me something warm to drink, Sam? It was a muddy drive up here."

"The stove's cold. I never got it going this morning."

"Seems like a good day for a fire, don't you think?"

"I didn't want to waste it. I thought I'd be leaving."

"Is that right?"

Sam finished lacing his boots, walked over and sat across the table from Mr. Fisher. "I was thinking I'd ride lines, but the rain slowed me down."

"Well, I can understand that."

"But I'll head out now."

"Don't, Sam. Sit here for a while. We could talk. Can't you dig us up a snack?"

Sam rocked back in his chair and looked at the ceiling. "What do you want?"

"Anything would be nice." Mr. Fisher looked at the cans on the shelves, the slab of bacon hung in its netting. "Didn't I pay for all this, anyway?"

"No, sir. I don't think so." Sam stepped to the counter, put a plate of slightly burned biscuits on the table, and went outside. He returned with two cans of lemon drink from the cold box. "Is this all right?"

"It's fine, Sam."

They ate in silence for a few minutes. Mr. Fisher took another biscuit and stood at the west window, leaned toward the glass, drummed his fingers once on a pane. Turning back to the room, he said, "These biscuits aren't bad. Did you make them?"

"Yesterday."

"Where'd you learn to cook?"

"I get hungry."

"Of course." He sat back down, finished his drink, turned the can slowly in his hands, inspecting the label, and then tossed the can toward the counter, where it hit and fell to the floor. "Listen, Sam. I want to talk to Blue. That's his truck out there, isn't it? I'd assumed he'd left town."

Sam stood up, walked to the row of hooks on the wall, took down his jacket, and put it on. He fumbled with the zipper. "I have to ride lines, Mr. Fisher. There's just a few hours of light left."

"Fine, if you're feeling up to it. We can talk about your position later. But I need to know where Blue is."

"He went out walking last night. I haven't seen him."

Sam stepped out the door, toward the corral. Mr. Fisher came out directly behind him.

"When you *do* see him, tell him I want to talk to him. I don't want things messed up. No lurking around. There actually *is* someone in charge here. Or I hope to be."

As Sam worked to get the saddle up on Starwood, Mr. Fisher drove away. Before Sam rode out from the cow camp, he ran back to the cabin and left a note on the table—"I'm looking for you. North. Then west."

When I came over the last ridge, I saw the cabin far below, and I walked straight toward it. The sun slanted into the valley and seemed to catch and swirl around the green. The marsh was tangled, the aspens ringed the pond, my truck sat at the end of the road—I was sure of each, but all I saw clearly was that dark box of logs, the clean square of the roof. Three nights, three days of walking. The miles still surged through my legs. Leaning against the door, I wondered, with the smooth, planed boards pressing me straight, how I'd found my way back. My palms and arms were cut and bruised from the times I'd fallen. Another huge circle that had brought me back to where I'd started.

But Sam hadn't taken my truck. So he waited for me, here, wrapped in a weight of blankets or standing beside the table, and if I stepped through the door he would help me, seat me, wash my hands, and we'd take an hour to lay a trail for ourselves, flipping through map after map, the patches of green soft among the winding snakes of white and tan, and then we'd be gone before night took the mountains again, before the heat evaporated. I'd sleep as he drove, awake to road streaming through the headlights, a hundred miles away and accelerating. It would be smooth. I opened the door. The cabin was empty.

I opened the bureau drawers, each filled with his clothes. Holding an armload of socks and shirts up to my nose, I inhaled and knew I smelled something of Sam through the clean. I stacked them on the bed and pulled out pants, sweaters, underwear, stacked them too in neat piles. And his maps—I tossed them on top of the shirts. Pulling the cases from the pillows, I started to pack them as if they were duffels—all the clothes, the maps, belts and coins and his sheathed knife. I knotted the top of each case and leaned them in the doorway.

There was plenty of food. I found a paper bag and filled it with cans and boxes. I ate an apple, snapping off huge, crisp chunks in my teeth—it hurt my stomach, but I followed it with pieces of bread and a handful of raisins. Out beside the cold box, I landed myself in the grass, flipped open the lid, and began to fill another paper bag with wet cans and plastic containers. I opened a can of cola, drank a few gulps too quickly, coughed some of it up, then finished it. The pain in my stomach seemed to push through to my spine and weigh down my legs, but I got to my feet, back into the cabin, gathered up the bags and pillowcases, and carried it all to my truck. Over the truck bed, a tarp had been laid, and I folded a corner aside and placed the sacks and Sam's clothes in among my boxes. I felt my pulse in my stomach. Holding onto the truck, I leaned toward the ground and gulped a few times, tried to catch my breath and control the spasms in my throat. I closed my eyes.

There was no sound. My crashing around must have set everything silent—the bullfrogs, the jays—and I waited for them all to calm, to take up their noise again, to get on with it. For a long time, I held myself there and listened.

I heard Starwood on the slope. I looked up. Her saddle had slipped halfway over to one side, and as she caught a rein under a hoof, her head jerked down. She stumbled into a trot, and the stirrups flopped against her belly with a painful thump.

And toward her, on the ground that rose between us, in the pale light beneath the aspens, Gilbert's green station wagon was parked among the white, scarred trunks. Grass in thick bunches pressed against the fenders and hid the tires, as if the car had been there since spring.

FIVE

I corralled Starwood, straightened her saddle, and got myself back to the cabin. From the center of the floor, looking wall to wall, I tried to recount the things I'd packed, add up the remains, figure where Sam had gone and if he'd taken anything with him, if he'd had a plan. On the floor beside the stove, I found a crumpled piece of paper. Smoothing it flat on the table, I read the words.

Then I was riding Starwood north from the cow camp. A white froth grew on her neck, broke free, and fell away. Heifers and calves crashed through underbrush, alarmed at my sudden passage.

I saw Sam perch bare-chested on a stool, back against a wooden counter. A chipped white enameled bowl behind him, an empty water glass beside the bowl. His collarbones formed a shadowed V, like wings, as he leaned forward, an elbow on a knee. He looked up at me as I stood against the closed door. There was no clock in the place. The green sheet of linoleum on the floor was streaked with red dried mud. The back room, visible through the far doorway, had been split into uneven halves. One side of that room was filled with a disintegrating sofa, thrown over on its back, legs and springs exposed. The other side was filled with a metal-frame bed, sturdy and slightly rusted, no mattress. Beside me, the woodstove had been pulled out from the wall, partway toward the door, and it rested there, unanchored, its pipe detached from the open circle of sky high on the wall. "Swallows," Sam said, and he nodded at the muddy floor and toward the far room. Above the bedframe, along the joint of wall and ceiling, swallows had built a row of their hollow mud nests. "Listen," he said, standing up toward me, then against me, silent. The sound of wind across the busted-out windows, loose door, and the sound of birds circling, their voices leaking with each stroke of their wings. "They want in," he said. "Open the door. Let's get out." We were gone, and from a distance we saw that the roof of the old cabin was peeling away, that a telephone pole without wires had sunk into the ground, no taller than a man now, and leaned toward a rocky, dry, late-summer creek bed. The birds swirled and disappeared into the cabin. We found what was left of a road and started walking. The ruts were shadows beneath tough new spiked plants. Where the road had been washed into a jagged gully by some old flood, we walked uphill a few paces to where the going was more narrow and then jumped across.

I saw us under a sun so blunt that our bodies, diminishing as we retreated, became as white and scattered as the salt leached from the walls of the gullies. Then again we were inside the cabin. Again outside where the sun was at zenith, fattening to reach the full circle of the horizon.

The long incline ended, and Starwood pulled up short. Gripping her mane, I leaned forward and looked across the valley to the Ramshorn. The peak was bright in sunset, the horizon red. Beneath a frail skin of sunlit evening lay the valley—knots of aspen and the snakes of the creek. There were trails over the edge, down in. Everything worked toward black. I might have waited for the moon, but it wasn't due that night.

Gilbert's mouth shaped his words—the smoothness, the ease of it. Beneath his game I could feel his stories, his stabs at me, as if he'd taken hold of the hair at the back of my head, jerked it, made me look up into rain. I opened my mouth.

A young woman grieved the death of her brother in a distant battle. She announced that she would marry any man who returned her dead brother's body.

A man began the journey. He labored across the plain. The sun rose straight ahead of him, day after day.

The body lay alone, far from any encampment or path. Blackened blood pooled on the soil. Arrowheads and bullets lay scattered among the roots of spring flowers. The man lifted the body, cradled it in his arms, and it seemed light, gentle, no burden. The wind was clean and the nights warm as he returned.

Finally, he stood outside her tent. She stepped out and faced him. At first she saw only her brother, his limbs hanging loosely, his hair long and bright. She held her palm to his forehead and felt the sun's heat on his skin. Taking tears from her eyes, she placed them on his cheeks.

Then she looked up at the man who had brought back the dead body. She reached out her hands and placed them on the man's shoulders, the shoulders that had supported her brother along the trail.

She did not see that the man was ungraceful, malformed. She saw only what he had done, and she loved him unselfishly.

There was a pinpoint of firelight far out in the valley. I twitched the reins, and Starwood moved forward. Down on the flats, she splashed through the creek, heaved up onto the bank, and paused. Her ears pricked, head turned toward the light. Fire burned in a ring of rocks, leaking an orange haze into the aspen leaves above. There was movement around the fire. We approached.

Firelight caught and sharpened in a shelter. A few feet above the ground, a pole had been wedged to span between two aspens. Propped against the pole, and descending away from the fire, were other poles—the top ends stuck high above the cross-piece like wild roof-beams. A dense mat of cut evergreen lay over the structure.

I saw a tanned-hide robe embroidered with stories in black, red, white, yellow, green. A kettle. A hairbrush. A long knife.

Gilbert faced me across the fire. His white shirt reached almost to his knees—the cut of shadow in the folds of cloth. "By the looks of you," he said, "you should be dead."

Beyond Gilbert, in the shelter, Sam lay beneath the robe and blankets. I looked far down at him. He was at the back edge of the firelight, settled in the lee of that tight ceiling. His eyes opened for a moment and wandered—he was sleeping, listening, heard me near, and then fell back into whatever dream—he looked dry, like ash.

Gilbert moved around the fire, dropped the kettle onto the coals at the side of the flames. Maybe he hadn't seen me. In a pot, there was a mash of something brown, maybe sweet or rich, with a spoon stuck in, but as I inhaled I smelled only myself—dust and tired sweat—then the fresh ooze of pitch. There was a stack of wood waiting to burn. Woodsmoke shifted enough to make Gilbert cough and wave his hands across his face. He stooped lower toward the fire, held his hair back against the nape of his neck, took up a stick with his free hand and nudged the kettle deeper into the hot bed. Then, between his palms, he rubbed some leaves, and the scraps fell into a tin cup.

There was no steady light. My eyes would close. I might still have been moving.

My own reek—I had worn those clothes for days—they clung to my joints, stuck to my creases. I snapped at buttons, opening them out.

My father went downstairs for dinner in the cafeteria. The nurse mumbled something as she poked around the bed, and then she was gone, too. My mother started talking—fever or dehydration. I could smell bleach and lemons.

You couldn't figure out how to work your mouth. Funny, me pinching your cheeks to make you pucker, then holding you to my nipple. You were hungry enough. You were all drool until you got it right, and then you were every bit of how I thought you'd be. Fat fingers. Fat everywhere. I poured lotion on your tummy, and it ran over your sides as I freed my hands and took hold of you. Slick and red, as wet and greased as newborn. I wanted to keep you fresh. You chewed on me. Your little body forced against my side as I held you to nurse—you could be sharp—you could be like a twinge I might have felt while carrying you inside, like a pain at wanting to know—how would you smell, why would you hold onto me, would your fingernails draw blood, would I know enough to clean your shit away, how soon before you were dead to me.

There were woods that you might remember—but you were too young. At places where the trees had been cleared for farms and the farms had been worked for a hundred or two hundred years and then the trees came back in, the woods were like a grove of poles. Poles and a sky of leaves. I could hardly push my way through—those poles were never thicker than my leg or maybe my waist. It was dark on the ground. I walked on rotted leaves and branches and a fern or two that seemed to have forced up from an ancient time, all wrong, too delicate. There were miles of those woods behind our house, and I took you walking out there, thinking I'd get lost. No sky but green. The sounds then were not much different from the sounds I hear right now. The rustle of cover. The creak of joints working. I had your breathing close to me. And then the other sounds that diced themselves through the woods and forgot their direction. Traffic—I'd never know which roads I heard. Always a dog yelping. The call of birds, high up and moving away, never approaching—invisible and smart. Nothing to aim for. No way to move quickly. It was sometimes, when we paused, as if all the sounds and bits of chatter and mysterious other noises that hung around us on a humid day were just silence. We heard only our thoughts of where we ought to be.

I remembered times at my summer camp, when I was old enough to be a counselor. I'd listen to all those young girls sleeping—heavy, even breathing from tiny bodies. They couldn't have been dreaming—too tired to have anything to dream about. Clusters of girls in the screen-window cabins in the woods. The air blew right through. You heard insects at the seams, trying to slip themselves in, and crickets going as steady as the starlight, the moonlight—a gray world. I got out and listened at each cabin—no shifting or voice—I was sure there wasn't even the sound of blinking eyes—anyone awake would be out and moving. You can't just stay locked in with all that empty sleep—clumps of it in rows. Those woods were rich and uneven. Huge oaks and alders and elms around the cabins, with trunks that threw out branches thick enough to hold us all. Moss and poison ivy and mats of ferns that gave out to grass where the sun would fall, too brightly. And coming up the hill through the woods, I'd smell the lawns spreading out just beyond the next break, and then I'd be running along the edge of the openness, where the main house stood highest in the center, in its circles of pines and honeysuckle and apples. No window was lit, but the house itself seemed bright white, its rows of black shutters the only shards of darkness. The owner would look out her window and see moonlight on the tidal river, far down through the swath where the forest had been cut for the view. She'd see the gravel lane that carved across the lawns, and the soft wave of the edge of the woods, ready to spill. Nothing much had changed there during almost two hundred years. The cabins of her camp—her support—were stashed in the trees. And I was back into the woods, close to the edge, down toward the river and its sharp mix of salt water, marsh grass that could cut your legs, even moose sometimes that would kill you if you gave them a chance. I'd stand at the bank of the river and look out at the flat islands where birds would flock at first light. Hundreds of birds—gulls and ducks and herons and plenty of stark white plumage. But at night, everything beautiful and bright was asleep. Depending on the moon, the water ran in from the ocean, or flowed away. I walked down along the river, my feet in the shallows. The bottom was sandy and clean, but I knew that out in the channel there were waving strings of green and bursts of dense orange scum and dots of silver fish that dove from shadows or broke into the air in fright. The islands became broader and rocky, choked with blueberries and thorny bushes. I was already past the four corners of the town, the church spire, post office, and seven tall white houses, all on one rolling lawn, all darkened. I never made it as far as the ocean. It could have been miles. No towns or fields or fences along the way. Just the river and the woods. Wild vines hanging into the water from the eaves sometimes. I never made it out to where I could hear the breakers. I thought I would take off my shoes and sit in the dunes, out of the wind in the dune grass, and watch for something to stir toward the gap between whitecaps and sky. If ships passed, they would be dark, no running lights. Deep inside them, in shuttered cabins, women in silk would light cigarettes beneath electrified crystal fixtures. And below the hull, in the incredible deep currents, narwhals would wander and giant ghosts of moonlight squid would hold to the bottom rocks. From that beach, I was sure, landed on a raft from a cruising submarine, an enemy had made his way up along the river. There was a hut I'd find, at the end of a path leading from the bank. Through a slit in the shutters I'd see his dangerous face and gold shoulders.

Halfway to somewhere.

From here I see a square of sky.

I was at the shore, at Grandmother Madeline's summer house. It was overcast, but hot, and I spent an afternoon sleeping on the beach. I got a terrible burn through the clouds. That evening, I covered myself with greasy lotion. There was supposed to be a dance. My dress was too stiff to pull over my head. I screamed for a while and gave up.

Men should learn to wear looser clothes. I walked along the

beach and the wind filled my shift—it floated, wouldn't hurt. Maybe the lights from the houses across the dunes reached me. Maybe people watched. I suppose I would have looked buffeted and unhappy. I liked the cold.

With the waves, I couldn't hear anything of the town, and then it was left behind. I came to a point where the rocks took the beach over and curved sharply into an inlet. I couldn't go any farther without leaving the ocean and heading up toward a river, so I stopped. Lights crossed a bridge, about a half mile in, and then they were gone again in the woods. I climbed out onto a rock—the waves washed right around it. Small boats with red and green running lights came in from the ocean and passed under the bridge. They were returning well after nightfall, when they should have long been anchored. I couldn't see anything but the lights bobbing. They had the town to guide them up the coast, then the bridge to draw them in. I couldn't do that—hold a wheel in pitch darkness and aim for broken strips of light. I heard the swells suck themselves up to a height, heard the wind tear the crests into froth, and then I heard the hollow of the trough, and knew how steeply it carved. Each crest, if I steered the boat, would fall out from under, who knew how deep.

I held my shirt open to allow cold air to my chest. Sleep was trying to take me, an upright sleep in which deep silence held the full reach of the Absaroka Range. I looked at the sky—too broad and crowded. Everything paused. I wouldn't even dream.

Then the fire threw sparks with a snap of gas and cracked wood, water rumbled in the creek, I heard the fall of hooves from the slopes around the valley, out along the tributaries, through the country, clearly. I heard a shifting almost too quiet to hear.

Gilbert stood up from beside the fire, and the light heated his stocky bare legs and glowed under his long shirt and changed it from white to the shadow of a part of him to red like weak dye bleeding. With the back of a hand pressed to his lips, he came around the fire—the slack fingers curled over the palm, pale beneath his black eyes. He took hold of my pant leg, held my calf to his side, slipped his hand under and freed my boot from the stirrup. I leaned. As if he would lift me from Starwood, he reached for my waist. His fingers hooked my belt, his head fell back and he watched me—if I let him, he would lean away and use the momentum to pull me with him. His mouth gaped. His tongue pressed in a wall behind his teeth. He wanted me to move. He looked straight at me. I thought I'd kick my boot back into the stirrup, but I just clenched my legs. His breath whistled through his throat—almost a melody—it came in shallow, wavering phrases, working around meaning, at the rhythm of his lungs. I looked away and waited for strength or my thoughts to gather.

Sam held his head up. His hair, matted black, brushed against the branches—he'd get pitch in his hair from those fresh cut ends. If he shimmied toward the fire a foot or two, the ceiling would be high enough for him to get up on his haunches. Then he could stand away from the shelter. Fully awake. Greet me.

His hands emerged and tried to lower the robe. He got it down his chest a few inches, no farther, and then his arms fell free across the designs. Bare arms, tracings of blue veins. His wrists looked tight and swollen.

His fingers seemed to scratch at rows of quills and over onto tiny beads. The hide had darkened with age to a damp earth brown, almost as dark as the thick fur that tufted from the other side, around the edges, that brushed against Sam's body. It had to have taken a month to complete the full design, and before that, the hunt and kill and the cure. Women in the smoky cool of a tipi through mornings and afternoons, in a circle with the hide between them. Someone had blessed each color and the pouches of weaving matter. A handful of beads like chips of rainfall, retrieved in trade from strangers who rose and fell like clouds over the plain, passing and changing or massing and clearing away. The women were silent. Sunlight fell from the smoke vent.

A bird spread its wings above the fat triangle of its tail. Groups of tents bounded by dark waves.

A man worked with the women. He was like them in dress, but his thick hands struggled to match the delicate stitches. On the final afternoon, toward evening, the women ran their hands through their hair to catch the oil and the scent, and then they placed their palms on the robe, pressed them there, before the man took it away. He carried it toward the fire, where a group of men warmed themselves.

The logs in the fire settled, and raw flames rose brightly. Sam let his head fall back, as if he hadn't broken from sleep at all.

"Lift him up to me," I said, and I twitched at Starwood enough to free myself from Gilbert's hands. She lurched past the shelter.

Gilbert tried to come around me again, skittering and jumping, staying clear of the hooves. I twisted my head to keep him in sight, but I lost him and jerked at the reins again. He smiled.

"You're going to hurt yourself," he shouted.

"Wake him up. I have to take him."

He tried for the reins, but his loose arms and the whip of his hair spooked Starwood. She backed against my urging, her hind footing wobbled, and she went directly down on four knees. For a long moment, my feet in their stirrups were flat on the ground—I might have been straddling a fallen log. Gilbert was slightly above me, the fire behind him, the roof poles reaching to cover us, the slant shadow in the aspens. I felt the heat of the fire. I was in the camp. I waited for Starwood to begin to kick herself to her feet, to roll and crush my leg. But as her nuzzle slowly lowered toward the dirt, preparing, Gilbert seized me under the arms, my feet were free from the stirrups, and I was on my butt beside the fire. Starwood heaved herself up, and Gilbert grabbed hold of her reins.

"You're a good girl," he said, and he ran his hands down her neck and slapped at her chest. "Let's give you a rest." She stood still for him as he uncinched the saddle and pulled it off. "You're nearly bloody," he said. He rubbed at the dark lines the saddle had chafed. "Will she hobble?"

I made to get up but couldn't force my legs under my weight. "Don't let her go."

"I won't. I'll hobble her if you tell me how."

"I want her saddled."

"She's all right. She just needs some rest. I'll wipe her down and picket her near the creek. Okay?" Dropping the bridle next to the saddle, he took a cloth and some rope from the shelter, looped one end of the rope around her neck, and led her away. "Don't you run off, now." He was already beyond the firelight.

Close down near the center, the flames were too bright to bring into focus without losing the edges in the red coals. The air was scorched—I tried not to breathe. I got up on my knees, squinted against the smoke, and backed away a foot or two, toward the cool.

I saw a cup of steaming brown liquid floating with flakes of leaf. A bowl of dirty roots, still caught on remnants of stems and green—white mule's-ear and tobaccoroot and arrowhead. Up the valley, in years past, I'd seen a stretch of blue camas so thick you could sit in one spot, and pull at what you could reach, and collect enough roots for a month.

I ate a mouthful of the mush in the blackened pot, scraped it off the spoon with my teeth. It was lukewarm and faintly bitter. I ate more, until I felt it gather in my stomach—a decent ache, a real discomfort.

There were piles of utensils. A pair of new leather work gloves with metal snaps to tighten them at the wrist. I crawled into the shelter, found a canteen, drank a few long swallows, and replaced it among the boxes of candles and the sewing kit.

I crouched beside Sam. I had to think of where I'd come, by what road, trail, how long or far. Sam was sleeping, would continue sleeping.

His shoulders were shiny with sweat. To prop his head, his clothes had been rolled into a ball. The cords in his neck shook with his pulse. Placing my hand on his forehead, I waited to feel his heat. He would have to be ready to move, soon, or I thought I'd fall asleep.

His head wrenched from under my hand, and as he turned back, his pupils surged wide open. "You look rough," he said. "Are you going to rest?" He raised a hand and rubbed his eyes, smoothed away the white crust at the corners of his mouth. "What are you going to do?"

"How do you feel, Sam?"

He stared at me for a moment, seemed to try to focus harder. As he raised his head a few inches, he said, "Will you fix the pillow?" I rearranged the clothes, and he settled again, higher, looking down over the robe toward the flames. "Oh," he said. He looked up at me. "I've been waiting for you?"

"I think you were *looking* for me."

"Where were you?"

"Are you all right, Sam?"

"I don't think so."

"Are you hurt?"

"The same thing."

"What happened?"

"Mr. Fisher came by. I went out. I thought you'd hurt yourself, Blue. I rode Starwood. When was that? A few days?"

"Maybe."

"She spooked. She threw me. Right out there somewhere. Smelled something she didn't know. Did you see her? She ran off."

"I found her, Sam."

"You know how cold it gets, Blue? It's like the air is gone. Pitch black with just the stars to look at. I heard things moving around. Couldn't tell what. I couldn't even tell if I was sleeping. I thought I dreamed that I was hot. I was on fire. It's strange. You know, I was sitting against a tree, looking at sunrise. Somewhere around here. I was waiting. The sun was stabbing me, it gave me a bad headache, and I started thinking that I had to get some water soon or move into shade." He closed his eyes.

For a night, at least, and hours more, Sam had leaned against one of those white knobby aspen pillars. In the darkness, he wouldn't have been much more than a shifting of scent for anything that passed. A coyote might not slow its lope, looking only in the vague direction, sensing a man. An owl might see him there, a colder shadow in the black shade the starlight threw. Maybe an eagle, rising over the ridge after the sun, would have scanned the valley and caught sight of Sam, there, at the edge of the grove where he'd fallen, as Sam opened his eyes and watched for something to approach. The increasing heat, the moisture drawn up into clouds. He looked out at the walls of the valley and their mottles of rusty rock and sage and flowers, the other groves of aspen that seemed to float in their paler shadows, the sunlight broken for a distant moment on the surface of the creek, the Ramshorn holding white ice out of reach on its raw face. Alone in this valley—maybe what he'd wanted since his first step west.

"You tell me about this, Blue," he said. "That Indian guy came up here with a big frame pack on, and he was dragging some sacks of stuff. He wants me to stay here. He said you'd come—I asked him."

Gilbert had laid Sam out flat, loosened his clothes, looked for wounds. Placed him out of sunlight while he built the shelter. Pulled Sam's shirt from his arms, pants from his legs. Crouched there beside Sam, unfolded the robe, prepared to wrap Sam in it, to shield him from the cold, but he waited. Sam shivered along the length of his body, open on the grass. There would have been words or songs, a probing for the cause of the pain, before Gilbert flung the robe to Sam's chin. Before they both rolled toward sleep.

I yanked at the robe, but Sam had hold of it. "He's been doing things," he said, pressing his eyes more firmly shut.

I wanted to peel away that robe and see that belly, know that the scar ran straight, stretched tight over the pressure of his gut. Grasping his shoulders, I tried to raise him, but he fought against me. He seemed to be forcing himself toward sleep.

"Lie down, Blue," he whispered. "I heard him tell it. Lie down here with me."

I stroked his forehead to make him know me, close, to keep him waking toward whatever I could think, but he shot his head up under my touch, grabbed at my thumb with his teeth, held it, hard, and set it loose.

"Go to sleep," he said. "It's night." He wouldn't rouse.

I could have fought with him to get him moving, out from that shelter, but I just slouched closer and watched. At some point I'd see the tension leave his shoulders, the muscles weaken, and he'd relax his hold.

"She's all clean and comfortable," Gilbert said from beyond the fire. He came around, hung from the crosspiece, and leaned into the shelter. "I knew you boys wouldn't get anywhere without me." His hair dangled. I watched it. He was dark and cleanly cut against the light, his legs spread and planted at the edge of the robe, his arms wide and gripping. Around him, the fall of his shirt seemed no more than fiery smoke. Clearly, every edge exposed. "He's a sight, Blue," he said. "A beauty."

I found my legs straightening, I lunged, took Gilbert's waist, and he folded over the brunt of my shoulder, his whole loose bulk, out onto the ground. Rock scraped my skull—I heard the gritty friction. Gilbert was on me. My legs kicked. He tangled away, to his feet, got over me, stood on my forearms as if he'd snap the bones. He shouted down at me, spit and echo. "Hey! You're too beat up for this."

"I want him out of here."

"You can't hardly stand."

"Get off me." I tried to kick up at his back. As he stepped forward, his whole body passed over me in the white bell of his shirt. "Have you hurt him?" I got up on my knees.

He stopped a few feet away, shook his head. "You don't know anything." Stooping, he gathered some sticks and threw them in the fire.

"He's hurt."

"I know."

"Let me take him."

"You can't. Be reasonable." He nudged my shoulder, pushed me sideways, settled me onto the ground. "Do what I say. Get out of your clothes." He turned his back, made a show of not looking.

The breeze shifted and brought the smoke across me, along with the warmth. I breathed that stinging gray for a while. Coughing, I fell back onto my elbows. The night was getting colder—my fingers wouldn't follow my thoughts.

Gilbert bent over me, stripped my clothes away. He wrapped me in a blanket, propped me by the fire, and handed me a cup of water. Then he took my clothes toward the creek.

I watched the flames and drank the cold, tasteless water.

He returned with my clothes in a wet clump and spread them on the rocks of the fire circle. They steamed where they hung toward the coals, and with a stick he kept shifting the dampness toward the heat.

"Let me tell you," he said. "Listen."

A man like you. I'll call him Daniel. I like the sound of it. You tell me where he's from. Somewhere far.

This Daniel walked out to where the mountains were beyond familiar. When night fell, with no moon, he had only memory to keep him going. He remembered seeing, in the last light, a valley of thick grass that stretched miles ahead, with a creek running toward a lake. The sound of flowing water kept him on the trail. Then the sky opened below him in the deep plain of the lake, and the same sky opened above, and the mountains circled around and separated one from the other. He was at the edge of the lake. He could roll on the black ground, feel the world roll, and when he stopped he wouldn't know which constellations to believe.

Across the lake, lights came into view, slightly more interesting than a hundred miles of stop-and-go animal trails and the endless varieties of shit in meadows. He hiked around the shore and approached a low stone building set in a group of canvas tents. It had been so dark in the wilds that the tents seemed almost unbearably bright in the light from the building's windows. He wanted to find an empty tent and crawl in and wait for shadows on the canvas, but someone opened the door and stepped out from the building, squinted toward him for a moment, and motioned for him to come inside.

The room was crowded with lanterns, tables, and stools, and a fire blazed high in the crude fireplace, and there were men, more than a dozen, in close quarters. Daniel could smell that they weren't clean. The noise they stirred didn't leave much room for clear thinking. The men ate from flat loaves of bread, plates of meat, were always passing from one to another, taking what they could. They all knew each other, thrown together in that camp—it was almost a town. A man brushed another on the ear, three leaned together and tried to drink from the same glass, one licked his fingers and smoothed his mustache. Daniel was half unsure. He knew he had to figure something fast or seem absent, had to settle on a move, but the man who had beckoned him in was pulling his pack from his back and turning him around. "I'll put it here, by the door, out of the way," the man said, naming himself Percy, newly west, and then laughed and walked away.

No reason to distinguish among the group, no man more or less than any of the others, but Daniel watched young Percy pour a glass from the keg of whiskey and return, hand the glass to him. Percy asked him where he'd come in from. Daniel turned toward the wall, drank a few gulps, turned back and said, "I would've made camp before nightfall, but you always think you'll get somewhere. I'm glad I kept going." He felt like a fool. He finished his drink, and Percy went off for more, called him over, and they sat together on the hearth. Daniel looked straight ahead into the crowd. Hard to think of how far each man must have come, across an ocean at some point, and tracing back through father to grandfather and further until no one knew who they were or why they felt they had to move on.

There was a shout from outside, and then a band of Indians burst in and were taken up in loud greetings and the building held more men and a new language. The Indians accepted the drink, and they wouldn't stay still. Daniel watched their muscles shift, their black hair. They were telling stories, he guessed—he could feel the words traveling great distances. Pausing on their way to hunt or raid, they had with them, moving away from them but always seeming close to their sides, a man who was not a man. They called him Rotten Bone. He took hold of a stranger, pulled him to his hips, moved on to another. The stories circled and soon the softness of Rotten Bone's robe flew around your neck and tangled with your legs and you felt the line of his crotch against yours. You fell back against the wall, taking his moves with you. Rotten Bone repeated a word continuously, and you watched the lips, smelled the breath like sage. The word entered you. You understood that your prick was hardening, and you smelled sweat, blankets, corn, something sweet as white grass. There were games to play, to catch you in loops. Rotten Bone's tongue danced along his teeth. You wanted to push your fingers in there. You wanted to hold onto that voice and let it soothe you.

But Daniel was left alone as that strange man took up a lantern, hooked the arm of a blue-eyed white man, and made an escape out the door. Daniel stepped to a window and cupped against his own reflection. The pair ran along the edge of the sky—their light swung. Then the light arced far out into the sky and drowned. Daniel tried to make out the stars, but they were shredded by ripples. He tried to make out the figures, but they'd settled into the blank blackness. No sound to it. Already gone—those scents.

He turned from the window and saw Percy pick up his backpack and step out the door. The other men leaned heavily on the tables, watching him, waiting, and finally one of them told him to go on out, follow Percy, he would bunk with him. Percy had offered, or someone had assumed.

Daniel walked outside. One of the tents was bright with its

239

own light. As he wandered toward it, he heard the other men stumble out behind him and head for their own tents.

Untying the tent flaps, he ducked inside. The tent was large, the ceiling high. There was a cot along each side and a lantern on an upturned section of log at the back. Lying on a cot, his blanket pulled to his ear, Percy had rolled toward the wall. At the foot of the empty cot was Daniel's own dusty pack. Quietly, he sat on the cot and took off his boots, socks, and pants, pulled off his jacket and shirt. His heart was running on, trying to warm him. He lay down and pulled the blanket over.

Maybe Percy wasn't asleep. Daniel wanted to speak, but his mind saw only silhouettes of sentences. He felt a sudden pain like a drop of water on a dry tongue. Maybe a swim in the lake at dawn—Percy would be running along the shore. Daniel tipped up on his elbow, trying to see him, to remember his face, but he was in shadow.

Daniel blew out the lantern. "Good night," he whispered, and then rolled toward the wall.

Daniel stared at nothing. He felt the soft pillow against his head, the sag of the cot, the scratchy blankets. He heard wind in the trees behind the camp. Pulling the blanket to his ear, he tried not to move. If he made no noise, the night would pass over and he'd sleep.

Listen.

Rotten Bone led that man along the shore. The lit windows of the camp were in the lake with the stars. Their clothes were gone, they'd torn them away, and Rotten Bone was on the ground and took hold of the man and pulled him in. They had nothing of each other's language.

I'll tell you. I was on a lava flow at midnight. The rocks hadn't had enough years yet to soften. Taking off my shirt, loosening my pants, I stretched out on my back. Beneath the few feet of rock that supported me, if I'd judged it right, a gaping tunnel ran from some deep place toward a shallow, broken opening on the plain. I shouted and tried to feel a hollow reverberation against my back. The earth wasn't moving. I pulled my pants off and raised my knees. The cold shrank my balls away and gave a hard point to my nipples. I tried to make the sounds I remembered. Gran and Gordon. Working toward a chant. Louder. No sign of weakness in the rock beneath me, no tremor that might have led to collapse and taken me down in. I couldn't hear a thing but my own voice, muddy, couldn't see anything but the stars, and even they were unclear—the cold had brought water to my eyes. I pushed and shouted and the rock cut my back, my neck, and my waist. I felt blood in my hair. The ground wouldn't give.

In the gatherings of soil, toward winter, somewhere out there in the Great Basin, a family dug into the ground, built a frame over the hole, and covered it with mud. Snow fell. At night, they huddled together in the darkness of their own accumulated stench, buried together for warmth. If the snow drifted, they were invisible—on a bright night, after the wind had died, you could walk a few yards from their shelter and not even a wisp of smoke would give them away. They wouldn't waste their supply of wood and risk moving their camp across the ice and crust—almost impossible to carve a new hole in the frozen ground. They would lie in the same direction, flat along the floor. The son groped for a sack, opened it, took out a handful of dried berries and chewed them, thought of a day with hot wind when he paused on a ridge and watched someone chased through the trees below, it looked like a game—he thought it should have been him who was chased, caught, lifted from the ground. The mother listened to him chew, swallow, remembered an early spring a life ago when the sun was strong and stayed strong, and the snow became a river, the whole earth for a wild stretch of days ran with water—it must have been some blessing they earned that freed them so early, something else that brought the snow back deeper the following years.

I have a robe that dresses me out—I'm tempting, a real startle. Gordon made it for me. It's decorated with symbols I don't know. Men could make a game of me. The robe would be off and padding the floor as I took them one by one, teasing them, choosing one for my husband. I would offer them luck and magic—the power was a gift promised to me on the first night Gordon shook me from my sleep. I remembered. I finally saw how he held my legs on his shoulders, bent over me, folded me into a silent, smothered bundle. He took me into his mouth where I thought it would hurt, but it seemed painless. I held onto him, let him bite at me and tell me I was magic, a gift from the birds, let him tell me we were what people like us used to be, we were together.

Gilbert pulled my clothes from the rocks and started folding them into a neat pile. He smoothed the shirt flat, pressed the collar between his palms. He buttoned the pants and shook them out, crisp. Then he ducked into the shelter and dropped the stack among the other clothes. Stripping off his shirt, he returned and sat beside the fire. His head hung forward as he combed his hair with his spread fingers. His skin was even, smooth, without variation. Slowly he rubbed the cold from his arms and thighs. I thought of how soon winter would begin to take the color from the mountains.

"Tell me what you've done to him," I said.

Gilbert didn't look up. "I've only taken care. He'll improve. I know enough."

"What do you know?"

"I know what I hear. It makes sense. I know what I taste. Crush something, put it on your tongue. I could begin to tell you things if you let me. I could just barely begin. Give me time."

"What? Tell me."

"I follow the land. From the start. It's all there."

"What are you going to do?"

"Blue. I won't hurt you."

On a late night when the northern sky is green, the fire will be higher than the roof poles. The aspen leaves will rattle in the wind like clouds of sound. Gilbert will have us standing so close to the flames that I think I'll singe. We're stripped, painted red, the paint cracks in the heat and peels away.

He took my blanket and wrapped it around himself, raised me to my feet and pushed me toward the shelter. I crouched down in and he pulled back the robe for me, rolled my clothes for a pillow, covered me to my neck. He left us and went to lie at the edge of the low, dying fire.

People had lived in that valley. I'd seen the signs—sharpened stones—brief summer camps.

At night, in their shelter, they'd listen and think they knew the source of each sound. Antelope, deer, moose. A bear that rushed at them sometimes. Birds that flew without light. They'd choose someone to stay awake and alert. What shapes do spirits take?

The fire dimmed until the ceiling of branches was a single shadow. Soon there'd be no point of flame to reach out to the edges of the valley. A man looking for us, riding up to the crest of the ridge, would see only outlines of mountains against stars. If he rode down into the valley, he might catch a breath of wood-smoke and follow it. Nothing to see—not unless he rode right to the edge of the fire circle—then he'd look down at a dull red space of coals, and he'd listen for breathing, for the beat of the heart of someone watching, someone who'd heard him approaching for the last mile, someone adjusted to the dark. But in against the aspens, night was heavier, the camp was settled, the shelter was solid, and no one would know how to look, how to see something that hadn't been built for generations.

Crossing the reservation, years ago, with an Indian outfitter named Bobby, a part-time rancher I'd met in dealings before, I headed across closed lands toward a wilderness trailhead. "There's rattlesnakes just at the start of the trail," Bobby said, "and some guys from the East saw a bear along those first meadows. But I'm sure you won't see any trouble." We could hardly speak over the roar of the engine. The truck strained up slopes dead dry on either side, through ruts a foot or two deep, and boulder creek beds in the shade of cottonwoods. Two hours of that road till we hit the first pines. I looked back and saw Crowheart Butte, a tiny shadow against the narrow green strip of the river and the badlands beyond. And then we stopped at the remains of the old ranger cabin. Bobby helped me on with my pack, repeated four times that he would return to pick me up in a week, at five o'clock, and said, "If you're not here to meet me, it might be the next day before I can find you. It would take even longer than we just took to get a horse trailer up this road, and I'm not gonna try it at night. So, the next day at the soonest. Don't do anything. Wait for me. But I don't know why I bother saying this. You'll be fine. It's nice in there. I go in sometimes myself and just lie around for a few days. It's the end of the world."

Twelve miles in, the lake was a long elbow of silvery blue water. All around, white falls threaded the broken walls, disappearing through patches of dense low vegetation, nothing growing tall as a man. Maybe five hundred feet up over the first lip of the walls, hidden in bowls, there would be glacial lakes. And then the circle of higher, terminal cliffs that cupped the whole head of the drainage—sheer and gray and veined from a million winter shatters, scabbed with huge patches of old snow. Each night, the moon rose over those cliffs and echoed and intensified. I set my tent at the upper shore, caught fish as big as my forearm.

I climbed the lower walls, holding to the vegetation while it lasted, then ascended beside the line of falling water, over the edge to a lake as pale as ice. I wandered across fields of boulders—saw sky reflected from standing water down in the gaps—broke through and trailed thick spider webs. A higher lake, smaller. Another, final lake, half caught in the downward slide of a snowfield. The water was pure white.

Black rosy finches hopped among the rocks, over the snow, around the lake. I tried to see where they'd take what they caught—a bug or a floating bit of seed—but I lost sight. They dipped and swooped and suddenly their forward motion had ceased somewhere back along the tracing of my sight. They knew I was watching.

Descending the cliffs to my camp, I dug into the slope and tried to keep my center of gravity low. I hadn't remembered the extreme steepness. My legs shook from the strain of holding against falling, and they ached long after I'd cooked dinner, eaten, scrubbed the pot, brought my sleeping bag from the tent and wrapped my shoulders, and settled against a rock, on a space of smooth pebbles, to watch the moon. As the night grew colder, I heard, above me, the cliffs crack and echo. I remember the moment of fright.

Bobby would be waiting for me, would come find me if I'd disappeared. If I'd fallen, he'd find me broken at the edge of the lake, lying where a waterfall broadened through vegetation. But if I'd lost my footing somewhere higher, he'd find my empty camp and never think to look over the lip, in the fields of rock that fell and rolled and gathered around the colder, whiter lakes.

Gilbert slept beside the fire. To find the cow camp, he would've asked someone in town, listened calmly to the directions, no matter how they'd been delivered. I couldn't remember if I'd left Sam's note on the table in the cabin, but even if I had, there were still miles of open country between us and anyone, a twisted jumble of blank faces and wide tracts of woods and no real trails. It would take the better part of another day for someone to return to town and van some horses up, to begin to scour such a spread of mountains. Sam would get stronger. Gilbert would dig in. I could rest.

I thought of winter. I thought of the fall of snow that would take the strata from the mountains and leave only bare light and shadow, blank depth. A cabin, renewed from a ruined foundation, could hold tight against the storms and weight of drifts. Even Gardelle wouldn't remember who had lived so high or which trails would lead to the door.

We'd walk on snowshoes bent from willow and secured with gut. Through woods where the snow had filtered down in an even layer. Across open ground, wary of a stream that melted the crust thin, out in the center where the land seemed to dip. Toward the Ramshorn, which lifted into the low clouds. A full-day hike until we saw Gilbert's camp—a fleck in a white valley. Scattered groves of aspen like crowdings of marble posts.

Gilbert had robes to warm us. He settled us down in the structure. The gray evening light reflected through the east door. A storm had begun—Gilbert shut it away. The small fire at the center of the room gave enough light, and the smoke rose straight into the spot of bleached sky in the ceiling, directly above.

Roasted camas roots pressed into cakes. Bags of dried gooseberries and Oregon grape. Gilbert would stand up from the meal. He'd have dreams to tell us.

Lime-Crazy made love indiscriminately. His brother, the chief, fined him for his sin, finally abandoned him on the hunt. But the people punished the chief for his harshness. Lime-Crazy returned and restored his brother to his position. Then Lime-Crazy made more love, and he was abandoned again. Lost to the White Owl, winter storm.

A quiver went across Sam's chest. I pressed my ear to his ribs, heard the pump of his heart, far down in. He shook again, his hands struggled to push at me. Under the robe, the crowded smell of our bodies, of the earth, the crushed grass. I laid my cheek on his belly. My tongue felt for the scar—a taste like sour blood or the leeched salt of old sweat—his fluids mixing. He tried to shift his weight, and his fingers dug at my scalp.

I heard, from a deep hollow, a sound like green bark stripped from a branch. I rolled away, reached for his scar, felt the even tension. Then I felt something tangle, and I heard the sound again. It seemed to echo.

I pushed the robe off. Sam curled away, pulling his knees toward his chest. His spine rose in a line of red bumps, his lower back was swirled with violet blood—the color seemed to rise from a distance beneath the surface.

Gilbert reached in past me, took up his medicine bag, and loosened the thong. The contents fell to the dirt in the rising firelight. Coins. An elk tail, one end strapped to a wooden handle. A small figure of a man made of sewn hide—it had darkened with soil and handling—yellow bits of feather for hair. Black leaves and red seeds. He squatted there, looking down at the scattered color. With an outstretched finger, he shifted the items, turned the coins, tried to separate the leaves from the seeds. "Listen," he said.

Sunrise was an hour away. Already I could smell how the heat would dry the air. Then the sage would be sharper, the spruces limber. I dragged the twisted wire and posts of the gate to the side and left it in a heap—I wasn't going to close it. The herd might pass through, down along the creek, but they wouldn't find much. I took a moment to tuck Sam more firmly into his blanket, and then put the truck in gear and continued. There was no chance of avoiding the ruts, whatever speed, so I drove fast. Sam didn't make a sound. He leaned hard into the padding I'd thrown against the door. He might have been asleep.

When we reached pavement, our movement seemed smooth and silent. Through the center of town, the only life was a street-light flickering outside the cafe. I headed onto the side streets. A tall black pickup was pulled up beside Sam's old trailer—a new tenant. Derek's car was gone, his dog chained to the screen door, asleep. The Talbots' house was dark. No one had risen. I could circle for an hour until windows lit and people looked out—they'd know my truck—but I pulled up to Jesse Byer's house. He was new, two years teaching chemistry at the school.

I shut off the engine. Sam roused and turned to look at me, focusing past me and then closing his eyes. "Get me out," he said, and shrugged back against the door.

"Wait here, Sam."

"I'm waiting."

I walked to the house, rang the bell. Somewhere down a hall a light came on. Jesse opened the door in a T-shirt and his shorts. Slumping against the doorjamb, he stared at me for a few seconds. "What is it?" he said.

"Don't you work at the clinic sometimes?"

"I'm an EMT. Certified. Volunteer."

"And you drive an ambulance?"

"No. But we have someone licensed to drive. Is someone hurt?"

I walked to the truck, and Jesse came with me. He strapped his chest with his arms and balanced on the balls of his feet. As I opened Sam's door a crack, I reached in and caught him as he began to fall, then held him there for Jesse to examine.

"Let's free him up," Jesse said, and helped me lift Sam and lay him flat on the lawn. "What happened?"

"He got thrown."

"Where's he hurt?"

"All through the gut, from what I can tell."

"Has he been moved a lot since the injury?"

"Yes." Miles on horseback, and the jolts of the road.

Jesse pulled the blanket away and loosened Sam's clothes, tipped him one way and the other, pressed his fingers around the scar. "This is Sam, huh?" he said. "I was the attendant after he got beat up." He held Sam's eyelids open, pinched his wrist, bent far over and pressed his ear to Sam's chest. Getting to his feet, he crossed his arms again and rocked a few times, forward and back, looking down at Sam. "Shit," he said. "Watch him. I'll be a minute." He ran into the house.

Crouching, I brushed the hair up off Sam's forehead, rested my hand there. "Are you all right?" I said.

"Funny."

"When you're stronger, Sam, I'll find you. Not now."

As Jesse ran back out of the house, I got into my truck and drove west toward Togwotee Pass.

The air was wet with minerals. Out on the elevated boardwalks, people wandered among the steaming pools and runoff. He listened to them talk—many were foreign. They leaned over railings and tried to peer through the mist into the gray cauliflower holes, the liquid like tropical sky. Whole fields flat with water that welled and hissed, gray matter brought up and deposited in soft-fringed sheets, bright tiny forests of yellow and orange algae. The people ran in step, teetered at the edge of a noisy eruption, trying to stay centered in the photograph. He watched as Echinus threw scalding water against the wind, and the crowd screamed and laughed and fell back. As he returned along the sandy trail toward the parking lot, the languages merged with the pressurized blare of the vent.

He drove in slow lines of cars. At the next crossroads, he found dinner and rented a tourist cabin for the night. The room was deep, with two double beds, hanging lamps and floor lamps, and a sliding glass door. He took a long shower, laid out clean clothes for the morning, dropped his towel, turned off the lights, and opened the broad panel of drapes. There were other cabins, cars parked, spindly pines, and a road passing through the woods a ways down the hill. He leaned against the glass and watched lights shift in windows, clouds blot the dark sky. A *family pulled in at the end of the row and began to unpack. Before they could look in his direction, he backed away and got into bed. The sheets were stiff and clean across his shoulders.*

He awoke and opened his eyes. He'd settled into a soft spot. In the darkness, he saw nothing for a while. He heard the sound of rushing water, steady, and he tried to think of where it flowed—a spring into a creek, down through a steep valley. If there were trails, if he was lost, if it was storm clouds that robbed the starlight—how long. The rhythm of walking still rocked him. He listened for movement. There—he saw pines swaying high against the sky, but he didn't hear them. And then, from down the valley, he saw lights approaching. A stream of people holding flashlights. They seemed to near, then veered into the woods, blocked from sight.

He sat up. Cars moved along the road. He tried to sleep again. He still heard the rush.